OLIVER TWIST

This Armada book belongs to:

wilmchursts

CHARLES DICKENS, born in Portsmouth in 1812, was the son of a clerk in the Navy pay office. His family was very poor, and while his father was in a debtor's prison, Charles was put to work in a blacking factory – an experience which he later wrote about in *David Copperfield*. Eventually, his father's financial troubles were resolved, and Charles was able to finish his schooling before beginning a career in a solicitor's office. He spent his spare time learning shorthand, and later became a reporter of debates in the House of Commons.

Between 1836 and his death in 1870, he wrote, among many others, such famous novels as *A Christmas Carol*, *Nicholas Nickleby*, *Great Expectations*, *A Tale of Two Cities* and, what is perhaps one of his most popular novels, *Oliver Twist*. Like most of his other books, this was first serialised in a magazine and a huge readership eagerly followed the fortunes of the workhouse boy who fell among criminals before finally finding happiness.

Doris Dickens, who abridged this story, is the great-granddaughter of Charles Dickens. She has abridged many of Dickens's novels for children.

IMPRIMÉ EN FRANCE

OLIVER TWIST

CHARLES DICKENS

Abridged and edited by
Doris Dickens

This abridged edition first published in
Armada in 1980 by
Fontana Paperbacks,
8 Grafton Street, London W1X 3LA.

Armada is an imprint of Fontana Paperbacks,
a division of the Collins Publishing Group.

This impression 1985

Made and printed for
William Collins Sons & Co. Ltd, Glasgow

CHAPTER 1

OLIVER TWIST IS BORN

In a certain town, which shall be nameless, there was a work-house, and in this workhouse was born the child whose name is at the head of this chapter.

For a time it was not certain that Oliver Twist was going to live. There was nobody by but an old woman, one of the inmates who was rendered rather misty by more beer than she was used to, and a parish surgeon who was paid a yearly sum to come when he was needed. Oliver lay gasping on a little flock mattress, but after a few struggles he breathed, sneezed and set up a loud cry.

At this, the patchwork coverlet, which was carelessly flung over the iron bedstead, rustled, the pale face of a young woman was raised feebly from the pillow, and a faint voice whispered, "Let me see the child and die."

The surgeon had been sitting with his face turned towards the fire, giving the palms of his hands a warm and a rub alternately. As the young woman spoke, he rose and, advancing to the bed's head, said, with more kindness than might have been expected of him:

"Oh, you must not talk about dying yet."

"Lor bless her dear heart, no!" exclaimed the nurse, hastily replacing in her pocket a green glass bottle, the contents of which she had been tasting in a corner with evident satisfaction. "Lor bless her dear heart, when she has lived as long as I have, sir, and had thirteen children of her own, and all of 'em dead except two, and them in the workus with me, she'll know better than to take on in that way, bless her dear heart! Think what it is to be a mother, there's a dear young lamb, do."

Her words had no effect. The patient shook her head, and stretched out her hand towards the child.

The surgeon placed it in her arms. She kissed it passionately on its forehead, passed her hands over her face, gazed wildly round, shuddered, fell back—and died. They tried to restore her circulation, but it was no use; the blood had stopped for ever.

"It's all over, Mrs Thingummy!" said the surgeon at last.

"Ah, poor dear, so it is!" said the nurse, picking up the cork of the green bottle, which had fallen out on the pillow, as she stooped to take up the child. "Poor dear!"

"You needn't mind sending for me if the child cries, nurse," said the surgeon, putting on his gloves. "It's very likely it *will* be troublesome. Give it a little gruel if it is." He put on his hat, and pausing by the bedside on his way to the door, added, "She was a good-looking girl, too. Where did she come from?"

"She was brought here last night," replied the old woman. "She was found lying in the street. She had walked some distance, for her shoes were worn to pieces, but where she came from, or where she was going to, nobody knows."

The surgeon leaned over the body, and raised the left hand.

"The old story," he said, shaking his head. "No wedding ring, I see. Ah! Good night!"

The medical gentleman walked away to dinner, and the nurse, after another drink from the green bottle, sat down on a low chair before the fire, and proceeded to dress the infant.

Wrapped in the blanket which, until now, had been his only covering, Oliver might have been the child of a nobleman or a beggar, but, now that he was clothed in the old calico robes which had grown yellow with use and age, he was labelled at once—a parish child—the orphan of a workhouse—the humble, half-starved drudge—to be cuffed and buffeted through the world—despised by all, and pitied by none.

Oliver cried lustily. If he could have known that he was an orphan, left to the tender mercies of churchwardens and workhouse overseers, perhaps he would have cried the louder.

CHAPTER 2

MR BUMBLE TAKES CHARGE

While he was very young, Oliver lived in a branch work-house some three miles away with twenty or thirty other babies in the care of an elderly female who was paid seven-pence-halfpenny per small head per week. This elderly female knew what was good for children, and she knew what was good for herself, so she kept the greater part of the weekly allowance for her own use, and kept the children short on food and clothing.

Oliver Twist's ninth birthday found him a pale, thin, some-what small child, which wasn't surprising, but he had a good sturdy spirit, and perhaps that is why he managed to have a ninth birthday at all. Anyhow, it *was* his ninth birthday, and he was keeping it in the coal-cellar with two other boys who, after sharing with him in a sound thrashing, had been locked up for daring to be hungry, when Mrs Mann, the lady of the house, was unexpectedly startled by the sight of Mr Bumble, the parish beadle, trying to undo the garden gate.

"Goodness gracious! Is that you, Mr Bumble, sir?" said Mrs Mann, thrusting her head out of the window and try-ing to sound pleased. "(Susan, take Oliver and them two brats upstairs, and wash 'em directly.) My heart alive! Mr Bumble, how glad I was to see you, sure-ly!"

Now Mr Bumble was a fat man, and peppery, so instead of responding pleasantly, he gave the little gate a tremendous shake and then a kick which could have proceeded from no leg but a beadle's.

"Lor, only think," said Mrs Mann, running out—for the three boys had been removed from the cellar by this time—"only think of that! That I should have forgotten that the gate was bolted on the inside, on account of them dear children! Walk in, sir. Walk in, pray, Mr Bumble, do sir."

"It is not respectful or proper conduct, Mrs Mann, to

keep the parish officers a-waiting at your garden gate when they come on business connected with the parish orphans," said Mr Bumble, grasping his cane. "I come on business now, and have something to say. Pray, lead the way in."

With great humility, Mrs Mann ushered the beadle into a small parlour with a brick floor, placed a seat for him and put his cocked hat and cane on the table before him.

"Now don't you be offended at what I'm a-going to say," said Mrs Mann sweetly. "You've had a long walk, you know, or I wouldn't mention it. Now, will you take a little drop of somethink, Mr Bumble?"

"Not a drop. Not a drop," said Mr Bumble, waving his right hand in a dignified but placid manner.

"I think you will," said Mrs Mann, who had noticed the tone of the refusal, and the gesture that had accompanied it. "Just a leetle drop, with a little cold water, and a lump of sugar."

Mr Bumble coughed.

"Now just a leetle drop," said Mrs Mann persuasively.

"What is it?" inquired the beadle.

"I'll not deceive you, Mr B.," replied Mrs Mann, as she opened a corner cupboard, and took down a bottle and glass. "It's gin—kept for medicinal reasons, of course."

"Of course," said Mr Bumble, eyeing the gin and water which Mrs Mann was mixing for him. He took the glass and raised it. "I drink your health with cheerfulness, Mrs Mann." And he swallowed half of it.

"And now about business," said the beadle, taking out a leathern pocket book. "The child that was half-baptised Oliver Twist is nine year old today."

"Bless him," put in Mrs Mann, inflaming her left eye with the corner of her apron.

"And in spite of a offered reward of ten pound, which was afterwards increased to twenty pound," said Mr Bumble, "we have never been able to discover who is his father, or what was his mother's name and state in life."

Mrs Mann raised her hands in astonishment, but added after a moment's thought, "How comes he to have any name at all, then?"

The beadle drew himself up with great pride, and said, "I invented it."

"You, Mr Bumble!"

8

"I, Mrs Mann. We name our foundlings in alphabetical order. The last was a S--Swubble, I named him. This was a T—Twist, I named *him*. The next one as comes will be Unwin, and the next Vilkins. I have got names ready made to the end of the alphabet, and all the way through it again, when we come to Z."

"Why, you're quite a literary character, sir!" said Mrs Mann.

"Well, well," said the beadle, evidently gratified with the compliment, "perhaps I may be. Perhaps I may be, Mrs Mann." He finished the gin and water, and added, "Oliver being now too old to remain here, the Board of Governors have decided to have him back in the workhouse. I have come out myself to take him there. So let me see him at once."

"I'll fetch him directly," said Mrs Mann, leaving the room. Oliver, having had by this time as much of the outer coat of dirt which encrusted his face and hands removed as could be scrubbed off in one washing, was led into the room.

"Make a bow to the gentleman, Oliver," said Mrs Mann.

Oliver made a bow, which was divided between the beadle on the chair, and the cocked hat on the table.

"Will you go along with me, Oliver?" said Mr Bumble, in a majestic voice.

Oliver was about to say that he would go along with anybody with great readiness, when, glancing upward, he caught sight of Mrs Mann, who had got behind the beadle's chair, and was shaking her fist at him with a furious countenance. He took the hint at once, for he had often felt that fist.

"Will *she* go with me?" inquired poor Oliver.

"No, she can't," replied Mr Bumble, "but she'll come and see you sometimes."

Oliver had enough sense to make a pretence of feeling great regret at going away, and, since he was hungry and had been ill-treated that very morning, he cried quite easily.

Mrs Mann gave him a thousand embraces, and, what Oliver wanted a great deal more, a piece of bread and butter, lest he should seem too hungry when he got to the workhouse.

With the slice of bread in his hand, and the little brown-cloth parish cap on his head, Oliver was then led away by Mr Bumble from the wretched home where he had never received one kind word or look in all his infant years. Yet he burst into tears as the cottage gate closed after him, for he was leaving his little companions in misery, the only friends he had ever known, and he was now alone in the great wide world.

CHAPTER 3

OLIVER ASKS FOR MORE

When they reached the workhouse, Oliver was handed over to the care of an old woman, but he had scarcely consumed a second slice of bread, when Mr Bumble returned, and, telling him that it was a Board night, informed him that the Board had said he was to appear before it at once.

He was taken into a large white-washed room, where eight or ten fat gentlemen were sitting round a table. At the top of the table, seated in an armchair rather higher than the rest, was a particularly fat gentleman with a very round, red face.

"What's your name, boy?" said this gentleman.

Oliver was frightened at the sight of so many gentlemen, and he answered in a very low and hesitating voice.

"The boy's a fool," said a gentleman in a white waistcoat.

"Boy," said the gentleman in the high chair, "listen to me. You know you're an orphan, I suppose?"

"What's that, sir?" inquired poor Oliver.

"The boy *is* a fool—I thought he was," said the gentleman in the white waistcoat.

"Hush!" said the gentleman who had spoken first. "You know you've got no father or mother, and that you were brought up by the parish, don't you?"

"Yes, sir," replied Oliver, weeping bitterly.

"Well, you have come to be educated, and taught a useful trade. Go with the beadle."

Oliver bowed by order of Mr Bumble, who gave him a smart rap behind with his cane, and was then hurried away to a large room, filled with workhouse boys, where, on a rough, hard bed, he sobbed himself to sleep.

After this, it was work every day, with intervals when Oliver and his companions were fed. They were allowed three meals of thin gruel a day, with an onion twice a week and half a roll on Sundays, and they were starving.

The room in which the boys were fed was a large stone hall with a copper at one end, out of which the master, dressed in an apron for the purpose, and assisted by one or two women, ladled the gruel at meal-times. Each boy had one porringer full and no more—except on occasions of great public rejoicings, when he had two ounces and a quarter of bread besides. The bowls never wanted washing. The boys polished them with their spoons till they shone, and then sat staring at the copper and sucking their fingers in case any splashes of gruel had been cast upon them.

Oliver Twist and his companions suffered the tortures of slow starvation for three months, but at last they got so ravenous and wild with hunger that one boy, who was tall for his age and hadn't been used to that sort of thing (for his father had kept a small cook-shop), hinted darkly that, unless he had another basin of gruel per day, he was afraid he might some night happen to eat the boy who slept next to him, who was younger and rather a weakly child. He had a wild, hungry eye, and the boys believed him. A council was held, lots were cast who should walk up to the master after supper that evening and ask for more, and it fell to Oliver Twist.

The evening arrived, and the boys took their places. The master, in his cook's uniform, stationed himself at the copper, his assistants ranged themselves behind him, the gruel was served out and a long grace was said. The gruel disappeared; the boys whispered to each other and winked at Oliver, while his neighbours nudged him. Child as he was, he was desperate with hunger, and reckless with misery. He rose from the table, and, advancing to the master, basin and spoon in hand, said, somewhat alarmed at his own daring, "Please, sir, I want some more."

The master was a fat, healthy man, but he turned very pale. He gazed in stupefied astonishment on the small rebel for some seconds, and then clung for support to the copper. The assistants were paralysed with wonder, the boys with fear.

"What?" said the master at length, in a faint voice.

"Please, sir," replied Oliver, "I want some more."

The master aimed a blow at Oliver's head with the ladle, seized him and shrieked aloud for the beadle.

The Board of Governors were sitting in solemn assembly, when Mr Bumble rushed into the room in great excitement, and addressing the gentleman in the armchair, said, "Mr Limbkins, I beg your pardon, sir! Oliver Twist has asked for more!" There was a general start of horror.

"For *more*?" said Mr Limbkins. "Compose yourself, Bumble, and answer me distinctly. Do I understand that he asked for more after he had eaten the supper allotted to him?"

"He did, sir," replied Bumble.

"That boy will be hung," said the gentleman in the white waistcoat. "I know that boy will be hung."

Nobody disagreed with him. A lively discussion took place. Oliver was ordered to be instantly shut away, and a notice was next morning pasted on the outside of the gate, offering a reward of five pounds to anybody who would take Oliver Twist off the hands of the parish. In other words, five pounds and Oliver Twist were offered to any man or woman who wanted an apprentice to any trade, business or calling.

"I never was more convinced of anything in my life," said the gentleman in the white waistcoat, as he knocked at the gate and read the notice the next morning. "I never was more convinced of anything in my life than I am that *that* boy will come to be hung."

CHAPTER 4

OLIVER GOES TO WORK

For a week, Oliver remained a close prisoner in the dark and lonely room to which he was sent as a punishment for asking for more. He cried bitterly all day, and when the long, dismal night came on, spread his hands before his face to shut out the darkness, and, crouching in a corner, tried to sleep, every now and then waking with a start and tremble, and drawing himself closer and closer to the wall for protection.

Mr Bumble was sent out every day to try and find someone who would take poor Oliver off the hands of the parish. He was returning after one of these expeditions, when he encountered at the gate no less a person than Mr Sowerberry, the parish undertaker.

Mr Sowerberry was a tall, gaunt, large-jointed mán, attired in a suit of threadbare black, with darned cotton stockings of the same colour, and shoes to match. His face was solemn, but suggested inward humour, and he was rather given to making jokes about his profession.

"I have taken the measure of the two women that died last night, Mr Bumble," said the undertaker.

"You'll make your fortune, Mr Sowerberry," said the beadle, as he thrust his thumb and forefinger into the snuff-box which the undertaker offered him. It was an ingenious little model of a coffin. "I say you'll make your fortune, Mr Sowerberry," repeated Mr Bumble, tapping the undertaker on the shoulder in a friendly manner with his cane.

"Think so?" said the undertaker. "The prices allowed by the Board are very small, Mr Bumble."

"So are the coffins," replied the beadle with a smile.

Mr Sowerberry was much tickled at this, and laughed a long time without stopping. "Well, well, Mr Bumble," he said at length, "there's no denying that, since the new system of feeding has come in, the coffins are something narrower and more shallow than they used to be, but we must have some profit, Mr Bumble. Well-seasoned timber is expensive, sir, and all the iron handles come by canal from Birmingham."

"Well, well," said Mr Bumble, "every trade has its drawbacks. A fair profit is, of course, allowable. By the bye, you don't know anybody who wants an apprentice do you? Liberal terms, Mr Sowerberry, liberal terms!" As Mr Bumble spoke, he raised his stick to the notice above him, and gave three distinct raps upon the words FIVE POUNDS which were printed on it in capital letters of gigantic size.

"As it happens, that's just the very thing I wanted to speak to you about," said the undertaker. "I pay a good deal towards the poor's rates, and I was thinking that if I pay so much towards 'em, I've a right to get as much out of 'em as I can, Mr Bumble, and so—and so—I think I'll take the boy myself." Mr Bumble grasped the undertaker by the arm, and led him into the building.

Mr Sowerberry was with the Board of Governors for five minutes, and it was arranged that Oliver was to go to him that evening "upon liking"—a phrase which means, in the case of a parish apprentice, that if the master finds, after a short trial, that he can get enough work out of a boy without putting too much food into him, he shall have him for a term of years, to do what he likes with.

That evening, Oliver, his cap pulled over his eyes and his few things in a brown-paper parcel in one hand, attached himself with the other hand to Mr Bumble's coat cuff, and was led away to a new scene of suffering.

Mr Bumble strode along with his head in the air, and, as it was a windy day, the skirts of his coat blew open, showing his smart waistcoat and plush knee-breeches and almost hiding Oliver from sight. As they neared their destination, he looked down at the boy to see if he was ready for inspection by his new master.

"Oliver!" said Mr Bumble.

"Yes, sir," replied Oliver in a low, trembling voice.

"Pull that cap off your eyes, and hold up your head, sir."

Although Oliver did as he was told at once, and passed the back of his free hand briskly across his eyes, he left a tear in them when he looked up at the beadle. As Mr Bumble gazed sternly upon him, it rolled down his cheek. It was followed by another and another. The child made a strong effort, but it was an unsuccessful one. Putting down his parcel, he covered his face with both hands, and wept until the tears sprang out from between his chin and bony fingers.

"Well!" exclaimed Mr Bumble, "of *all* the ungratefullest boys as ever I see, Oliver, you are the——"

"No, no, sir," sobbed Oliver, clinging to the hand which held the well-known cane. "No, no, sir! I will be good indeed. Indeed, indeed I will, sir! I am a very little boy, sir, and it is so—so——"

"So what?" inquired Mr Bumble in amazement.

"So lonely, sir! So very lonely!" cried the child. "Everybody hates me. Oh, sir, don't, don't pray be cross to me!" The child beat his hands upon his heart, and looked in his companion's face with tears of real agony.

Mr Bumble regarded Oliver's piteous look with some astonishment for a few seconds, hemmed three or four times in a husky manner, and, after muttering something about a troublesome cough, bade Oliver dry his eyes, pick up his things and be a good boy. Then, taking his hand, he walked on with him in silence.

The undertaker, who had just put up the shutters of his shop, was making some entries in his day book by the light of a suitably dismal candle, when Mr Bumble entered.

"Aha!" said the undertaker, looking up from the book and pausing in the middle of a word. "Is that you, Bumble?"

"No one else, Mr Sowerberry," replied the beadle. "Here! I've brought the boy." Oliver made a bow.

"Oh! That's the boy, is it?" said the undertaker, raising the candle above his head, to get a better view of Oliver. "Mrs Sowerberry, will you have the goodness to come here a moment, my dear?"

Mrs Sowerberry emerged from a little room behind the shop, and presented the form of a short, thin, squeezed-up woman with a vixenish countenance.

"My dear," said Mr Sowerberry respectfully, "this is the boy from the workhouse that I told you of." Oliver bowed again.

"Dear me!" said the undertaker's wife, "he's very small."

"Why, he *is* rather small," replied Mr Bumble, looking at Oliver as if it was his fault he was no bigger, "he *is* small. There's no denying it. But he'll grow, Mrs Sowerberry—he'll grow."

"Ah! I dare say he will," replied the lady peevishly, "on our food and our drink. I see no saving in parish children, not I, for they almost cost more to keep than they're worth. However, men always think they know best. There! Get downstairs, little bag o' bones." With this, the undertaker's wife opened a side door and pushed Oliver down a steep flight of stairs into a stone cell, damp and dark, forming the ante-room to the coal-cellar, and named "kitchen". In it sat a slatternly girl, in shoes down at heel, and blue worsted stockings very much out of repair.

"Here, Charlotte," said Mrs Sowerberry, who had followed Oliver down, "give this boy some of the cold bits that were put by for Trip. He hasn't come home since the morning, so he may go without 'em. I dare say the boy isn't too dainty to eat 'em—are you, boy?"

Oliver, whose eyes had glistened at the mention of meat, answered that he was not, and a plateful of coarse broken pieces was set before him which he devoured with all the ferocity of famine.

"Well," said the undertaker's wife, when Oliver had finished his supper, "have you finished?"

There being nothing eatable within his reach, Oliver replied that he had.

"Then come with me," said Mrs Sowerberry, taking up a dim and dirty lamp, and leading the way upstairs. "Your bed's under the counter. You don't mind sleeping among the coffins, I suppose? But it doesn't matter whether you do or don't, for you can't sleep anywhere else. Come, don't keep me here all night!"

Oliver lingered no longer, but meekly followed his new mistress.

CHAPTER 5

NOAH CLAYPOLE—A BULLY

Oliver, being left to himself in the undertaker's shop, set the lamp down on a workman's bench and gazed timidly about him with a feeling of awe and dread. An unfinished coffin on black trestles, which stood in the middle of the shop, looked so gloomy and death-like that a cold tremble came over him every time his eyes wandered in the direction of the dismal object, from which he almost expected to see some frightful form slowly raise its head, to drive him mad with terror.

Against the wall were ranged, in regular array, a long row of elm boards cut into the same shape, looking, in the dim light, iike high-shouldered ghosts with their hands in their breeches pockets. Coffin-plates, elm-chips, bright-headed nails and shreds of black cloth lay scattered on the floor, and there was a picture on the wall behind the counter of a hearse drawn by four black horses. The shop was close and hot. The atmosphere seemed tainted with the smell of coffins. The space beneath the counter, into which his flock mattress was thrust, looked like a grave. Oliver's heart was heavy, and he wished, as he crept into his narrow bed, that it really *was* his coffin, and that he could be laid in a calm and lasting sleep in the churchyard ground, with the tall grass waving gently above his head, and the sound of the old deep bell to soothe him in his sleep.

He was awakened in the morning by a loud kicking at the outside of the shop door. Before he could pull on his clothes, this was repeated in an angry and hasty manner, about twenty-five times. When he began to undo the door-chain, the legs stopped, and a voice began.

"Open the door, will yer?" cried the voice which belonged to the legs which had kicked at the door.

"I will directly, sir," replied Oliver, undoing the chain and turning the key.

"I suppose yer the new boy, ain't yer?" said the voice through the key-hole.

"Yes, sir," replied Oliver.

"How old are yer?" inquired the voice.

"Ten, sir," replied Oliver.

"Then I'll whop yer when I get in," said the voice. "You just see if I don't, that's all, my work'us brat!" And having made this obliging promise, the voice began to whistle.

Oliver drew back the bolts with a trembling hand and opened the door.

For a second or two, he glanced up the street, and down the street, and over the way, believing that the unknown person who had spoken to him through the key-hole had walked a few paces off to warm himself, for nobody did he see but a big charity-boy, sitting on a post in front of the house, eating a slice of bread and butter which he cut into wedges, the size of his mouth, with a clasp knife, and then ate with great skill.

"I beg your pardon, sir," said Oliver at length, seeing that no other visitor made his appearance, "did you knock?"

"I kicked," replied the charity-boy.

"Did you want a coffin, sir?" inquired Oliver innocently. At this the charity-boy looked monstrous fierce, and said that Oliver would want one before long, if he cut jokes with his superior in that way.

"Yer don't know who I am, I suppose, Work'us?" said the charity-boy, descending from the top of the post.

"No, sir," rejoined Oliver.

"I'm Mister Noah Claypole," said the charity-boy, "and you're under me. Take down the shutters, yer idle young ruffian!" With this, Mr Claypole kicked Oliver and entered the shop with a dignified air which did him great credit. It is difficult for a large-headed, small-eyed youth of lumbering make and heavy countenance, to look dignified under any circumstances, but it is more especially so, when added to these personal attractions are a red nose and yellow leather breeches.

Noah Claypole went down the stairs to breakfast, and Oliver, having taken down the heavy shutters, followed him.

"Come near the fire, Noah," said Charlotte. "I saved a nice little bit of bacon for you from master's breakfast. Oliver, shut that door at Mr Noah's back, and take them bits that I've put out on the cover of the bread-pan. There's your tea. Take it away to that box, and drink it there, and make haste, for they'll want you to mind the shop. D'ye hear?"

"D'ye hear. Work'us?" said Noah Claypole.

"Lor, Noah!" said Charlotte. "What a rum creature you are! Why don't you let the boy alone?"

"Let him alone!" said Noah. "Why, everybody lets him alone enough, for the matter of that. Neither his father nor his mother will ever interfere with him. All his relations let him have his own way pretty well. Eh, Charlotte? He! He! He!"

"Oh, you queer soul!" said Charlotte, bursting into a hearty laugh, in which she was joined by Noah. After this, they both looked scornfully at poor Oliver Twist, as he sat shivering on the box in the coldest corner of the room and ate the stale bits of food which had been specially put by for him.

Noah was a charity-boy, but not a workhouse orphan. His mother was a washerwoman and his father a drunken soldier, discharged with a wooden leg and small pension. The shop-boys in the neighbourhood had long been in the habit of shouting "Charity-boy!" at Noah when they saw him in the street; he had borne it without reply, but now that fortune had cast in his way a nameless orphan, at whom even the poorest could point the finger of scorn, he made Oliver pay for his own suffering.

Oliver had been living at the undertaker's some three weeks

or a month. Mr and Mrs Sowerberry—the shop being shut up —were taking their supper in the little back parlour when Mr Sowerberry remarked, "A very good-looking boy, that young Twist, my dear."

"He needs be, for he eats enough," replied the lady.

"There's an expression of melancholy in his face, my dear," resumed Mr Sowerberry, "which is very interesting. He would make a delightful mute, my love."

Mrs Sowerberry looked up with an expression of considerable wonderment. Mr Sowerberry noticed it, and before she could contradict him, went on, "I don't mean a regular mute to follow grown-up people's coffins, my dear, but for children's funerals. You may depend upon it, it would have a superb effect."

Mrs Sowerberry was much struck by the novelty of this idea, but, as it would have been beneath her dignity to have said so, she merely inquired, with much sharpness, why her husband had not thought of it before.

Mr Sowerberry rightly understood by this that she approved of the suggestion, and it was speedily decided that Oliver should make a start as soon as possible.

CHAPTER 6

OLIVER TEACHES NOAH A LESSON

The month's trial over, Oliver was formally apprenticed. He had acquired a great deal of experience, for the oldest inhabitants recollected no period during which more infants had died of measles. Many were the mournful processions which little Oliver headed, in a hat-band reaching down to his knees, and he was much admired.

Noah Claypole treated him far worse than before, now that his jealousy was roused by seeing the new boy promoted to the black stick and hat-band, while he, the old one, was still in his muffin-cap and leather breeches. Charlotte treated him badly because Noah did, and Mrs Sowerberry was his decided enemy because Mr Sowerberry was, on the whole, his friend, so between these three on one side, and a glut of funerals on the other, Oliver was not altogether as comfortable as he might have been.

One day Oliver and Noah had gone down to the kitchen at the usual dinner-hour, when Charlotte was called upstairs, and Noah decided to use the time they had to wait to tease Oliver in his usual vicious way. He put his feet on the tablecloth and pulled Oliver's hair, and twitched his ears, said that he was a sneak and that he would be glad to see him hanged whenever that desirable event should take place. Finding that he could not make Oliver cry, he got rather personal.

"Work'us," said Noah, "how's your mother?"

"She's dead," replied Oliver. "Don't you say anything about her to me!"

Oliver's colour rose as he said this, he breathed quickly and there was a curious movement of the mouth and nostrils which made Noah think he was going to cry. Under this impression, he returned to the attack.

"What did she die of, Work'us?" said Noah.

"Of a broken heart, some of our old nurses told me," replied Oliver, more as if he were talking to himself than answering Noah. "I think I know what it must be to die of that."

"Tol de rol lol lol, right fol lairy, Work'us," said Noah, as a tear rolled down Oliver's cheek. "What's set you a-snivelling now?"

"Not *you*," replied Oliver, hastily brushing the tear away. "Don't think it."

"Oh, not me, eh!" sneered Noah.

"No, not you," replied Oliver sharply. "There, that's enough. Don't say anything more to me about her; you'd better not!"

"Better not!" exclaimed Noah. "Well! Better not! Work'us, don't be impudent. *Your* mother, too! She was a nice 'un, she was. Oh lor!" And here, Noah nodded his head expressively, and curled up his small red nose.

"Yer know, Work'us," continued Noah, made bold by Oliver's silence, and speaking in a jeering tone of pretending pity, "yer know, Work'us, it can't be helped now, and of course yer couldn't help it then, and I'm very sorry for it, and I'm sure we all are, and pity yer very much. But yer must know, Work'us, yer mother was a regular right-down bad'un."

"What did you say?" inquired Oliver, looking up very quickly.

"A regular right-down bad'un, Work'us," replied Noah coolly. "And it's a great deal better, Work'us, that she died when she did, or else she'd have been doing hard labour in prison, or transported, or hung, which is more likely than either, isn't it?"

Crimson with fury, Oliver jumped up, overthrew the chair and table, seized Noah by the throat, shook him in the violence of his rage till his teeth chattered in his head, and, collecting his whole force into one heavy blow, felled him to the ground.

"He'll murder me!" blubbered Noah. "Charlotte! Missis! Here's the new boy a-murdering of me! Help! Help! Oliver's gone mad! Char-lotte!"

Noah's shouts were responded to by a loud scream from Charlotte and a louder one from Mrs Sowerberry. Charlotte rushed into the kitchen by a side door, while Mrs Sowerberry paused on the staircase till it was quite certain that it was safe to come down.

"Oh, you little wretch!" screamed Charlotte, seizing Oliver with her utmost force. "Oh you little un-grate-ful, mur-de-rous, hor-rid villain!"

And between every syllable, Charlotte gave Oliver a blow with all her might, accompanying it with a scream.

Charlotte's fist was by no means a light one, but, in case she needed help, Mrs Sowerberry plunged into the kitchen, and assisted to hold Oliver with one hand, while she scratched his face with the other. Taking advantage of the situation, Noah rose from the ground and pummelled him from behind.

This was rather too violent exercise to last long. When they were all wearied out, and could tear and beat no longer, they dragged Oliver, struggling and shouting, into the dust-cellar, and there locked him up. This being done, Mrs Sowerberry sank into a chair and burst into tears.

"Bless her, she's going off!" said Charlotte. "A glass of water, Noah dear. Make haste."

"Oh, Charlotte," said Mrs Sowerberry, speaking as well as she could, through too little breath, and too much cold water, which Noah had poured over her head and shoulders. "Oh,

21

Charlotte, what a mercy we have not all been murdered in our beds!"

"Ah, mercy indeed, ma'am," was the reply. "I hope this'll teach master not to have any more of these dreadful creatures, that are born to be murderers and robbers from their very cradle. Poor Noah! He was all but killed, ma'am, when I come in."

"Poor fellow!" said Mrs Sowerberry, looking piteously on the charity-boy.

Noah, whose top waistcoat button might have been somewhere on a level with the crown of Oliver's head, rubbed his eyes with the insides of his wrists and performed some affecting tears and sniffs.

"What's to be done?" exclaimed Mrs Sowerberry. "Your master's not at home; there's not a man in the house, and he'll kick that door down in ten minutes." Oliver's vigorous plunges and bangs rendered this highly likely.

"Dear, dear! I don't know, ma'am," said Charlotte, "unless we send for the police-officers."

"Or the soldiers," suggested Noah.

"No, no," said Mrs Sowerberry. "Run to Mr Bumble, Noah, and tell him to come here at once, and not to lose a minute. Never mind your cap. Make haste! You can hold a knife to that black eye as you run along. The cold will keep the swelling down."

Noah did not stop to answer, but started off at his fullest speed, and very much astonished the people who were out walking, to see a charity-boy tearing through the streets, with no cap on his head, and a clasp-knife at his eye.

CHAPTER 7

A BEATING

Noah Claypole ran along the streets at his swiftest pace, and paused not once for breath until he reached the workhouse gate. Having rested there for a minute or so, to collect a good burst of sobs and an impressive show of tears and terror, he knocked loudly and presented such a miserable face to the aged inmate who opened it that even he, who saw nothing but miserable faces around him at the best of times, stepped back in astonishment.

"Why, what's the matter with the boy?" said the old man.

"Mr Bumble! Mr Bumble!" cried Noah, in tones so loud and agitated that they not only caught the ear of Mr Bumble himself, who happened to be near by, but alarmed him so much that he rushed into the yard without his cocked hat.

"Oh, Mr Bumble, sir!" said Noah. "Oliver, sir—Oliver has——"

"What? What?" said Mr Bumble, with a gleam of pleasure in his metallic eyes. "Not run away; he hasn't run away, has he, Noah?"

"No, sir, no. Not run away, sir, but he's turned wicious," replied Noah. "He tried to murder me, sir, and then he tried to murder Charlotte, and then missis. Oh, what a dreadful pain it is! Such agony, please, sir!" Here Noah writhed and twisted his body like an eel, and when he observed a gentleman in a white waistcoat crossing the yard, wailed more tragically than ever, hoping to attract his attention.

The gentleman had not walked three paces, when he turned angrily round and inquired what that young cur was howling for, and why Mr Bumble did not give him something to cry about.

"It's a poor boy from the free-school, sir," replied Mr Bumble, "who has been nearly murdered—all but murdered—sir, by young Oliver Twist."

"By Jove!" exclaimed the gentleman in the white waistcoat, stopping short. "I knew it! I always knew that that audacious young savage would come to be hung!"

"He has likewise attempted, sir, to murder the female servant," said Mr Bumble, with a face of ashy paleness.

"And his missis," added Noah.

"And his master, too, I think you said, Noah," suggested Mr Bumble.

"No, he's out, or he would have murdered him," replied Noah. "He said he wanted to."

"Ah, said he wanted to, did he, my boy?" inquired the gentleman in the white waistcoat.

"Yes, sir," replied Noah. "And please, sir, missis wants to

know whether Mr Bumble can spare time to step up there now, and flog him—'cause master's out."

"Certainly, my boy, certainly," said the gentleman in the white waistcoat, smiling and patting Noah's head, which was about three inches higher than his own. "You're a good boy—a very good boy. Here's a penny for you. Bumble, just step up to Sowerberry's with your cane, and see what's best to be done. Don't spare him, Bumble."

"No, I will not, sir," replied the beadle, adjusting the wax-end which was twisted round the bottom of his cane.

Mr Bumble and Noah Claypole betook themselves with all speed to the undertaker's shop, where matters had not at all improved. Mr Sowerberry had not yet returned, and Oliver continued to kick strongly at the cellar door. Mr Bumble kicked the door from the outside, and then, putting his mouth to the keyhole, said in a deep, impressive voice, "Oliver!"

"Let me out," replied Oliver from the inside.

"Do you know this here voice, Oliver?" said Mr Bumble.

"Yes," replied Oliver.

"Ain't you afraid of it? Ain't you a-trembling while I speak?" said Mr Bumble.

"No!" replied Oliver boldly.

Mr Bumble stepped back from the keyhole, drew himself up to his full height, and looked from one to another of the three bystanders in astonishment.

At this moment Mr Sowerberry returned, and Oliver's behaviour having been explained to him by Mrs Sowerberry and Charlotte, and made to sound as wicked as possible, he unlocked the cellar-door in a twinkling, and dragged his rebellious apprentice out by the collar.

Oliver's clothes had been torn in the beating he had received, his face was bruised and scratched, and his hair scattered over his forehead. The angry flush had not disappeared, however, and when he was pulled out of his prison he scowled boldly at Noah and looked quite undismayed.

"You are a nice young fellow, ain't you?" said Mr Sowerberry, giving Oliver a shake, and a box on the ear.

"He called my mother names," replied Oliver.

"Well, and what if he did, you little ungrateful wretch?" said Mrs Sowerberry. "She deserved what he said, and worse."

"She didn't," said Oliver.

"She did," said Mrs Sowerberry.

"It's a lie," said Oliver.

Mrs Sowerberry burst into a flood of tears.

This flood of tears left Mr Sowerberry no choice. He at once gave Oliver a beating, which satisfied even Mrs Sowerberry and rendered Mr Bumble's caning which followed rather unnecessary. For the rest of the day, Oliver was shut up in the back kitchen, in company with a pump and a slice of bread, and at night Mrs Sowerberry looked into the room, and, amidst the jeers and pointings of Noah and Charlotte, ordered him upstairs to his dismal bed.

It was not until he was left alone in the silence and stillness of the gloomy workshop that Oliver gave way to his feelings. Now, when there were none to see nor hear him, he fell upon his knees on the floor, and hiding his face in his hands, wept such tears to God as few so young have ever had cause to pour out before him.

For a long time, Oliver remained motionless in this attitude. The candle was burning low in the socket when he rose to his feet. Having gazed cautiously around him, and listened intently, he gently undid the fastening of the door and looked out.

It was a cold, dark night. The stars seemed, to the boy's eyes, farther from the earth than he had ever seen them before. There was no wind, and the sombre shadows thrown by the trees upon the ground looked sepulchral and deathlike, from being so still. He softly reclosed the door, and, tying up in a handkerchief, by the light of the dying candle, the few articles of clothing he had, sat himself down upon a bench to wait for morning.

CHAPTER 8

ON THE ROAD TO LONDON

With the first ray of light that struggled through the crevices in the shutters, Oliver arose, and again unbarred the door. One timid look around—one moment's pause of hesitation—then he had closed it behind him, and was in the open street.

Oliver looked to the right and to the left, uncertain which way to run. He remembered having seen the wagons, as they went out, toiling up the hill. He took the same route, and after walking for over an hour reached the high-road.

It was eight o'clock now. Though he was nearly five miles away from the town, he ran, and hid behind the hedges, by turns, till noon, fearing that he might be pursued and over-taken. Then he sat down to rest by the side of a milestone, and began to think, for the first time, where he had better go and try to live.

The stone by which he was seated told him, in large characters, that it was just seventy miles from that spot to London. London!—that great place! Nobody—not even Mr Bumble—could ever find him there! He had often heard the old men in the workhouse, too, say that no lad of spirit need starve in London, and that there were ways of living in that vast city which those who had been bred up in country parts had no idea of. It was the very place for a homeless boy, who would die in the streets unless someone helped him. As these things passed through his thoughts, he jumped to his feet and again walked forward.

He had gone four miles before he recollected how much he must undergo before he could hope to reach his destination. As he began to realise this, he slackened his pace a little, and thought about the means of getting there. He had a crust of bread, a rough shirt, and two pairs of stockings in his bundle. He had a penny, too, in his pocket, which Mr Sowerberry had given him one day after he had done especially well at some funeral.

"A clean shirt," thought Oliver, "is a comfortable thing, and so are two pairs of darned stockings, and so is a penny, but they are small helps to a sixty-five miles' walk in winter-time." After a good deal of thinking, which brought no solution to his problem, Oliver changed his little bundle over to the other shoulder and trudged on.

Oliver walked twenty miles that day, and all that time tasted nothing but the crust of dry bread, and a few drinks of water which he begged at the cottage-doors by the roadside. When the night came, he turned into a meadow, and, creeping close under a hay-rick, decided to lie there until morning. He felt frightened at first, for the wind moaned dismally over the empty fields, and he was cold and hungry, and more alone than he had ever felt before. Being very tired, however, he soon fell asleep and forgot his troubles.

He felt cold and stiff when he got up next morning, and was so hungry that he was obliged to exchange the penny for a small loaf in the very first village through which he passed. He had only walked twelve miles, when night closed in again. His feet were sore, and his legs so weak that they trembled beneath him. Another night passed in the bleak, damp air, made him worse; when he set forward on his journey next morning, he could hardly crawl along.

He waited at the bottom of a steep hill till a stage-coach came up, and then begged of the outside passengers, but there were very few who took any notice of him, and even those told him to wait till they got to the top of the hill, and then let them see how far he could run for a halfpenny. Poor Oliver tried to keep up with the coach a little way, but was unable to do it, because he was so tired, and his feet were so sore. When the outside passengers saw this, they put their halfpence back into their pockets again, declaring that he was an idle young dog and didn't deserve anything; and the coach rattled away and left only a cloud of dust behind. If it had not been for one or two kinder people who saw Oliver struggling through their villages and gave him food, he would surely have fallen dead upon the King's highway.

CHAPTER 9

INTRODUCING THE ARTFUL DODGER

Early on the seventh morning after he had left Mr Sowerberry's, Oliver limped slowly into the little town of Barnet. The window-shutters were closed; the street was empty; not a soul had awakened to the business of the day. The sun was rising in all its splendid beauty, but the light only served to show the boy his own lonesomeness and desolation, as he sat, with bleeding feet and covered with dust, upon a doorstep.

27

By degrees, the shutters were opened, the window-blinds were drawn. up, and people began passing to and fro. Some few stopped to gaze at Oliver for a moment or two, or turned round to stare at him as they hurried by, but no one asked if he needed help or troubled themselves to inquire how he came there. He had no heart to beg, and there he sat.

After a while, he noticed that a boy who had passed him some minutes before had returned and was staring at him from the opposite side of the way. Oliver paid no attention at first, but the boy continued to stare until Oliver raised his head and returned his steady look. Upon this, the boy crossed over and, walking close up to Oliver, said, "Hullo, my covey! What's the row?"

He was about his own age, but one of the queerest-looking boys that Oliver had ever seen. He was a snub-nosed, flat-browed, common-faced boy, and as dirty a child as one would wish to see, but he had about him all the airs and manners of a man.

He was short for his age, with rather bow-legs, and little sharp, ugly eyes. His hat was stuck on the top of his head so lightly that it threatened to fall off every moment, and would have done so, very often, if he had not given his head a sudden twitch every now and then, and brought it back to its old place again.

This boy wore a man's coat which reached nearly to his heels. He had turned the cuffs back, half-way up his arm to get his hands out of the sleeves, so that he could thrust them into the pockets of his corduroy trousers, and there he kept them. He was, altogether, as roistering and swaggering a young gentleman as ever stood four feet six, or something less, in his boots.

"Hullo, my covey! What's the row?" said this strange young gentleman to Oliver.

"I am very hungry and tired," replied Oliver, the tears standing in his eyes as he spoke. "I have walked a long way. I have been walking for seven days."

"You want grub," said the young gentleman, "and you shall have it. I'm at low-water-mark myself—only one bob and a magpie, but, *as* far *as* it goes, I'll fork out for you. Up with you on your pins. There! Now then!"

Assisting Oliver to rise, the young gentleman took him to a nearby chandler's shop, and pulling out a shilling and a halfpenny, which was all he had, purchased some ham and a half-quartern loaf, the ham being kept clean by making a hole in the loaf, pulling out a portion of the crumb, and stuffing it inside. Taking the bread under his arm, the young gentleman turned into a small public-house and led the way to a tap-room in the rear of the premises. Here the mysterious youth ordered a pot of beer, and told Oliver to start eating. Oliver made a long and hearty meal, during which the strange boy eyed him from time to time with great attention.

"Going to London?" said the strange boy, when Oliver had finished eating.

"Yes."

"Got any lodgings?"

"No."

"Money?"

"No."

The strange boy whistled, and put his arms into his pockets, as far as the big sleeves would let them go.

"Do you live in London?" inquired Oliver.

"Yes I do, when I'm at home," replied the boy. "I suppose you want some place to sleep in tonight, don't you?"

"I do indeed," answered Oliver. "I have not slept under a roof since I left the country."

"Don't fret your eyelids on that score," said the young gentleman. "I've got to be in London tonight, and I know a 'spectable old genelman as lives there, what'll give you lodgings for nothink; and never ask for the change—that is, if any genelman he knows interduces you. And don't he know me? Oh no! Not in the least! By no means. Certainly not!"

The young gentleman smiled, as if to show that he was joking, and finished the beer as he did so.

This unexpected offer of shelter was too tempting to be resisted, although Oliver's new friend, who was called Jack Dawkins, bore the nickname of "The Artful Dodger", and had a rather flighty manner of speech.

As Jack Dawkins, for reasons of his own, did not wish to enter London before nightfall, it was nearly eleven o'clock when they reached the turnpike at Islington. They crossed from the Angel into St John's Road, went down the small street which ends at Sadler's Wells Theatre, then through a maze of streets until they reached Little Saffron Hill, and so into Saffron Hill the Great, along which the Dodger scudded at a rapid pace, telling Oliver to follow close at his heels.

The street was narrow and muddy, and the air was filled with filthy smells. Even at that time of night, children were crawling in and out of doors or screaming from the insides of the houses and shops. The public houses were filled with drunken men and women, and suspicious-looking people were to be seen setting out on far from harmless errands.

Oliver was just considering whether he hadn't better run away, when they reached the bottom of the hill. His companion, catching him by the arm, pushed open the door of a house near Field Lane, and, drawing him into the passage, closed it behind them.

"Now then!" cried a voice from below, in reply to a whistle from the Dodger.

"Plummy and Slam!" was the reply.

This seemed to be some watchword or signal that all was right, for the light of a feeble candle gleamed on the wall at the far end of the passage, and a man's face peeped out, from where a balustrade of the old kitchen staircase had been broken away.

"There's two of you," said the man, thrusting the candle forward, and shading his eyes with his hand. "Who's the other one?"

"A new pal," replied Jack Dawkins. "Is Fagin upstairs?"

"Yes, he's sortin' the wipes. Up with you!" The candle was drawn back, and the face disappeared.

Oliver, groping his way with one hand, and having the other firmly grasped by his companion, climbed with much difficulty the dark and broken stairs, which the Dodger mounted with an ease and speed that showed he knew them well. He threw open the door of a back-room and drew Oliver in after him.

The walls and ceiling of the room were perfectly black with age and dirt. There was a table before the fire upon which were a candle, stuck in a ginger-beer bottle, two or three pewter pots, a loaf and butter, and a plate. In a frying pan, which was on the fire, and which was secured to the mantel-shelf by a string, some sausages were cooking, and standing over them, with a toasting-fork in his hand, was a very old shrivelled Jew, whose villainous-looking face was hidden by a quantity of matted red hair. He was dressed in a greasy flannel gown, with his throat bare, and seemed to be dividing his attention between the frying-pan and a clothes-horse, over which a great number of silk handkerchiefs were hanging. Several rough beds made of old sacks were huddled side by side on the floor. Seated round the table were four or five boys, none older than the Dodger, smoking long clay pipes and drinking spirits with the air of middle-aged men. These all crowded round Jack Dawkins as he whispered a few words to the Jew, and then turned round and grinned at Oliver. So did the old man himself, toasting-fork in hand.

"This is him, Fagin," said the Dodger, "my friend Oliver Twist."

Fagin grinned, and, making a low bow to Oliver, took him by the hands and hoped he would have the honour of his friendship.

At this, the boys with the pipes came round him, and shook both his hands very hard—especially the one in which he he held his little bundle. One was very anxious to hang his cap up for him, and another put his hands in Oliver's pockets, in order that, as he was very tired, he might not have the trouble of emptying them himself when he went to bed. At length, Fagin rapped the boys with the toasting-fork, and they left him in peace.

"We are very glad to see you, Oliver, very," said Fagin. "Dodger, take off the sausages, and draw a stool near the fire for Oliver. Ah, you're staring at the pocket-handkerchiefs, eh, my dear? There are a good many of 'em, ain't there? We've just looked 'em out, ready for the wash, that's all, Oliver, that's all. Ha! Ha! Ha!"

The last part of his speech was hailed by a boisterous shout from all the pupils of the merry old gentleman, in the midst of which, they went to supper.

Oliver ate his share, and the old man then mixed him a glass of hot gin and water, telling him he must drink it up straight-away, because another boy wanted the glass. Oliver did as he was asked. Immediately afterwards he felt himself gently lifted on to one of the sacks, and then he sank into a deep sleep.

CHAPTER 10

OLIVER LEARNS A NEW TRADE

It was late next morning when Oliver awoke from a sound, long sleep. There was no other person in the room but the old man, who was boiling some coffee in a saucepan for breakfast, and whistling softly to himself as he stirred it round and round with an iron spoon. He would stop every now and then to listen when there was the least noise below, and when he had satisfied himself, he would go on, whistling and stirring again as before.

Although Oliver had roused himself from sleep, he was not thoroughly awake. He saw Fagin through half-closed eyes, heard his low whistling, and recognised the sound of the spoon grating against the saucepan's sides, and yet, at the same time, he seemed to be still in his dreams among all the people of his past life.

When the coffee was done, the old man drew the saucepan to the hob. Hesitating for a few minutes, as if he did not quite well know what to do, he turned round and looked at Oliver, and called him by his name. Oliver did not answer, and seemed to be asleep.

Satisfied, Fagin stepped gently to the door, which he fastened. He then drew forth, as it seemed to Oliver, from beneath a trap-door in the floor, a small box, which he placed carefully on the table. His eyes glistened as he raised the lid and looked in. Dragging an old chair to the table, he sat down, and took from the box a magnificent gold watch, sparkling with jewels.

"Ah!" said Fagin, shrugging up his shoulders, and making a hideous grin. "Clever dogs! Clever dogs! Staunch to the last! Never told where the jewels were. Never peached upon old Fagin! And why should they? It wouldn't have saved them from hanging. No, no, no! Fine fellows! Fine fellows!"

Muttering such thoughts aloud, the old man once more hid

the watch in a place of safety. At least half a dozen more were drawn in turn from the same box, and looked at with equal pleasure, besides rings, brooches, bracelets and other articles of jewellery, of such magnificent materials and costly workmanship that Oliver had no idea even of their names.

Fagin replaced these trinkets, and glanced at Oliver. The boy's eyes were fixed on his in silent curiosity, and it was enough to show the old man that he had been observed. He closed the lid of the box with a loud crash and, laying his hand on a bread knife which was on the table, started furiously up. He trembled very much, though, for, even in his terror, Oliver could see that the knife quivered in the air.

"What do you watch me for?" said Fagin. "Why are you awake. What have you seen? Speak out, boy! Quick—quick, for your life!"

"I wasn't able to sleep any longer, sir," replied Oliver meekly. "I am very sorry if I have disturbed you, sir."

"You were not awake an hour ago?" said Fagin, scowling fiercely on the boy.

"No! No, indeed!" replied Oliver.

"Are you sure?" cried Fagin, with a still fiercer look than before, and a threatening attitude.

"Upon my word I was not, sir," replied Oliver earnestly. "I was not indeed, sir."

"Tush, tush, my dear!" said the old man, abruptly resuming his old manner, and playing with the knife a little before he laid it down, as if to make believe that he had caught it up in mere sport. "Of course I know that, my dear. I only tried to frighten you. You are a brave boy, Oliver!" Fagin rubbed his hands with a chuckle, but glanced uneasily at the box just the same.

"Did you see any of these pretty things, my dear?" said the old man, laying his hand upon it after a short pause.

"Yes, sir," replied Oliver.

"Ah!" said Fagin, turning rather pale. "They—they're mine, Oliver, my little property. All I have to live upon in my old age. The folks call me a miser, my dear. Only a miser, that's all."

Oliver thought the gentleman must be a decided miser to live in such a dirty place, with so many watches, but thinking that perhaps his fondness for the Dodger and the other boys cost him a good deal of money, he only cast a respectful look at Fagin, and asked if he might get up.

"Certainly, my dear, certainly," replied the old gentleman. "There's a pitcher of water by the door. Bring it here, and I'll give you a basin to wash in, my dear."

Oliver got up, walked across the room and stooped for an instant to raise the pitcher. When he turned his head, the box was gone.

He had scarcely washed himself, and made everything tidy —by emptying the basin out of the window, in obedience to Fagin's directions—when the Dodger returned, accompanied by a very sprightly young friend, whom Oliver had seen smoking on the previous night, and who was now formally introduced to him as Charley Bates. The four sat down to breakfast on the coffee, and some hot rolls and ham which the Dodger had brought home in the crown of his hat.

"Well," said Fagin, glancing slyly at Oliver, and addressing himself to the Dodger. "I hope you've been at work this morning, my dears."

"Hard," replied the Dodger.

"As nails," added Charley Bates.

"Good boys, good boys!" said Fagin. "What have *you* got, Dodger?"

"A couple of pocket-books," replied that young gentleman.

"Lined?" inquired Fagin with eagerness.

"Pretty well," said the Dodger, producing two pocket-books, one green and the other red.

"Not so heavy as they might be," said Fagin, after looking at the insides carefully, "but very neat and nicely made. Clever workman, ain't he, Oliver?"

"Very, indeed, sir," said Oliver. At which Charley Bates laughed uproariously, very much to the amazement of Oliver, who saw nothing to laugh at in anything that had passed.

"And what have you got, my dear?" said Fagin to Charley Bates.

"Wipes," replied Charley, at the same time producing four pocket-handkerchiefs.

"Well," said Fagin, inspecting them closely, "they're very good ones, very. You haven't marked them well, though, Charley, so the marks shall be picked out with a needle, and we'll teach Oliver how to do it. Shall us, Oliver, eh? Ha! Ha! Ha!"

"If you please, sir," said Oliver.

"You'd like to be able to make pocket-handkerchiefs as easy as Charley Bates, wouldn't you, my dear?" said Fagin.

"Very much indeed, if you'll teach me, sir," replied Oliver.

Charley Bates burst into another laugh which, meeting the coffee he was drinking and carrying it down the wrong way, very nearly ended in his early suffocation.

"He is so jolly green!" said Charley when he recovered, as an apology to the company for his unpolite behaviour.

The Dodger said nothing, but he smoothed Oliver's hair over his eyes, and said he'd know better by-and-bye. Oliver began to grow rather pink, and couldn't imagine why they seemed to be laughing at him.

When the breakfast was cleared away, the merry old gentleman and the boys played at a very curious and uncommon game, which was performed in this way. The merry old gentleman, placing a snuff-box in one pocket of his trousers, a note-case in the other, and a watch in his waistcoat pocket, with a guard-chain round his neck, and sticking a mock diamond pin in his shirt, buttoned his coat round him, and, putting his spectacle-case and a handkerchief in his pockets, trotted up and down the room with a stick, in imitation of the manner in which old gentlemen walk about the streets any hour in the day. Sometimes he stopped at the fire-place, and sometimes at the door, making believe that he was staring with all his might into shop-windows. At such times he would look constantly round him, for fear of thieves, and would keep slapping all his pockets in turn, to see that he hadn't lost anything, in such a very funny and natural manner that Oliver laughed until the tears ran down his face. All this time, the two boys followed him closely about, getting out of his sight so nimbly every time he turned round that it was impossible to follow their movements. At last, the Dodger trod upon his toes, or ran upon his boot accidentally, while Charley Bates stumbled up against him behind, and in that one moment they took from him, with the most extraordinary speed, snuff-box, note-case, watch-guard, chain, shirt-pin, pocket-handkerchief, even the spectacle-case. If the old gentleman felt a hand in any one of his pockets, he cried out where it was, and then the game began all over again.

When this game had been played a great many times, a

couple of young ladies called to see the boys; one of them was named Bet, and the other Nancy. They wore a good deal of hair, not very neatly turned up behind, and were rather untidy about the shoes and stockings. They were not exactly pretty, perhaps, but they had a great deal of colour in their faces, and looked quite stout and hearty. They were remarkably free and agreeable in their manners, and Oliver thought them very nice girls indeed. After a time spent in drinking spirits and joking together, the Dodger and Charley and the two young ladies went off together, having been kindly provided by Fagin with money to spend.

"There, my dear," said Fagin, "that's a pleasant life, isn't it? They have gone out for the day."

"Have they finished work, sir?" inquired Oliver.

"Yes," said Fagin, "that is, unless they should unexpectedly come across any when they are out, and they won't neglect it if they do, my dear, depend upon it. Make 'em your models, my dear. Make 'em your models"—tapping the fire-shovel on the hearth to add force to his words. "Do everything they bid you, and take their advice in all matters—especially the Dodger's, my dear. He'll be a great man himself, and will make you one, too, if you copy him.—Is my handkerchief hanging out of my pocket, my dear?" said Fagin, stopping short.

"Yes, sir," said Oliver.

"See if you can take it out, without my feeling it, as you saw them do, when we were at play this morning."

Oliver held up the bottom of the pocket with one hand, as he had seen the Dodger hold it, and drew the handkerchief lightly out of it with the other.

"Is it gone?" cried the old gentleman.

"Here it is, sir," said Oliver, showing it in his hand.

"You're a clever boy, my dear," said Fagin, patting Oliver on the head approvingly. "I never saw a sharper lad. Here's a shilling for you. If you go on in this way, you'll be the greatest man of the time. And now come here, and I'll show you how to take the marks out of the handkerchiefs."

Oliver wondered what picking the old gentleman's pocket had to do with his chances of being a great man, but thinking that Fagin, being so much older than himself, must know best, he followed him quietly to the table and was soon learning his new lesson.

CHAPTER 11

ARRESTED!

For many days, Oliver remained in Fagin's room, picking the marks out of the pocket-handkerchiefs (of which a great number were brought home), and sometimes taking part in the game already described, which the two boys and their master played regularly every morning. At length, he began to long for fresh air, and begged the old gentleman more than once to allow him to go out to work with his two companions.

At length one morning he was given permission, and the three boys left the house; Charley Bates, the Dodger with his coat sleeves tucked up and his hat cocked as usual, and Oliver between them, wondering where they were going, and what they would do first.

They sauntered along in such a lazy way that Oliver soon began to think his companions were going to deceive the old gentleman by not going to work at all. The Dodger had a vicious habit, too, of pulling the caps from the heads of small boys and tossing them over area railings, while Charley Bates stole odd apples and onions from the food stalls, and thrust them into enormous pockets. These things looked so bad that Oliver was on the point of saying that he was going back on his own, when he noticed a very mysterious change of behaviour on the part of the Dodger.

They were just emerging from a narrow court not far from the open square in Clerkenwell, which is still called "The Green", when the Dodger made a sudden stop, and, laying his finger on his lips, drew his companions back again, with the greatest caution.

"What's the matter?" demanded Oliver.

"Hush!" replied the Dodger. "Do you see that old cove at the bookstall?"

"The old gentleman over the way?" said Oliver. "Yes, I see him."

37

·"He'll do," said the Dodger.

"A prime plant," observed Charley Bates.

Oliver looked from one to the other with the greatest surprise, but, without any explanation, the two boys walked stealthily across the road and slunk close behind the old gentleman towards whom his attention had been directed. Oliver walked a few paces after them and, not knowing whether to advance or retire, stood looking on in silent amazement.

The old gentleman was a very respectable-looking personage, with a powdered head and gold spectacles. He was dressed in a bottle-green coat with a black velvet collar, wore white trousers, and carried a smart bamboo cane under his arm. He had taken up a book from the stall, and there he stood, reading away, as hard as if he were in his arm-chair in his own study.

What was Oliver's horror and alarm as he stood a few paces off, looking on with his eyelids as wide as they could possibly go, to see the Dodger plunge his hand into the old gentleman's tail-coat pocket, and draw from it a handkerchief! To see him hand the same to Charley Bates; and finally to behold them both running away round the corner at full speed.

In an instant the whole mystery of the handkerchiefs, and the watches, and the jewels and the Jew, rushed upon Oliver's mind. He stood for a moment, with the blood so tingling through all his veins from terror that he felt as if he were in a burning fire. Then, confused and frightened, he took to his heels and, not knowing what he did, made off as fast as he could lay his feet to the ground.

This was all done in a minute's space. In the very instant when Oliver began to run, the old gentleman, putting his hand to his pocket, and missing his handkerchief, turned sharp round. Seeing the boy scudding away at such a rapid pace, he very naturally shouted. "Stop thief!" with all his might, and made off after him, book in hand.

But the old gentleman was not the only person who raised the hue and cry. The Dodger and Charley Bates, unwilling to attract public attention by running down the open street, had merely retired into the very first doorway round the corner. They no sooner heard the cry, and saw Oliver running, than, guessing exactly how the matter stood, they dashed out, and, shouting "Stop Thief!" too, joined in the pursuit like good citizens.

Oliver was terrified. Away he went like the wind, with the old gentleman and the two boys roaring and shouting behind him.

"Stop thief! Stop thief!" There is magic in the sound. The cry is taken up by a hundred voices, and more join in at every turning. Away they fly, splashing through the mud, and rattling along the pavements. Up go the windows, out run the people, onward bear the mob, a whole audience desert the Punch and Judy Show, and, joining the rushing throng, swell the shout, and lend fresh vigour to the cry, "Stop thief! Stop thief!"

Stopped at last! A clever blow. The breathless child is down upon the pavement, and the crowd eagerly gather round him, each newcomer jostling and struggling with the others to catch a glimpse.

"Stand aside!"

"Give him a little air!"

"Nonsense! He don't deserve it."

"Where's the gentleman?"

"Here he is, coming down the street."

"Make room there for the gentleman!"

"Is this the boy, sir?"

"Yes."

Oliver lay covered with mud and dust, and bleeding from the mouth, looking wildly round upon the heap of faces that surrounded him, when the old gentleman was dragged and pushed into the circle by the foremost of the pursuers.

"Yes," said the gentleman, "I'm afraid it is the boy."

"Afraid!" murmured the crowd. "That's a good 'un!"

"Poor fellow!" said the gentleman, "he has hurt himself."

"*I* did that, sir," said a great lubberly fellow, stepping forward, "and preciously I cut my knuckles agin' his mouth. *I* stopped him, sir."

The fellow touched his hat with a grin, expecting a reward, but the old gentleman, eyeing him with an expression of dislike, looked anxiously round, as if he were thinking of running away himself. At that moment, a police officer made his way through the crowd and seized Oliver by the collar.

"Get up," said the man roughly.

"It wasn't me, sir. Indeed, indeed, it was two other boys,"

cried Oliver, looking wildly round. "They are here somewhere."

"Oh no, they ain't," said the officer. This was actually true, for the Dodger and Charley Bates had run off down the first convenient alley-way they came to. "Get up, will you!"

"Don't hurt him," said the old gentleman.

"Oh no, I won't hurt him," replied the officer, tearing Oliver's jacket half way off his back to prove it. "Will you stand upon your legs, you young devil!"

Oliver, who could hardly stand, tried to raise himself to his feet, and was at once lugged along the streets by the jacket-collar, at a rapid pace. The gentleman walked on with them by the officer's side, and as many of the crowd as could manage it got a little ahead, and stared back at Oliver from time to time. Boys shouted in triumph, and on they went.

CHAPTER 12

OLIVER IN COURT

The theft had been committed not far from a police-office that had a very bad name. Oliver was taken there immediately and was led beneath a low archway, and up a dirty alleyway into the premises by a backway, to avoid the crowd. It was a small paved yard into which they turned, and here they encountered a stout man with a bunch of whiskers on his face, and a bunch of keys in his hand.

"What's the matter now?" said the man carelessly.

"A young pickpocket," replied the man who had Oliver in charge.

"Are you the gentleman that's been robbed, sir?" inquired the man with the keys.

"Yes, I am," replied the old gentleman, "but I am not sure that this boy actually took the handkerchief. I—I would rather not press the case."

"Must go before the magistrate now, sir," replied the man.

"His worship will be able to see him in half a minute. Now, young gallows!"

This was an invitation for Oliver to enter through a door which he unlocked as he spoke, and which led into a stone cell. Here he was searched, and, nothing being found upon him, locked up.

The old gentleman looked almost as miserable as Oliver when the key grated in the lock. He turned with a sigh to the book which he had been reading when he was robbed.

"There is something in that boy's face," said the old gentleman to himself, as he walked slowly away, tapping his chin with the cover of the book in a thoughtful manner, "something that touches and interests me. *Can* he be innocent? He looked like—bless my soul! Where have I seen something like that look before?"

The old gentleman walked with the same thoughtful face into a small room opening from the yard and was, for a time, lost in his memories. He was roused by a touch on the shoulder, and a request from the man with the keys to follow him into the office. He got up hastily and was at once ushered into the imposing presence of the renowned Mr Fang, the police magistrate.

The office was a front parlour with a panelled wall. Mr Fang sat behind a bar at the upper end, and on one side of the door was a sort of wooden pen in which poor little Oliver was already standing, trembling very much at the awfulness of the scene.

Mr Fang was a lean, long-backed, stiff-necked, middle-sized man, with no great quantity of hair, and what he had, grew on the back and sides of his head. His face was stern, and much flushed, and looked as if he were in the habit of drinking rather more than was exactly good for him. He was out of temper that morning and scowled at the old gentleman, who had advanced to his desk and announced himself as Mr Brownlow, at the same time handing over his card.

"Officer!" said Mr Fang, "what's this fellow charged with?"

"He's not charged at all, your worship," replied the officer. "He appears against the boy, your worship."

His worship knew this perfectly well, but it was a good annoyance and a safe one.

"Swear this person!" said Mr Fang, looking at the clerk and ignoring Mr Brownlow.

Mr Brownlow's indignation was greatly roused, but reflecting, perhaps, that it might harm the boy if he protested at the magistrate's behaviour, he took the oath as directed.

"Now," said Fang, "what's the charge against this boy? What have you got to say, sir?"

"I was standing at a bookstall——" Mr Brownlow began.

"Hold your tongue, sir," said Mr Fang. "Policeman! Where's the policeman? Here, swear this policeman. Now, policeman, what is this?"

The policeman related how Oliver had been handed into his charge, how he had searched him, and found nothing on his person, and how that was all he knew about it.

"Are there any witnesses?" inquired Mr Fang.

"None, your worship," replied the policeman.

Mr Fang sat silent for some minutes, and then, turning round to Mr Brownlow, said in a towering rage, "You have been sworn. Do you mean to state what your complaint against this boy is, or do you not?"

With many interruptions, and repeated insults, Mr Brownlow managed to state his case, saying that, in the surprise of the moment, he had run after the boy because he saw him running away. He hoped that if the magistrate believed him connected with thieves, though not actually the thief himself, he would not be too hard upon him.

"He has been hurt already," said the old gentleman, "and I fear," he added with great energy, looking towards Oliver, "I really feel that he is ill."

"Oh yes, I dare say!" said Mr Fang with a sneer. "None of your tricks here, you young vagabond; they won't do. What's your name?"

Oliver tried to reply, but his tongue failed him. He was deadly pale, and the whole place seemed turning round and round.

"What's your name, you hardened scoundrel?" demanded Mr Fang. "Officer, what's his name?"

This was addressed to a bluff old fellow in a striped waistcoat, who was standing by the bar. He bent over Oliver and repeated the inquiry. Receiving no answer, and knowing that this would only infuriate the magistrate still more, and cause him to be harder on Oliver, he hazarded a guess.

"He says his name's Tom White, your worship," said this kind-hearted officer.

42

At this moment, Oliver raised his head, and, looking round with imploring eyes, asked for water.

"Stuff and nonsense!" said Mr Fang. "Don't try to make a fool of me."

"I think he really is ill, your worship," protested the officer.

"I know better," said Mr Fang.

"Take care of him, officer," said the old gentleman, putting out his hands, "he'll fall down."

"Stand away, officer," cried Fang. "Let him, if he likes."

Oliver promptly fell to the floor in a faint. The men in the office looked at each other, but no one dared to stir.

"I knew he was shamming," said Fang, as if this proved it. "Let him lie there; he'll soon be tired of that."

"How do you propose to deal with the case, sir?" inquired the clerk in a low voice.

"Without delay," replied Mr Fang. "He goes to prison for three months—hard labour, of course. Clear the office."

The door was opened for this purpose, and a couple of men were preparing to carry the unconscious boy to his cell when an elderly man of decent but poor appearance, clad in an old suit of black, rushed hastily into the office and advanced towards the magistrate.

"Stop, stop! Don't take him away! For heaven's sake, stop a moment!" cried the newcomer, breathless with haste.

"Who is this? Who is this? Turn this man out. Clear the office!" cried Mr Fang.

"I *will* speak," cried the man. "I will not be turned out. I saw it all. I keep the bookstall. I demand to be sworn. I will not be put down. Mr Fang you must hear me. You must not refuse, sir."

The man was right. His manner was determined, and the matter was growing rather too serious to be hushed up.

"Swear the man," growled Mr Fang with a very ill grace. "Now, man, what have you got to say?"

"This," said the man: "I saw three boys, two others and the prisoner here, loitering on the opposite side of the way, when this gentleman was reading. The robbery was committed by another boy. I saw it done, and I saw that this boy was perfectly amazed and stupefied by it." Having by this time recovered a little breath, the worthy book-stall keeper proceeded to explain exactly how the robbery took place.

43

"Why didn't you come here before?" said Fang after a pause.

"I hadn't a soul to mind the shop," replied the man. "Everybody who could have helped me had joined in the pursuit. I could get nobody until five minutes ago, and I've run here all the way."

"The prosecutor was reading, was he?" inquired Fang after another pause.

"Yes," replied the man. "The very book he has in his hand."

"Oh, that book, eh?" said Fang. "Is it paid for?"

"No, it is not," replied the man with a smile.

"Dear me, I forgot all about it!" exclaimed the absent-minded old gentleman innocently.

"A nice person to bring a charge against a poor boy!" said Fang, with a comical effort to look humane. "You may think yourself very lucky that the owner of the book does not appear to wish to prosecute you. Let this be a lesson to you, my man, or the law will overtake you yet. The boy is discharged. Clear the office!"

The order was obeyed, and the indignant Mr Brownlow was ushered out with the book in one hand, and the bamboo cane in the other, in a perfect frenzy of rage and defiance. He reached the yard, and his anger vanished in a moment. Little Oliver Twist lay on his back on the pavement, with his shirt unbuttoned, his forehead bathed with water, his face a deadly white, and a cold tremble convulsing his whole body.

"Poor boy, poor boy!" said Mr Brownlow, bending over him. "Call a coach, somebody, pray. Directly!"

A coach was obtained and, Oliver having been carefully laid on one seat, the old gentleman got in and sat himself on the other.

"May I accompany you?" said the book-stall keeper, looking in.

"Bless me, my dear sir," said Mr Brownlow quickly. "I forgot you. Dear, dear! I have this unhappy book still! Jump in. Poor boy! There is no time to lose."

The book-stall keeper got into the coach, and away they drove.

CHAPTER 13

AT MR BROWNLOW'S

The coach rattled away, left the bookseller near his stall with his book returned and then covered nearly the same ground as that which Oliver had walked across when he first entered London in company with the Dodger. When it reached the Angel at Islington, however, it turned a different way and stopped at length before a neat house in a quiet, shady street near Pentonville. Here Oliver was immediately put to bed and cared for with the utmost kindness.

For many days he remained unconscious. The sun rose and sank, and rose and sank again, and many times after that, and still the boy lay stretched on his uneasy bed, dwindling away beneath the dry and wasting heat of fever.

Weak and thin and pale, he awoke at last from what seemed to have been a long and troubled dream. Feebly raising himself in the bed, with his head resting on his trembling arm, he looked anxiously around.

"What room is this? Where have I been brought to?" said Oliver. "This is not the place I went to sleep in."

He uttered these words in a feeble voice, being very faint and weak, but they were overheard at once. The curtain at the bed's head was hastily drawn back, and a motherly old lady, very neatly and precisely dressed, rose as she undrew it from an armchair close by, in which she had been sitting at needlework.

"Hush, my dear," said the old lady softly. "You must be very quiet, or you will be ill again. Lie down again, there's a dear!" With those words, the old lady very gently placed Oliver's head upon the pillow, and, smoothing his hair from his forehead, looked so kindly and lovingly in his face that he could not help placing his little withered hand in hers and drawing it round his neck.

"Save us!" said the old lady, with tears in her eyes. "What

a grateful little dear he is! What would his mother feel if she had sat by him as I have, and could see him now!"

"Perhaps she does see me," whispered Oliver. "She is in Heaven, but perhaps she *has* sat by me. I almost feel as if she had."

"That was the fever, my dear," said the old lady mildly. She wiped her eyes again, and then her spectacles, which lay on the counterpane, as if they were part of her eyes, and brought some cool stuff for Oliver to drink. Then, patting him on the cheek, she told him he must lie very quiet, or he would be ill again.

So Oliver kept very still, partly because he was anxious to obey the kind old lady, and partly, to tell the truth, because he was completely exhausted with what he had already said. He soon fell into a gentle doze, from which he was awakened by the light of a candle, which, being brought near the bed, showed him a gentleman with a very large and loud-ticking gold watch in his hand, who felt his pulse and said he was a great deal better.

"You *are* a great deal better, are you not, my dear?" said the gentleman.

"Yes, thank you, sir," replied Oliver.

"Yes, I know you are," said the gentleman. "You're hungry too, aren't you?"

"No, sir," answered Oliver.

"Hem!" said the gentleman. "No, I know you're not. He is not hungry, Mrs Bedwin," said the gentleman, looking very wise.

The old lady bent her head respectfully, as if she seemed to say that she thought the doctor was a very clever man. The doctor appeared to think so too.

"You feel sleepy, don't you, my dear?" said the doctor.

"No, sir," replied Oliver.

"No," said the doctor with a very shrewd and satisfied look. "You're not sleepy. Nor thirsty. Are you?"

"Yes, sir, rather thirsty," answered Oliver.

"Just as I expected, Mrs Bedwin," said the doctor. "It's very natural that he should be thirsty. You may give him a little tea, ma'am, and some dry toast without any butter. Don't keep him too warm, ma'am, but be careful that you don't let him be too cold; will you have the goodness?"

The old lady dropped a curtsey. The doctor, after tasting

the cool stuff, and expressing his approval of it, hurried away, his boots creaking in a very important and wealthy manner as he went downstairs.

Oliver dozed off again, woke and said his prayers, and then, turning his face upon the pillow, fell into a deep, tranquil sleep.

It had been bright day for hours, when Oliver opened his eyes. He felt cheerful and happy and knew that he was going to be well again.

In three days' time, he was able to sit in an easy chair, well propped up with pillows, and, as he was still too weak to walk, Mrs Bedwin had him carried downstairs into the little house-keeper's room which belonged to her. Having him sat here, by the fireside, the good lady sat herself down, too, and, being in a state of considerable delight at seeing him so much better, at once began to cry most violently.

"Never mind me, my dear," said the old lady. "I'm only having a regular good cry. There! It's all over now, and I'm quite comfortable."

"You're very, very kind to me, ma'am," said Oliver.

"Well, never you mind that, my dear," said the old lady; "that's got nothing to do with your broth, and it's full time you had it, for the doctor says Mr Brownlow can come in to see you this morning, and we must get up our best looks, be-cause the better we look, the more he'll be pleased." And with this, the old lady started to warm up, in a little saucepan, a basin full of good broth.

"Are you fond of pictures, dear?" she inquired, seeing that Oliver had fixed his eyes most intently on a portrait which hung against the wall, just opposite his chair.

"I don't quite know, ma'am," said Oliver, without taking his eyes from the canvas. "I have seen so few, that I hardly know. What a beautiful face that lady's is. Is it a likeness of someone?"

"Yes," said the old lady, looking up for a moment from the broth. "That's a portrait."

"Whose, ma'am?" asked Oliver.

"Why, really, my dear, I don't know," answered the old lady in a good-humoured manner. "It's not a likeness of any-body that you or I know, I expect."

"Its eyes look so sorrowful, and, where I sit, they seem fixed upon me. It makes my heart beat," said Oliver in a low voice, "as if it was alive, and wanted to speak to me, but couldn't."

"Lord save us!" exclaimed the old lady, "don't talk in that way, child. You're weak and nervous after your illness. Let me wheel your chair round to the other side, and then you won't see it. There!" said the old lady, turning his chair. "You don't see it now at all events."

Oliver *did* see it in his mind's eye as distinctly as if he had not altered his position, but he thought it better not to worry the kind old lady, so he said no more about it. He got through his broth with extraordinary speed, and had scarcely swallowed the last spoonful, when there came a soft rap at the door. "Come in," said the old lady, and in walked Mr Brownlow.

Now the old gentleman came in as brisk as need be, but he had no sooner raised his spectacles on his forehead, and thrust his hands behind the skirts of his dressing-gown to take a good long look at Oliver, than his face changed and tears came into his eyes.

"Poor boy, poor boy!" said Mr Brownlow, clearing his throat. "I'm rather hoarse this morning, Mrs Bedwin. I'm afraid I have caught cold."

"I hope not, sir," said Mrs Bedwin. "Everything you have had has been well aired, sir."

"I don't know, Bedwin. I don't know," said Mr Brownlow. "I rather think I had a damp napkin at dinner-time yesterday. But never mind that. How do you feel, my dear?"

"Very happy, sir," replied Oliver, "and very grateful indeed, sir, for your goodness to me."

"Good boy," said Mr Brownlow stoutly. "Have you given him any nourishment, Bedwin?"

"He has just had a basin of beautiful strong broth, sir," replied Mrs Bedwin.

"Ugh!" said Mr Brownlow with a slight shudder. "A couple of glasses of port wine would have done him a great deal more good. Wouldn't they, Tom White, eh?"

"My name is Oliver, sir," replied the little invalid with a look of astonishment.

"Oliver," said Mr Brownlow, "Oliver what? Oliver White, eh?"

"No, sir, Oliver Twist."

"Queer name!" said the old gentleman. "What made you tell the magistrate your name was White?"

"I never told him so, sir," returned Oliver in amazement.

This sounded so like a falsehood that the old gentleman looked somewhat sternly at Oliver, but it was impossible to doubt him. There was truth in every line of his thin, worn face.

"Some mistake," said Mr Brownlow, but he continued to look at Oliver.

"I hope you are not angry with me, sir," said Oliver, raising his eyes beseechingly.

"No, no," replied the old gentleman. "Why, what's this? Bedwin, look there!"

As he spoke, he pointed hastily to the picture above Oliver's head, and then to the boy's face. There was its living copy. The eyes, the head, the mouth. Every feature was the same, and so, for the instant, was the expression.

Oliver did not know the cause of this sudden exclamation, for, not being strong enough to bear the start it gave him, he fainted away.

But to return to the Dodger and Charley Bates. While the general attention was fixed on Oliver, they had made immediately to their home by the shortest possible way.

It was not until the two boys had scoured, with great rapidity, through a most intricate maze of narrow streets and alleyways, that they ventured to halt beneath a low and dark archway. Having remained silent there, just long enough to recover breath to speak, Charlie Bates uttered an exclamation of amusement and delight, and, bursting into an uncontrollable fit of laughter, flung himself upon a doorstep, and rolled about on it.

"What's the matter?" inquired the Dodger.

"Ha! Ha! Ha!" roared Charley Bates.

"Hold your noise," said the Dodger, looking cautiously round. "Do you want to be grabbed, stupid?"

"I can't help it," said Charley. "I can't help it! To see him splitting away at that pace, and me with the wipe in my pocket singing out arter him—oh, my eye!" Charley again rolled upon the doorstep, and laughed louder than before.

"What'll Fagin say?" inquired the Dodger, taking advantage of the next interval of breathlessness to ask the question.

"What?" repeated Charley Bates.

"Ah, what?" said the Dodger.

"Why, what should he say?" inquired Charley, stopping rather suddenly in his merriment, for the Dodger's manner was impressive. "What should he say?"

The Dodger whistled for a couple of minutes, then, taking off his hat, scratched his head and nodded three times.

"What do you mean?" said Charley.

"Toor rul lol loo, gammon and spinach, the frog he wouldn't, and high cockolorum," said the Dodger, with a slight sneer on his face.

Charley Bates felt that this explanation was not satisfactory, and again said, "What do you mean?"

The Dodger made no reply, but, putting his hat on again and gathering the skirts of his long-tailed coat under his arm, thrust his tongue into his cheek, slapped the bridge of his nose some half-dozen times in a familiar but expressive manner, and, turning on his heel, slunk down the street. Charley Bates followed him with a thoughtful countenance.

The noise of their footsteps on the creaking stairs a few minutes later roused the merry old gentleman as he sat over the fire with a cold sausage and a small loaf in his left hand, a pocket-knife in his right and a pewter pot on the trivet. There was a rascally smile on his white face, as he turned round and looked sharply out from under his thick, red eyebrows, bent his ear towards the door and listened.

"Why, how's this?" muttered Fagin, changing countenance. "Only two of 'em? Where's the third? They can't have got into trouble. Hark!"

The footsteps approached nearer; they reached the landing. The door was slowly opened, and the Dodger and Charley Bates entered, closing it behind them.

CHAPTER 14

ENTER BILL SIKES

"Where's Oliver?" said Fagin, rising with a threatening look. "Where's the boy?"

The young thieves eyed their master as if they were alarmed at his manner, and looked uneasily at each other, but they made no reply.

"What's become of the boy?" said Fagin, seizing the Dodger tightly by the collar, and cursing horribly. "Speak out, or I'll throttle you!" He shook the Dodger so much that his keeping in his big coat at all seemed perfectly miraculous.

"Why, the police have got him, and that's all about it," said the Dodger sullenly. "Let go o' me, will you!" And swinging himself at one jerk clean out of the big coat, which he left in Fagin's hands, the Dodger snatched up the toasting fork and made a lunge at the merry old gentleman's waistcoat. Fagin stepped back with surprising agility and, seizing a beer pot, prepared to hurl it at the Dodger's head, but Charley Bates at this moment distracting his attention by a terrific shout, he suddenly swung round, and flung it full at the other boy.

"Why, what the blazes is in the wind now?" growled a deep voice. "Who pitched that 'ere at me? It's well it's the beer and not the pot as hit me, or I'd have settled somebody. What's it all about, Fagin? Damme if my neck-handkerchief ain't lined with beer! Come in, you sneaking varmint. What are you stopping outside for, as if you was ashamed of your master? Come in!"

The man who growled out these words was a stoutly-built fellow of about five-and-thirty, in a black velveteen coat, very soiled drab breeches, lace-up half boots and grey cotton stockings which enclosed a bulky pair of legs with large, swelling calves. He had a brown hat on his head, and a dirty handkerchief round his neck, with the long frayed ends of which he smeared the beer from his face as he spoke. He disclosed, when he had done so, a broad, heavy countenance with a beard of three days' growth, and two scowling eyes, one of which looked as if it had been recently damaged by a blow.

"Come in, d'ye hear?" growled this ruffian.

A white shaggy dog, with his face scratched and torn in twenty different places, skulked into the room.

"Why didn't you come in afore?" said the man. "You're getting too proud to own me afore company, are you? Lie down!"

This command was accompanied with a kick, which sent the animal to the other end of the room. He appeared well used to it, however, for he coiled himself up in a corner very quietly, without uttering a sound, and, winking his very shifty-looking eyes twenty times in a minute, appeared to occupy himself in looking round the apartment.

"What are you up to? Ill-treating the boys, you covetous, avaricious, in-sa-ti-a-ble old fence?" said the man, seating himself without haste. "I wonder they don't murder you! *I* would, if I was them. If I'd been your 'prentice, I'd have done it long ago."

"Hush! Hush! Mr Sikes," said the old man, trembling. "Don't speak so loud."

"None of your mistering," replied the ruffian. "You always mean mischief when you start that. You know my name. Out with it! I shan't disgrace it when the time comes."

"Well, well then, Bill Sikes," said Fagin humbly, "you seem out of humour, Bill."

"Perhaps I am," replied Sikes. "I should think *you* was rather out of sorts, too, throwing pewter pots at people. Give me a glass o' liquor, and mind you don't poison it." This was said in jest, but if the speaker could have seen the evil leer with which Fagin bit his pale lip as he turned round to the cupboard, he might have felt uneasy.

After swallowing two or three glasses of spirits, Sikes started talking to the boys, and they told him of Oliver's capture, with such altercations and improvements on the truth as the Dodger thought wise.

"I'm afraid," said Fagin, "that he may say something which will get us into trouble."

"That's very likely," returned Sikes with a malicious grin. "You're blown upon, Fagin."

"And I'm afraid, you see," added the old gentleman, speaking as if he had not noticed the interruption, and regarding the other closely as he did so—"I'm afraid that if the game was up with us, it might be up with a good many more, and then it would come out rather worse for you than it would for me, my dear."

Sikes turned round with a startled look, but the old gentleman's shoulders were shrugged up to his ears, and his eyes were vacantly staring at the opposite wall. There was a long pause.

"Somebody must find out what's been done at the police-office," said Bill Sikes, in a much lower tone than he had taken since he came in.

Fagin nodded his agreement.

"If he hasn't peached, and is committed to prison, there's no fear till he comes out again," said Sikes, "and then he must be taken care on. You must get hold of him somehow."

Again Fagin nodded.

There was a silence. Nobody wanted to go anywhere near the police-office.

The sudden entrance of Nancy and Bet suggested a way out of the difficulty. "The very thing!" said Fagin. "Bet will go. won't you, my dear?"

"Wheres?" inquired Bet.

"Only just up to the police-office, my dear," said Fagin, coaxingly.

"I'm blessed if I do," said Bet.

Fagin's face fell. He turned from Bet, who was gorgeously attired in a red gown, green boots and yellow curl-papers, to her friend.

"Nancy, my dear," said Fagin, in a soothing manner, "what do *you* say?"

"That it won't do, so it's no use a-trying it on, Fagin," replied Nancy.

"What do you mean by that?" said Sikes, looking up in a surly manner.

"What I say, Bill," replied Nancy calmly.

"Why, you're just the very person for it," reasoned Sikes. "Nobody about here knows anything of you."

"And as I don't want 'em to, neither," replied Nancy in the same calm manner, "it's rather more no than yes with me, Bill."

"She'll go, Fagin," said Sikes.

"No she won't, Fagin," said Nancy.

"Yes she will, Fagin," said Sikes.

And he was right. By means of alternate threats, promises and bribes, Nancy was finally persuaded to go. Accordingly, with a clean white apron tied over her gown, and her curl-papers tucked up under a straw bonnet—both articles of dress being provided by Fagin from his large stock of stolen goods—Nancy prepared to issue forth on her errand.

"Stop a minute, my dear," said Fagin, producing a little covered basket. "Carry that in one hand. It looks more respectable, my dear."

"Give her a door-key to carry in her t'other one, Fagin," said Sikes, "for the look of the thing."

"Yes, that's very good," said Fagin, hanging a large street-door key on the forefinger of the young lady's right hand. "There! Very good! Very good indeed, my dear!"

"Oh, my brother! My poor, dear, sweet, innocent little brother!" exclaimed Nancy, bursting into tears. "What has become of him? Where have they taken him to? Oh, do have pity, and tell me what's been done with the dear boy, gentlemen. Do, gentlemen, if you please, gentlemen!"

Having uttered these words in a heartbroken tone to the utmost delight of her hearers, Miss Nancy paused, winked to the company, nodded smilingly round, and disappeared.

"Ah, she's a clever girl, my dears," said the old gentleman, turning round to his young friends, and shaking his head gravely, as if to counsel them to follow the bright example they had just beheld.

"She's a honour to her sex," said Sikes, filling his glass, and smiting the table with his enormous fist. "Here's her health, and wishing they was all like her."

Meanwhile Nancy was making the best of her way to the police-office. Entering by the back way, she immediately encountered the bluff officer in the striped waistcoat, and, with the most piteous wailings and lamentations, demanded her own dear brother.

"I haven't got him, my dear," said the old man.

"Where is he?" screamed Nancy in a distracted manner.

"Why, the gentleman's got him," replied the officer.

"What gentleman? Oh, gracious heavens! What gentleman?" cried Nancy.

The old man told her all that had happened to Oliver since he had been arrested for another boy's crime, and that he believed the gentleman had taken him somewhere in Pentonville, for he had heard that word mentioned in the directions given to the coachman.

In a state of distress, Nancy staggered to the gate, but, as soon as she was out of sight, she broke into a swift run and, keeping to the back streets, returned to Fagin's home.

Bill Sikes no sooner heard Nancy's account of the expedition, than he called up the white dog, and, putting on his hat, hastened away without troubling to wish the company good-morning.

"We must know where he is, my dears. He must be found," said Fagin, greatly excited. "Charley, do nothing but skulk about, till you bring home some news of him! Nancy, my dear, I must have him found. I trust to you, my dear—to you and the Artful for everything! Stay, stay," he added, unlocking a drawer with a shaking hand. "There's money, my dears. I shall shut up this place tonight. You'll know where to find me. Don't stop here a minute. Not an instant, my dears!"

With these words, Fagin pushed them from the room, and, carefully double-locking and barring the door behind them, drew from its place of concealment the box which Oliver had seen. Then he hastily proceeded to hide the stolen watches and jewellery beneath his clothing.

A rap at the door startled him in this occupation.

"Who's there?" he cried in a shrill tone.

"Me!" replied the voice of the Dodger through the key-hole.

"What now?" cried the old man impatiently.

"Is he to be kidnapped to the other place, Nancy says?" inquired the Dodger.

"Yes," replied Fagin, "wherever she lays hands on him. Find him, find him out, that's all! I shall know what to do next, never fear."

The boy murmured a reply which showed that he understood, and hurried downstairs after his companion.

"He has not peached so far," said the old man out loud. "If he means to blab on us to his new friends, we may stop his mouth yet."

CHAPTER 15

OLIVER GOES ON AN ERRAND

Oliver soon recovered from the fainting fit caused by Mr Brownlow's sudden exclamation. He was still too weak to get up for breakfast, but when he came down into the housekeeper's room the next day he looked eagerly at the wall, in the hope of seeing again the face of the beautiful lady. To his disappointment, however, he saw that the picture had been removed.

"Ah!" said the housekeeper, watching the direction of Oliver's eyes. "It is gone, you see."

"I see it is, ma'am," replied Oliver. "Why have they taken it away?"

"It has been taken down, child, because Mr Brownlow said that, as it seemed to worry you, perhaps it might prevent your getting well, you know," rejoined the old lady.

"Oh no, indeed. It didn't worry me, ma'am," said Oliver. "I liked to see it. I quite loved it."

"Well, well," said the old lady good-humouredly, "you get well as fast as ever you can, dear, and it shall be hung up again, I promise you. Now, let us talk about something else."

They were happy days, those of Oliver's recovery. Everything was so quiet and neat and orderly, everybody so kind and gentle, that after the noise and commotion in the midst of which he had always lived, it seemed like Heaven itself. He was no sooner strong enough to put his clothes on properly than Mr Brownlow caused a complete new suit, and a new cap and a pair of shoes, to be provided for him. As Oliver was told that he might do what he liked with the old clothes, he gave them to a servant who had been very kind to him, and she sold them to a man who called at the door. Oliver was delighted to think he would never have to wear them again. He had never had a new suit before.

One afternoon, about a week after the affair of the picture, as he was sitting talking to Mrs Bedwin, there came a message down from Mr Brownlow that if Oliver Twist felt pretty well, he would like to see him and talk to him a little while. Oliver made himself tidy, went downstairs, and knocked at the study door. On Mr Brownlow calling him to come in, he found himself in a little back room, quite full of books, with a window looking into some pleasant gardens. There was a table drawn up before the window, at which Mr Brownlow was seated reading. When he saw Oliver, he pushed the book away from him, and told him to come near the table and sit down.

"Now," said Mr Brownlow, speaking in a kind but serious manner. "I want you to pay great attention, my boy, to what I am going to say. I shall talk freely to you, because I am sure you are well able to understand me as many older persons would be."

"Oh, don't tell me you are going to send me away, sir!" exclaimed Oliver, alarmed at the serious tone of Mr Brownlow's words. "Don't turn me out of doors to wander in the streets again. Let me stay here and be a servant. Don't send me back to the wretched place I came from. Have mercy upon a poor boy, sir!"

"My dear child," said Mr Brownlow, moved by the warmth of Oliver's sudden appeal, "you need not be afraid of my deserting you unless you give me cause."

"I never, never will, sir!" cried Oliver.

"I hope not," rejoined Mr Brownlow. "I do not think you ever will. Now, let me hear your story, where you came from, who brought you up, and how you got into the company in which I found you. Speak the truth, and you shall not be friendless while I live."

For a few minutes, Oliver could not speak through his tears. He was on the point of beginning to relate how he had been brought up in the workhouse, when a peculiarly impatient little double-knock was heard at the street door, and the servant, running upstairs, announced Mr Grimwig.

"Is he coming up?" inquired Mr Brownlow.

"Yes, sir," replied the servant. "He asked if there were any muffins in the house, and when I told him yes, he said he had come to tea."

Mr Brownlow smiled and, turning to Oliver, said that Mr

Grimwig was an old friend of his, and he must not mind his being a little rough in his manners, for he was really a worthy creature, as he had reason to know.

"Shall I leave the room, sir?" inquired Oliver.

"No," replied Mr Brownlow, "I would rather you remained here."

At that moment, there walked into the room, supporting himself by a thick stick, a stout old gentleman, rather lame in one leg, who was dressed in a blue coat, striped waistcoat, nankeen breeches and gaiters, and a broad-brimmed white hat, with the sides turned up with green. A very small-plaited shirt frill stuck out from his waistcoat, and a very long steel watch-chain, with nothing but a key at the end, dangled loosely below it. Mr Grimwig had a manner of screwing his head on one side when he spoke, and of looking out of the corner of his eyes at the same time, which reminded one of a parrot. In this attitude, he fixed himself, the moment he made his appearance, and, holding out a small piece of orange peel at arm's length, exclaimed in a growling, discontented voice, "Look at this! Isn't it a most wonderful and extraordinary thing that I can't call at a man's house without finding a piece of this poor surgeon's friend on the staircase? I've been lamed with orange peel once, and I know orange peel will be my death at last. It will, sir; orange peel will be my death, or I'll be content to eat my own head, sir!"

Mr Grimwig struck his stick upon the ground, then, seeing Oliver, retreated a pace or two exclaiming, "Hallo! Who's that?"

"This is young Oliver Twist, whom we were speaking about," said Mr Brownlow.

Oliver bowed.

"You don't mean to say that's the boy who had the fever, I hope?" said Mr Grimwig, taking another pace backwards. "Wait a minute! Don't speak! Stop!" continued Mr Grimwig abruptly, losing all dread of the fever in his triumph at the discovery. "That's the boy who had the orange! If that's not the boy, sir, who had the orange, and threw this bit of peel upon the staircase, I'll eat my head, and his, too."

"No, no, he has not had one," said Mr Brownlow, laughing. "Come, put down your hat, and speak to my young friend."

Mr Grimwig, still keeping his stick in his hand, sat down and, opening a double eye-glass, which he wore attached to a broad black riband, took a view of Oliver, who coloured and bowed again.

"That's the boy, is it?" said Mr Grimwig, at length.

"That is the boy," replied Mr Brownlow.

"How are you, boy?" said Mr Grimwig.

"A great deal better, thank you, sir," replied Oliver.

Mr Brownlow, seeing that his odd friend might be about to say something disagreeable, asked Oliver to find Mrs Bedwin and tell her they were ready for tea; which, as he did not half like the visitor's manner, he was very happy to do.

"He is a nice-looking boy, is he not?" inquired Mr Brownlow.

"I don't know," replied Mr Grimwig peevishly.

"Don't know?"

"No. I don't know. I never see any difference in boys. I only know two sorts of boys. Mealy boys, and beef-faced boys."

"And which is Oliver?"

"Mealy. I know a friend who has a beef-faced boy; a fine boy, they call him, with a round head and red cheeks, and glaring eyes, a horrid boy, with a body and limbs that appear to be swelling out of the seams of his blue clothes. He has the voice of a sea captain, and the appetite of a wolf. I know him! The wretch!"

"Come," said Mr Brownlow, "that does not describe young Oliver Twist, so you needn't be angry with him."

"It may not," replied Mr Grimwig, who liked being contrary. "He may be worse. Where does he come from? Who is he? What is he?" Chuckling maliciously, he went on to demand with a sneer whether the housekeeper was in the habit of counting the silver at night, because, if she didn't find a tablespoon or two missing some sunshiny morning, why, he would be content to eat his head.

All this, Mr Brownlow, knowing his friend's peculiarities, bore with good humour. As Mr Grimwig, at tea, was graciously pleased to say how good the muffins were, matters went on very smoothly, and Oliver, who made one of the party, began to feel more at his ease than he had yet done in the fierce old gentleman's presence.

"And when are you going to hear a full, true, and particular account of the life and adventures of Oliver Twist?" asked

Grimwig of Mr Brownlow, at the conclusion of the meal, looking sideways at Oliver as he resumed the subject.

"Tomorrow morning," replied Mr Brownlow. "I would rather he was alone with me at the time. Come and see me tomorrow morning at ten o'clock, Oliver."

"Yes, sir," replied Oliver. He answered with some hesitation, because he was confused by Mr Grimwig's looking so hard at him.

"I'll tell you what," whispered that gentleman to Mr Brownlow; "he won't come and see you tomorrow morning. I saw him hesitate. He is deceiving you, my good friend."

"I'll swear he is not," replied Mr Brownlow warmly.

"If he is not," said Mr Grimwig, "I'll eat my head," and down went the stick.

"I'll answer for that boy's truth with my life!" said Mr Brownlow, knocking the table.

"And I for his falsehood with my head!" rejoined Mr Grimwig, knocking the table also.

"We shall see," said Mr Brownlow, checking his rising anger.

"We will," replied Mr Grimwig, with a provoking smile, "we will."

As fate would have it, Mrs Bedwin chanced to bring in, at that moment, a small parcel of books, which Mr Brownlow had that morning purchased from the identical book-stall keeper, who has already appeared in this story. Having laid them on the table, she prepared to leave the room.

"Stop the boy, Mrs Bedwin!" said Mr Brownlow; "there is something to go back."

"He has gone, sir," replied Mrs Bedwin.

"Call after him," said Mr Brownlow. "It's important. He is a poor man, and they are not paid for. There are some books to be taken back, too."

The street door was opened. Oliver ran one way, and the servant girl ran another, and Mrs Bedwin stood on the step and screamed for the boy, but there was no boy in sight. Oliver and the girl returned, in a breathless state, to report that there were no tidings of him.

"Dear me, I am very sorry for that," exclaimed Mr Brownlow. "I particularly wished those books to be returned tonight."

"Send Oliver with them," said Mr Grimwig, with a meaning smile. "He will be sure to deliver them safely, you know."

"Yes, do let me take them, if you please, sir," said Oliver. "I'll run all the way, sir."

Mr Brownlow was just going to say that Oliver should not go out on any account, when a most malicious cough from Mr Grimwig made him change his mind. Oliver should prove to Mr Grimwig the injustice of his suspicions.

"You *shall* go, Oliver," said the old gentleman. "The books are on a chair by my table. Bring them down."

Oliver, delighted to be of use, brought down the books under his arm, and waited, cap in hand, to hear what message he was to take.

"You are to say," said Mr Brownlow, glancing steadily at Grimwig, "you are to say that you have brought those books back, and that you have come to pay the four pound ten I owe him. This is a five-pound note, so you will have to bring me back ten shillings change."

"I won't be ten minutes, sir," replied Oliver eagerly. Having buttoned up the bank-note in his jacket pocket and placed the books carefully under his arm, he made a respectful bow and left the room. Mrs Bedwin followed him to the street-door, giving him many directions about the nearest way, and the name of the bookseller, and the name of the street, all of which Oliver said he clearly understood. Having added many warnings to be sure and not take cold, the old lady at length permitted him to depart.

"Bless his sweet face!" said the old lady, looking after him. "I can't bear, somehow, to let him go out of my sight."

At this moment, Oliver looked gaily round and nodded before he turned the corner. The old lady smilingly nodded back and, closing the door, went back to her own room.

"Let me see; he'll be back in twenty minutes at the longest," said Mr Brownlow, pulling out his watch, and placing it on the table. "It will be dark by that time."

"Oh! You really expect him to come back, do you?" inquired Mr Grimwig.

"Don't you?" asked Mr Brownlow, smiling.

"No," said Mr Grimwig, smiting the table with his fist. "I do not. The boy has a new suit of clothes on his back, a set of valuable books under his arm, and a five-pound note in his pocket. He'll join his old friends and thieves, and laugh at you. If ever that boy returns to this house, sir, I'll eat my head."

With these words, he drew his chair closer to the table, and there the two friends sat, in silent expectation, with the watch between them.

Mr Grimwig was not by any means a bad-hearted man, and though he would have been really sorry to see his respected friend duped and deceived, he really did most earnestly and strongly hope at that moment that his judgment would be proved correct and that Oliver Twist might not come back.

It grew so dark that the figures on the watch face could scarcely be seen, but there the two old gentlemen continued to sit in silence, with the watch between them.

CHAPTER 16

OLIVER IS KIDNAPPED

In the dingy parlour of a low public-house, in the filthiest part of Little Saffron Hill, a dark and gloomy den, where a flaring gaslight burnt all day in the winter-time, and where no ray of sun ever shone in the summer, there sat, brooding over a little pewter measure and a small glass which smelt strongly of drink, a man in a velveteen coat, drab breeches, half boots and stockings. It was Bill Sikes.

"Keep quiet, you varmint! Keep quiet!" said Sikes, suddenly breaking silence and aiming a kick at the dog, which had done nothing to annoy him. Growling viciously, the dog made for Sikes, who seized a poker and began to attack him. At that moment the door opened and the dog darted out of the room as Fagin came silently in.

"What the devil do you come in between me and my dog for?" said Sikes with a fierce gesture.

"I didn't know, my dear; I didn't know," replied Fagin humbly.

"Didn't know, you white-livered thief!" growled Sikes. "Couldn't you hear the noise?"

"Not a sound of it, as I'm a living man, Bill," replied Fagin.

"Oh no! You hear nothing, you don't," retorted Sikes with a fierce sneer. "Sneaking in and out, so as nobody hears how you come or go! Well, what have you got for me?"

"It's all passed safe through the melting-pot," replied Fagin, "and this is your share. It's rather more than it ought to be, my dear, but as I know you'll do me a good turn another time, and——"

"Stow that gammon," cut in the robber impatiently. "Where is it? Hand over!"

"Yes, yes, Bill. Give me time, give me time," replied Fagin soothingly. "Here it is! All safe!" As he spoke, he drew forth an old cotton handkerchief from inside his coat, and, untying a large knot in one corner, produced a small brown paper packet. Sikes, snatching it from him, hastily opened it, and proceeded to count the golden sovereigns it contained.

"This is all, is it?" inquired Sikes.

"All," replied Fagin.

"You haven't opened the parcel and swallowed one or two as you come along, have you?" inquired Sikes, suspiciously. "Don't put on an injured look at the question you've done it many a time. Jerk the tinkler."

A young Jew answered Fagin's ring of the bell, and Bill Sikes pointed to his empty glass. The young man took the hint and went out with it, returning almost immediately with a new measure.

"Is anybody here, Barney?" inquired Fagin.

"Not a shoul," replied Barney, whose words, whether they came from the heart or not, made their way through the nose.

"Nobody?" inquired Fagin, in a tone of surprise, which perhaps might mean that Barney was at liberty to tell the truth.

"Nobody but Biss Dadsy," replied Barney.

"Nancy!" exclaimed Sikes. "Where? Strike me blind if I don't honour that girl for her native talents."

"She's bid havid a plate of boiled beef id the bar," replied Barney.

"Send her here," said Sikes, pouring out a glass of liquor. "Send her here."

Barney went out and presently returned, ushering in Nancy, who was decorated with the bonnet, apron, basket, and street-door key complete.

"You are on the scent, are you, Nancy?" inquired Sikes offering her his drink.

"Yes I am, Bill," replied the young lady, emptying the glass, "and tired enough of it I am, too. The young brat's been ill and confined to the crib, but he's up and about now, and I'll chance my luck presently."

Nancy pulled her shawl over her shoulders and declared it was time to go. She and Sikes went away together, followed at a little distance, by the dog, who slunk out of a backyard as soon as his master was out of sight.

Fagin thrust his head out of the room door when Sikes had left it, looked after him as he walked up the dark passage, shook his clenched fist, muttered a deep curse, and then, with a horrible grin, seated himself at the table, where he was soon deeply absorbed in details of wanted criminals in the pages of the *Hue-and-Cry*.

Meanwhile, Oliver Twist, little dreaming that he was within so very short distance of Fagin, was on his way to the bookstall. When he got into Clerkenwell, he accidentally turned down a bye-street which was not exactly on his way, but not discovering his mistake until he had got half-way down it, and knowing it must lead in the right direction, he did not think it worthwhile to turn back, and so marched on, as quickly as he could, with the books under his arm.

He was walking along thinking of his new friends and how happy and contented he ought to feel, when he was startled by a young woman screaming out very loud, "Oh, my dear brother!" And he had hardly looked up, to see what the matter was, when he was stopped by having a pair of arms thrown tight round his neck.

"Don't!" cried Oliver, struggling. "Let go of me. Who is it? What are you stopping me for?"

The only reply to this was a great number of loud wails from the young woman who had embraced him, and who had a little basket and a street-door key in her hand.

"Oh, my gracious!" said the young woman, "I've found him! Oh, Oliver! Oh you naughty boy, to make me suffer sich distress on your account! Come home, dear, come. Oh, I've found him. Thank gracious goodness heavins, I've found him!" The young woman burst into another fit of crying, and became so dreadfully hysterical that a couple of women came up and asked if they should send for a doctor.

"Oh no, no, never mind," said the young woman, grasping Oliver's hand. "I'm better now. Come home directly, you cruel boy! Come!"

"What's the matter, ma'am?" inquired one of the women.

"Oh, ma'am," replied the young woman, "he ran away, near a month ago, from his parents, who are hardworking and respectable people, and went and joined a set of thieves and bad characters, and almost broke his mother's heart."

"Young wretch!" said one woman.

"Go home do, you little brute," said the other.

"I am not a brute," replied Oliver, greatly alarmed. "I don't know her. I haven't any sister, or father and mother either. I'm an orphan; I live at Pentonville."

"Only hear him, how he braves it out!" cried the young woman.

"Why, it's Nancy!" exclaimed Oliver, who now saw her face for the first time, and started back in astonishment.

"You see, he knows me!" cried Nancy, appealing to the bystanders. "He can't help himself. Make him come home, there's good people, or he'll kill his dear mother and father and break my heart!"

"What the devil's this?" said a man, bursting out of a beer-shop with a white dog at his heels. "Young Oliver! Come home to your poor mother, you young dog! Come home at once."

"I don't belong to them. I don't know them. Help! Help!" cried Oliver, struggling in the man's powerful grasp.

"Help!" repeated the man. "Yes, I'll help you, you young rascal! What books are these? You've been a-stealing 'em, have you? Give 'em here." With these words, the man tore the volumes from his grasp, and struck him on the head.

"That's right!" cried a looker-on from a garret-window. "That's the only way of bringing him to his senses!"

"To be sure!" said a sleepy-faced carpenter, casting an approving look at the garret-window.

"It'll do him good," said the two women.

"And he shall have it, too!" rejoined the man, giving Oliver another blow, and seizing him by the collar. "Come on, you young villain! Here, Bull's-eye, mind him, boy! Mind him!"

Oliver was helpless. In another moment he was dragged into a labyrinth of dark narrow streets, and was forced along them at a pace which rendered his few cries useless. It mat-

C

tered little indeed whether anyone heard them or not, for there was nobody to care for them, had they been ever so loud.

The gas-lamps were lighted; Mrs Bedwin was waiting anxiously at the open door; the servant had run up the street twenty times to see if there were any traces of Oliver; and still the two old gentlemen sat, perseveringly, in the dark parlour with the watch between them.

CHAPTER 17

NANCY DEFENDS OLIVER

The narrow streets and alleyways led to a large open space. Stalls for animals were scattered around, showing that it was used as a cattle market. Sikes slackened his pace when they reached this spot, because Nancy was unable to keep up any longer the rapid rate at which he had been walking up until now. Turning to Oliver, he roughly commanded him to take hold of Nancy's hand.

"Do you hear?" growled Sikes, as Oliver hesitated and looked round.

They were in a dark corner, quite out of the track of way-farers. Oliver saw that resistance would be useless. He held out his hand, which Nancy clasped tight in hers.

"Give me the other," said Sikes, seizing Oliver's free hand. "Get on, young 'un."

With Bull's-eye leading the way, they crossed Smithfield, although it might have been Grosvenor Square, for all Oliver knew. The night was dark and foggy. The lights in the shops could scarcely struggle through the heavy mist, which thickened every moment and shrouded the streets and houses in gloom, rendering the strange place still stranger to Oliver's eyes, and making his uncertainty the more dismal and depressing.

They walked on by lonely and dirty ways, for a full half-hour, meeting very few people, and those appearing from their looks to follow much the same occupation as Sikes himself. At length they turned into a very filthy, narrow street, nearly full of old-clothes shops, and the dog, running forward, stopped before the door of a shop that was closed and apparently empty. The house was in a ruinous condition, and on the door was nailed a board, stating that it was to let, which looked as if it had hung there for many years.

"All right," said Sikes, glancing cautiously round.

Nancy stooped below the shutters, and Oliver heard the sound of a bell. They crossed to the opposite side of the street, and stood for a few moments under a lamp. A noise, as if a sash window were gently raised, was heard, and soon afterwards the door softly opened. Sikes seized the terrified boy by the collar, and all three were quickly inside the house.

The passage was perfectly dark. They waited, while the person who had let them in chained and barred the door.

"Anybody here?" inquired Sikes.

"No," replied a voice, which Oliver thought he had heard before.

"Is the old 'un here?" asked the robber.

"Yes," replied the voice, "and precious down in the mouth he has been. Won't he be glad to see you? Oh no!"

The voice and style of speech seemed familiar to Oliver's ears, but it was impossible to distinguish even the form of the speaker in the darkness.

"Let's have a glim," said Sikes, "or we shall go breaking our necks, or treading on the dog. Look after your legs if you do!"

"Stand still a moment, and I'll get you one," replied the voice. They waited, and in another minute the form of Jack Dawkins, otherwise the Artful Dodger, appeared. He bore in his right hand a tallow candle stuck in the end of a cleft stick. He grinned at Oliver and, turning away, beckoned the visitors to follow him down a flight of stairs. They crossed an empty kitchen, and, opening the door of a low, earthy-smelling room, which seemed to have been built in a small backyard, were received with a shout of laughter.

"Oh my wig, my wig!" cried Charley Bates, from whose lungs the laughter had proceeded. "Here he is, here he is! Oh, Fagin, look at him! Fagin, do look at him! I can't bear it; it is such a jolly game, I can't bear it. Hold me, somebody, while I laugh it out."

Charley Bates laid himself flat on the floor and kicked for joy, while Fagin, taking off his nightcap, made a great number of low bows to the bewildered boy, and the Artful, who seldom gave way to merriment when it interfered with business, rifled Oliver's pockets with great thoroughness.

"Look at his togs, Fagin!" said Charley, putting the light so close to Oliver's new jacket as nearly to set him on fire. "Look at his togs! Superfine cloth, and the heavy swell cut! Oh, my eye, what a game! And his books, too! Nothing but a gentleman, Fagin!"

"Delighted to see you looking so well, my dear," said Fagin, bowing with mock humility. "The Artful shall give you another suit, my dear, for fear you should spoil that Sunday one. Why didn't you write, my dear, and say you were coming? We'd have got something warm for supper."

At that moment the Dodger drew forth the five pound note which Mr Brownlow had given to Oliver to pay for the books.

"Hallo! What's that?" inquired Sikes, stepping forward as the old gentleman seized the note. "That's mine, Fagin."

"No, no, my dear," said Fagin. "Mine, Bill, mine. You shall have the books."

"If that ain't mine," said Bill Sikes, putting on his hat with a determined air, "mine and Nancy's that is, I'll take the boy back again. Hand over, will you?"

"This is hardly fair, Bill, hardly fair, is it, Nancy?" inquired Fagin.

"Fair or not fair," retorted Sikes, "hand over, I tell you! Do you think Nancy and me has got nothing else to do with our precious time, but to spend it in scouting arter and kidnapping every young boy as gets grabbed through you? Give it here, you avaricious old skeleton, give it here!"

With this, Sikes plucked the note from between Fagin's finger and thumb, and, looking the old man coolly in the face, folded it up small and tied it in his neckerchief.

"That's for our share of the trouble," said Sikes, "and not half enough, neither. You may keep the books if you're fond of reading. If you ain't, sell 'em."

"They're very pretty," said Charley Bates, who, with many grimaces, had been pretending to read one of the books. "Beautiful writing, isn't it, Oliver?"

"They belong to the old gentleman," cried Oliver, "to

the good, kind, old gentleman who took me into his house, and had me nursed when I was near dying of fever. He'll think I stole them. The old lady, all of them who were so kind to me, will think I stole them. Oh, do have mercy upon me, and send the books and money back!"

"The boy's right," remarked Fagin, looking secretively round, and knitting his shaggy eyebrows into a hard knot. "You're right, Oliver, you're right. They *will* think you have stolen them. Ha! Ha!" chuckled Fagin, rubbing his hands. "It couldn't have happened better, if we had chosen our time!"

"Of course it couldn't," replied Sikes, "I knowed that, directly I see him coming through Clerkenwell, with the books under his arm. It's all right enough. They're soft-hearted psalm-singers, or they wouldn't have taken him in at all, and they'll ask no questions about him, for fear they should be obliged to prosecute, and so get him locked up. He's safe enough."

Oliver had looked from one to the other, while these words were being spoken, as if he were bewildered, and could scarcely understand what passed, but when Sikes finished speaking, he jumped suddenly to his feet and tore wildly from the room, uttering shrieks for help, which made the bare old house echo to the roof.

"Keep back the dog, Bill!" cried Nancy, springing before the door, and closing it, as Fagin and the two boys darted out in pursuit. "Keep back the dog. He'll tear the boy to pieces."

"Serve him right!" cried Sikes, struggling to get away from the girl's grasp. "Stand off from me, or I'll split your head against the wall."

"I don't care for that, Bill. I don't care for that," screamed the girl, struggling violently with the man. "The child shan't be torn down by the dog unless you kill me first."

"Shan't he!" said Sikes, setting his teeth. "I'll soon do that, if you don't keep off."

The housebreaker flung the girl from him to the further end of the room, just as Fagin and the two boys returned, dragging Oliver among them.

"What's the matter here?" said Fagin, looking round.

"The girl's gone mad, I think," replied Sikes savagely.

"No she hasn't," said Nancy, pale and breathless from the scuffle. "No she hasn't, Fagin. Don't think it."

"Then keep quiet, will you?" said Fagin with a threatening look.

"No, she won't do that neither," replied Nancy, speaking very loud. "Now then, what do you think of that?"

Fagin knew enough of Nancy to realise that she would be better left alone at present. He turned his attention to Oliver.

"So you wanted to get away, my dear, did you?" said Fagin, taking up a jagged and knotted club which lay in a corner of the fireplace. "Eh?"

Oliver made no reply, but he watched Fagin and breathed quickly.

"Wanted to get assistance, called for the police, did you?" sneered Fagin, catching the boy by the arm. "We'll cure you of that, my young master."

He inflicted a smart blow on Oliver's shoulders with the club, and was raising it for a second, when the girl, rushing forward, wrested it from his hand. She flung it into the fire, with a force that brought some of the glowing coals whirling out into the room.

"I won't stand by and see it done, Fagin," cried the girl. "You've got the boy, and what more would you have? Let him be—let him be—or I shall put that mark on some of you, that will bring me to the gallows before my time."

The girl stamped her foot violently on the floor as she uttered this threat, and, with her hands clenched, looked alternately at Fagin and Sikes, her face quite colourless from the passion of rage into which she had gradually worked herself.

"Why, Nancy!" said Fagin in a soothing tone, after a pause, during which he and Sikes had stared at one another, rather taken aback; "you—you're more clever than ever to-night. Ha! Ha! my dear, you are acting beautifully."

"Am I?" said the girl. "Take care I don't overdo it. You will be the worse for it, Fagin, if I do, and so I tell you in good time to keep clear of me."

The old man shrank back and cast a glance half imploring, half cowardly at Sikes.

"What do you mean by this?" said Sikes. "What do you mean by it? Damn my eyes and burn my body! Do you know who you are, and what you are?"

"Oh yes, I know all about it," replied Nancy, laughing hysterically, and shaking her head from side to side, with a poor pretence of indifference.

"Well then, keep quiet," rejoined Sikes, with a growl like that he was accustomed to use when addressing his dog, "or I'll quiet you for a good long time to come. You're a nice one to take his side! A fine person for the child, as you call him, to make a friend of!"

"God Almighty, help me, I am!" cried the girl passionately, "and I wish I had been struck dead in the street before I had lent a hand in bringing him here. He's a thief, a liar, a devil, all that's bad, from this night forth. Isn't that enough for the old wretch, without blows?"

"Come, come, Sikes," said Fagin reprovingly as he motioned towards the boys, who were listening eagerly to all that passed. "We must have civil words, civil words, Bill."

"Civil words!" cried the girl. "Civil words, you villain! Yes, you deserve 'em from me. I thieved for you when I was a child not half as old as this!" pointing to Oliver. "I have been in the same trade, and in the same service for twelve years since. Don't you know it? Speak out! Don't you know it?"

"Well, well," replied Fagin, trying to pacify her, "and if you have, it's your living!"

"Aye, it is!" returned the girl, "it is my living and the cold, wet, dirty streets are my home, and you're the wretch that drove me to them long ago, and that'll keep me there, day and night, day and night, till I die!"

"I shall do you a mischief!" put in Fagin, stung by these reproaches, "a mischief worse than that, if you say much more!"

The girl said nothing more, but made a rush at the old man. Sikes caught her by the wrists, she made a few feeble struggles, and fainted.

"She's all right now," said Sikes, laying her down in a corner. "She's uncommon strong in the arms when she's up in this way."

Fagin wiped his forehead and smiled, as if it were a relief to have the disturbance over, but neither he, nor Sikes, nor the dog, nor the boys, seemed to consider what had passed at all unusual.

"It's the worst of having to do with women," said Fagin,

picking his club out of the fireplace, "but they're clever, and we can't get on in our line without 'em. Charley, show Oliver to bed."

"I suppose he'd better not wear his best clothes tomorrow, Fagin, had he?" inquired Charley Bates.

"Certainly not," replied the old gentleman, returning the grin with which Charley put the question.

Charley Bates led Oliver into a kitchen, where there were two or three of the beds on which he had slept before, and here, with many uncontrollable bursts of laughter, he produced the identical old suit of clothes which Oliver had been so pleased to leave off at Mr Brownlow's, and which had been sold by the maid to someone who had, by chance, showed them to Fagin, thus giving him his first clue to Oliver's whereabouts.

"Pull off the smart ones," said Charley, "and I'll give 'em to Fagin to take care of. What fun it is!"

Poor Oliver unwillingly obeyed, Charley, rolling up the new clothes under his arm, departed from the room, leaving Oliver in the dark, and locking the door behind him.

The noise of Charley's laughter, and the voice of Miss Betsy, who arrived at just the right time to throw water over her friend, and assist her recovery, might have kept many people awake under more happy circumstances than those in which Oliver was placed. But he was sick and weary, and he soon fell sound asleep.

CHAPTER 18

FAGIN AND SIKES PLAN A ROBBERY

About noon next day, when the Dodger and Charley Bates had gone out, Fagin gave Oliver a lecture on the crying sin of ingratitude towards those who had befriended him when he was homeless. He told Oliver the story of another young lad under his protection who had gone to the police and had subsequently been committed to the Old Bailey, found guilty on evidence supplied by his old master, and finally hanged.

Oliver's blood ran cold as he listened to Fagin's words, and the old gentleman smiling hideously, patted him on the head and said that if he kept himself quiet, and applied himself to business, he saw they would be very good friends yet. Then, taking his hat, and covering himself with an old, patched great-coat, he went out, and locked the room door behind him.

And so Oliver remained all that day and for the greater part of the days following, seeing nobody between early morning and midnight, and left during the long hours to his own thoughts, which, turning to his kind friends and what they must be thinking of him, were sad indeed.

After a week or so, Fagin left the room door unlocked, and he was at liberty to wander about the house.

It was a very dirty place. The rooms upstairs had great high wooden chimney pieces and large doors with panelled walls and cornices to the ceilings, which, although they were black with neglect and dust, were ornamented in various ways. Oliver thought that, a long time ago, it must have belonged to better people, and had perhaps been quite handsome, dismal and dreary as it looked now.

Spiders had built their webs in the angles of the walls and ceilings, and sometimes, when Oliver walked softly into a room, the mice would scamper across the floor, and run back terrified to their holes. Apart from the mice, there was neither sight nor sound of any living thing, and often, when it grew dark, and he was tired of wandering from room to room, he would crouch in the corner of the passage by the street-door, to be as near living people as he could, and would remain there, listening and counting the hours, until Fagin or the boys returned.

One chill, damp, windy night, Fagin, leaving Oliver with Dodger and Charley Bates, buttoned his great-coat tight round his shrivelled body, pulled the collar up over his ears so as completely to hide the lower part of his face, and emerged from his den. He paused on the step as the door was locked and chained behind him, and, having listened while the boys made all secure, and until he could no longer hear their retreating footsteps, slunk down the street as quickly as he could.

The house to which Oliver had been taken was in the neighbourhood of Whitechapel. Fagin stopped for an instant at the corner of the street, and, glancing suspiciously round, crossed the road and struck off in the direction of Spitalfields.

He kept on his course, through many winding and narrow ways, until he reached Bethnal Green; then, turning suddenly off to the left, he soon became involved in a maze of mean and dirty streets. Fagin was quite familiar with the district, and he hurried without hesitation through several alleys and streets, and at length turned into one, lighted only by a single lamp at the farther end. At the door of the house in this street, he knocked, and, having exchanged a few muttered words with the person who opened it, he walked upstairs.

A dog growled as he touched the handle of a room door, and a man's voice demanded who was there.

"Only me, Bill. Only me, my dear," said the old man, looking in.

"Bring in your body, then," said Sikes. "Lie down, you stupid brute! Don't you know the devil when he's got a greatcoat on?"

Apparently the dog had been somewhat deceived by Fagin's outer garment, for, as the old man unbuttoned it, and threw it over the back of a chair, he retired to the corner from which he had risen, wagging his tail as he went, to show that he was as well satisfied as it was in his nature to be.

"Well?" said Sikes.

"Well, my dear," replied Fagin. "—Ah! Nancy."

This was said with slight embarrassment, for Fagin and Nancy had not met since she had interfered on behalf of Oliver. However, Nancy took her feet off the fender, pushed back her chair, and bade Fagin draw up his, saying it was a cold night and no mistake.

"It *is* cold, Nancy dear," said the old man as he warmed his skinny hands over the fire. "It seems to go right through one," he added, touching his side.

"It must be a piercer, if it finds its way through *your* heart," said Sikes. "Give him something to drink, Nancy. Burn my body, make haste! It's enough to turn a man ill, to see his lean old carcase shivering in that way, like a ugly ghost just rose from the grave."

Nancy quickly brought a bottle from a cupboard and Sikes, pouring out a glass of brandy, bade Fagin drink it off.

"Quite enough, quite, thankye, Bill," replied the old man, putting down the glass after just setting his lips to it.

"What! You're afraid of our getting the better of you, are you?" inquired Sikes, fixing his eyes on Fagin. "Ugh!"

With a hoarse grunt of contempt, he seized the glass and threw the remainder of its contents into the ashes, filling it again for himself.

"There," said Sikes, smacking his lips. "Now I'm ready."

"For business?" inquired Fagin.

"For business," replied Sikes. "So say what you've got to say."

"About the crib at Chertsey, Bill," said Fagin, drawing his chair forward, and speaking in a very low voice.

"Yes, what about it?" inquired Sikes.

"Ah! You know what I mean, my dear," said the old man. "He knows what I mean, Nancy, don't he?"

"No, he don't," sneered Sikes. "Or he won't, and that's the same thing. Speak out, and call things by their right names. Don't sit there, winking and blinking, and talking to me in hints, as if it wasn't you that thought about the robbery in the first place. What d'ye mean?"

"Hush, Bill, hush!" said Fagin. "Somebody will hear us, my dear. Somebody will hear us."

"Let 'm hear," said Sikes. "I don't care." But, as he *did* care, he dropped his voice as he said the words, and grew calmer.

"There, there," said Fagin coaxingly. "It was only my caution, nothing more. Now, my dear, about that house at Chertsey: when is it to be done, Bill, eh? When is it to be done? Such silver-plate, my dear, such silver-plate!" said Fagin, rubbing his hands and arching his eyebrows in a rapture of anticipation.

"Not at all," replied Sikes coldly.

"Not to be done at all!" echoed Fagin, leaning back in his chair.

"No, not at all," rejoined Sikes. "At least, it can't be an inside job, as we expected."

"Then it hasn't been properly gone about," said the old man, turning pale with anger. "Don't tell me!"

"But I will tell you," retorted Sikes. "Who are you that's not to be told? I tell you that Toby Crackit has been hanging about the place for a fortnight, and he can't get one of the servants into a line."

"Do you mean to tell me, Bill," said Fagin, "that neither of the two men in the house can be got over?"

"Yes, I do mean to tell you so," replied Sikes. "The old lady has had 'em these twenty years, and if you were to give 'em five hundred pound, they wouldn't be in it."

"But do you mean to say, my dear," said Fagin, "that the women can't be got over?"

"Nor them neither," replied Sikes.

"Not by flash Toby Crackit? Think what women are, Bill."

"No, not even by flash Toby Crackit," replied Sikes. "He says he's worn sham whiskers, and a canary waistcoat, the whole blessed time he's been loitering down there, and it's all of no use."

"He should have tried mustachios and a pair of military trousers, my dear," said Fagin.

"He did," rejoined Sikes, "and they weren't of any more use, neither."

Fagin thought for a while and finally said with a deep sigh that if flash Toby Crackit reported aright, he feared the game was up.

"And yet," said the old man, "it's a sad thing, my dear, to lose so much when we had set our hearts upon it."

"So it is," said Sikes. "Worse luck!"

A long silence followed, during which Fagin was plunged in deep thought. Sikes eyed him from time to time, but Nancy, apparently afraid of irritating the housebreaker, sat with her eyes fixed upon the fire, as if she had been deaf to all that passed.

"Fagin," said Sikes, abruptly breaking the silence, "is it worth an extra fifty if it's done from outside?"

"Yes," said the old man, as suddenly rousing himself.

"Is it a bargain?" inquired Sikes.

"Yes, my dear, yes," rejoined Fagin, his eyes glistening, and every muscle in his face working with excitement.

"Then," said Sikes, "let it come off as soon as you like. Toby and me were over the garden wall the night before last, sounding the panels of the doors and shutters. The house is barred up at night like a jail, but there's one place we could get in."

"Is there no other help wanted, but yours and Toby's?" said the old man.

"None," said Sikes, "except the right tools and a young boy. The first we've got; the second you must find us."

Fagin thought for a while, then nodded his head towards Nancy, who was still gazing at the fire, and signed to Bill to send her out of the room. Sikes shrugged his shoulders impatiently, as if he thought the precaution unnecessary, but complied, nevertheless, by asking Nancy to fetch him a jug of beer.

"You don't want any beer," said Nancy, folding her arms and staying where she was.

"I tell you I do!" replied Sikes.

"Nonsense," rejoined the girl. "Go on, Fagin. I know what he's going to say, Bill. He needn't mind me."

Fagin still hesitated. Sikes looked from one to the other in some surprise.

"Why, you don't mind the old girl, do you, Fagin?" he asked at length. "You've known her long enough to trust her. She ain't one to blab. Are you, Nancy?"

"I should think not!" replied Nancy, drawing her chair up to the table and putting her elbows upon it. "Go on, Fagin, tell Bill about Oliver?"

"Ha! You're a clever one, my dear; the sharpest girl I ever saw!" said Fagin, patting her on the neck. "Oliver's the boy for you, Bill. It's time he began to work for his bread. Besides, the others are all too big."

"Well, he is just the size I want," said Sikes thoughtfully.

"And will do everything you want, Bill, my dear," said Fagin. "He can't help himself. That is, if you frighten him enough."

"Frighten him!" echoed Sikes. "It'll be no sham frightening, mind you. If there's anything wrong about him when we once get into the work, in for a penny, in for a pound. You won't see him alive again, Fagin. Think of that before you send him."

"When is it to be done?" asked Nancy.

"Ah, to be sure," said the old man. "When is it to be done, Bill?"

"I planned with Toby, the night arter tomorrow," rejoined Sikes, "if he heard nothing from me to the contrary."

"Good," said Fagin. "There's no moon."

"No," replied Sikes.

"It's all arranged about bringing off the swag, is it?" asked Fagin.

Sikes nodded.

"And about——"

"Oh, ah, it's all planned," said Sikes, interrupting him. "Never mind particulars. You'd better bring the boy here tomorrow night. I shall get out of the town an hour after daybreak. Then you hold your tongue and keep the melting-pot ready, and that's all you'll have to do."

After some discussion, it was decided that Nancy should go to Fagin's the next evening when the night had set in, and bring Oliver away with her, Fagin craftily observing that if he showed any reluctance, he would be more willing to accompany the girl who had so recently interfered on his behalf, than anybody else.

Matters settled, Sikes now proceeded to drink brandy at an alarming rate, and the old man prepared to take his leave.

The girl went to the door with him.

"Good night, Nancy," said Fagin, muffling himself up as before.

"Good night."

Their eyes met, and Fagin scrutinised her narrowly. There was no flinching about the girl. She was as true and earnest in the matter as Toby Crackit himself could be.

The old man took his way through mud and mire to his gloomy abode, where the Dodger was sitting up, impatiently awaiting his return.

"Is Oliver a-bed? I want to speak to him," was the first remark as they descended the stairs.

"Hours ago," replied the Dodger, throwing open a door. "Here he is."

The boy was lying fast asleep, on a rough bed upon the floor, so pale with anxiety and sadness, and the closeness of his prison, that he looked as if his young and gentle spirit had but an instant fled to Heaven.

"Not now," said Fagin, turning softly away. "Tomorrow. Tomorrow."

CHAPTER 19

OLIVER WITH BILL AND NANCY

When Oliver awoke in the morning, he was a good deal surprised to find that a new pair of shoes, with strong thick soles, had been placed at his bedside, and that his old shoes had been removed. At first, he was pleased with the discovery, hoping that it might be the forerunner of his release; but such thoughts were quickly banished on his sitting down to breakfast along with Fagin, who told him, in a tone and manner which increased his alarm, that he was to be taken to the home of Bill Sikes that night.

"To—to—stop there, sir?" asked Oliver anxiously.

"No, no, my dear. Not to stop there," replied Fagin. "We shouldn't like to lose you. Don't be afraid, Oliver; you shall come back to us again. Ha! ha! ha! We won't be so cruel as to send you away, my dear. Oh no, no!"

The old man, who was stooping over the fire toasting a piece of bread, looked round as he teased Oliver thus, and chuckled as if to show that he knew he would still be very glad to get away if he could.

"I suppose," said Fagin, fixing his eyes on Oliver, "you want to know what you're going to Bill's for—eh, my dear?"

Oliver blushed to find that the old thief had been reading his thoughts, but boldly said, Yes, he did want to know.

"Why, do you think?" inquired Fagin, avoiding the question.

"Indeed, I don't know, sir," replied Oliver.

"Bah!" said the old man, turning away with a disappointed countenance from a close study of the boy's face. "Wait till Bill tells you then."

Fagin seemed much vexed by Oliver's not expressing any greater curiosity on the subject, but the truth is that, although Oliver felt very anxious, he was too much confused by the earnest cunning of the old man's looks, and by the questions in his own mind, to make any further inquiries just then. He had no other opportunity, for Fagin remained very surly and silent till night, when he prepared to go out.

"You may burn a candle," said Fagin, putting one upon the table. "Presently, they will come to fetch you. Good night, Oliver and take heed, take heed of Bill! He's a rough man, and thinks nothing of blood when his own is up. Whatever happens, say nothing and do what he bids you. Mind!" A ghastly grin came over his face, and, nodding his head, Fagin left the room.

Oliver leaned his head upon his hand when the old man disappeared, and pondered with a trembling heart on the words he had just heard. Then, falling upon his knees, he prayed to Heaven in a low and broken voice, that he might be rescued from his present dangers, and that help might come to him now when, desolate and deserted, he stood alone in the midst of wickedness and guilt.

He had concluded his prayer, but still remained with his head buried in his hands, when a rustling noise aroused him.

"What's that?" he cried, jumping up and catching sight of a figure standing by the door. "Who's there?"

"Me. Only me," replied a tremulous voice.

Oliver raised the candle above his head, and looked towards the door. It was Nancy.

"Put down the light," said the girl, turning away her head. "It hurts my eyes."

Oliver saw that she was very pale, and gently inquired if she were ill. The girl threw herself into a chair, with her back towards him, but made no reply.

"God forgive me!" she cried after a while. "I never thought of this."

"Has anything happened?" asked Oliver. "Can I help you? I will if I can. I will indeed."

The girl beat her hands upon her knees, and her feet upon the ground, and, suddenly stopping, drew her shawl close round her, and shivered with the cold.

Oliver stirred the fire. Drawing her chair close to it, she sat there for a little time without speaking, but at length she raised her head and looked round.

"I don't know what comes over me sometimes," said she, affecting to busy herself in arranging her dress. "It's this damp, dirty room, I think. Now, Nolly dear, are you ready?"

"Am I to go with you?" asked Oliver.

"Yes, I have come from Bill," replied the girl. "You are to come with me."

"What for?" asked Oliver, stepping back.

"What for?" echoed the girl, raising her eyes, and turning them away again, the moment they encountered the boy's face. "Oh! For no harm."

"I don't believe it," said Oliver, who had watched her closely.

"Have it your own way," rejoined the girl, making the pretence of a laugh. "For no good, then."

Oliver could see that he had some power over the girl's better feelings, and, for an instant, thought of appealing to her for help. But then the thought darted across his mind that it was barely eleven o'clock, and that many people were still in the streets, and he might find someone who would believe his tale. He stepped forward, and said, somewhat hastily, that he was ready.

Nancy eyed him narrowly while he spoke, and showed by her looks that she guessed what had been passing in his thoughts.

"Hush!" said the girl, stooping over him, and pointing to the door as she looked cautiously round. "You can't help yourself. I have tried hard for you, but all to no purpose. You are hedged round and round. If ever you are to get loose from here, this is not the time. No more. Give me your hand."

She caught the hand which Oliver instinctively placed in hers, and, blowing out the light, drew him after her up the stairs. The door was opened quickly by someone shrouded in the darkness, and was as quickly closed, when they had passed out. A hackney-cabriolet was in waiting; the girl pulled Oliver in with her, and drew the curtains close. The driver needed no directions, but drove off at full speed, without the delay of an instant. All was so quick and hurried that Oliver scarcely had time to recollect where he was, or how he came there, when the carriage stopped at the house which Fagin had visited the night before.

Nancy held him tightly, they entered the house, and the door was shut.

"This way," said the girl, releasing her hold for the first time. "Bill!"

"Hallo!" replied Sikes, appearing at the head of the stairs with a candle. "Oh! That's the time of day. Come on!"

This was an uncommonly hearty welcome from such a man as Sikes. Nancy, appearing pleased, greeted him cordially.

"Bull's-eye's gone home with Charley," said Sikes, as he lighted them up. "He'd have been in the way."

"That's right," rejoined Nancy.

"So you've got the kid," said Sikes, when they had all reached the room, closing the door as he spoke.

"Yes, here he is," replied Nancy.

"Did he come quiet?" inquired Sikes.

"Like a lamb," rejoined Nancy.

"I'm glad to hear it," said Sikes, looking grimly at Oliver, "for his own sake. Come here, young 'un, and let me read you a lecture, which is as well got over at once."

Thus addressing his new pupil, Sikes pulled off Oliver's cap and threw it into a corner. Then, taking him by the shoulder, he sat himself down by the table, and stood the boy in front of him.

"Now, first, do you know what this is?" inquired Sikes, taking up a pocket pistol which lay on the table.

Oliver replied that he did.

"Well then, look here," continued Sikes. "This is powder, that 'ere's a bullet, and this is a little bit of old hat for waddin'."

Oliver murmured that he understood, and Sikes proceeded to load the pistol, very carefully and deliberately.

"Now it's loaded," said Sikes when he had finished.

"Yes, I see it is, sir," replied Oliver.

"Well," said the robber, grasping Oliver's wrist and putting the barrel so close to his temple that they touched—at which moment the boy could not keep back a start—"if you speak a word when you're out o'doors with me, except when I speak to you, that bullet will be in your head without notice. So, if you do make up your mind to speak without leave, say your prayers first. And now that he's thoroughly up to it, Nancy, let's have some supper, and get a snooze before starting."

Nancy quickly laid the cloth and, disappearing for a few minutes, presently returned with a pot of beer and a dish of sheep's heads, which Sikes washed down by swallowing all the beer at one gulp, while Oliver ate and drank—as may be imagined, practically nothing.

Supper being ended, Sikes drank a couple of glasses of spirits and water and threw himself on the bed, ordering Nancy to call him at five precisely. Oliver stretched himself, in his clothes, on a mattress upon the the floor, and the girl, making up the fire, sat before it, in readiness to rouse them at the appointed time.

For a long time Oliver lay awake, thinking it possible that Nancy might use the opportunity to whisper him some further advice, but the girl sat brooding over the fire, without moving, save now and then to trim the light. Weary with watching and anxiety, he at length fell asleep.

When he awoke, the table was covered with tea-things, and Sikes was thrusting various articles into the pockets of his great-coat, which hung over the back of a chair. Nancy was busily engaged in preparing breakfast. It was not yet daylight, for the candle was still burning, and it was quite dark outside. A sharp rain, too, was beating against the window panes, and the sky looked black and cloudy.

"Now then!" growled Sikes, as Oliver started up, "half-past five! Look sharp, or you'll get no breakfast, for it's late as it is."

Oliver was not long in getting ready. Having taken some breakfast, he replied to a surly inquiry from Sikes by saying that he was ready.

Nancy, scarcely looking at the boy, threw him a handkerchief to tie round his throat, and Sikes gave him a large rough cape to button over his shoulders. Thus attired, he gave his hand to the robber, who, merely pausing to show him with a threatening gesture that he had that same pistol in a side-pocket of his great-coat, clasped it firmly in his, and, exchanging a farewell with Nancy, led him away.

Oliver turned, for an instant, when they reached the door, in the hope of meeting a look from the girl. But she had resumed her old seat in front of the fire, and sat perfectly motionless before it.

CHAPTER 20

A LONG JOURNEY

It was a cheerless morning when they got into the street, blowing and raining hard, and the clouds looking dull and stormy. The night had been very wet, and large pools of water had collected in the road. The sombre light of the coming day made the street lamps look pale, without shedding any warmer or brighter tints upon the wet housetops and dreary streets. There appeared to be nobody stirring in that part of the town. The windows of the houses were all closely shut, and the streets through which they passed were noiseless and empty.

By the time they had turned into the Bethnal Green Road, the day had fairly begun to break. Many of the lamps were already extinguished, a few country wagons were slowly toiling on towards London, and now and then, a stage-coach, covered with mud, rattled briskly by. The public-houses, with gas-lights burning inside, were already open. By degrees, other shops began to be unclosed, and a few scattered people were met with. Then came straggling groups of labourers going to their work; then men and women with fish-baskets on their heads, donkey-carts laden with vegetables, chaise-carts filled with livestock or whole carcases of meat, milk-women with pails, an unbroken throng of people, trudging out with various supplies to the eastern suburbs of the town. As they approached the City, the noise and traffic gradually increased, and when they threaded the streets between Shoreditch and Smithfield, it had swelled into a roar of sound and bustle. It was as light as it was likely to be, till night came on again, and the busy morning of half the London population had begun.

Turning down Sun Street and Crown Street, and crossing Finsbury Square, Bill Sikes went by way of Chiswell Street into Barbican, thence into Long Lane, and so into the crowds at Smithfield Market.

Dragging Oliver after him, he elbowed his way among

the people, paying very little attention to the sights and sounds around him. He nodded once or twice to a passing friend, and, resisting their invitations to take a morning drink with them, pressed steadily onward until they were clear of the turmoil, and had made their way through Hosier Lane into Holborn.

"Now, young 'un," said Sikes, looking up at the clock of St Andrew's Church, "hard upon seven! You must step out. Come, don't lag behind already, Lazylegs!" He gave Oliver's wrist a jerk, and the boy, quickening his pace into a kind of trot, between a fast walk and a run, kept up with the rapid strides of the housebreaker as well as he could.

They held their course at this rate until they had passed Hyde Park Corner and were on their way to Kensington. Then Sikes relaxed his pace, until an empty cart, which had been some little distance behind, came up. Seeing "Hounslow" written on it, he asked the driver with as much politeness as he could assume if he would give them a lift as far as Isleworth.

"Jump up," said the man. "Is that your boy?"

"Yes, he's my boy," replied Sikes, looking hard at Oliver, and putting his hand casually into the pocket where the pistol was.

"Your father walks rather too quick for you, don't he, my man?" inquired the driver, seeing that Oliver was out of breath.

"Not a bit of it," replied Sikes, "he's used to it. Here, take hold of my hand, Ned. In with you!"

Thus addressing Oliver, he helped him into the cart, and the driver, pointing to a heap of sacks, told him to lie down there, and rest himself.

As they passed the different milestones, Oliver wondered more and more where his companion meant to take him. Kensington, Hammersmith, Chiswick, Kew Bridge, Brentford, were all passed, and yet they went on steadily as if they had only just begun their journey. At length, they came to a public-house called the Coach and Horses, a little way beyond which, another road appeared to turn off. And here, the cart stopped and Sikes and Oliver jumped down.

Sikes waited until the cart was out of sight, and then, telling Oliver he might look about him if he wanted, once again led him onward on his journey.

They turned round to the left, a short way past the public-house, and then, taking a right-hand road, walked on for a long time, passing many large gardens and gentlemen's houses on both sides of the way, and stopping for nothing but a little beer until they reached a town. Here, against the wall of a house, Oliver saw written up in rather large letters, "Hampton". They lingered about in the fields for some hours. At length, they came back into the town, and, turning into an old public-house with a faded signboard, ordered some dinner by the kitchen fire.

The kitchen was an old, low-roofed room, with a great beam across the middle of the ceiling, and benches, with high backs to them, by the fire, on which were seated several rough men in smocks, drinking and smoking. They took no notice of Oliver, and very little of Sikes, and, as Sikes took very little notice of them, he and Oliver sat in a corner by themselves, without being much troubled by their company.

They had some cold meat for dinner, and sat so long after it, while Sikes indulged himself with three or four pipes, that Oliver began to feel quite certain they were not going any further. Being much tired with the walk, and getting up so early, he dozed a little at first, then, quite overpowered by fatigue and the fumes of the tobacco, fell asleep.

It was quite dark when he was awakened by a push from Sikes. Rousing himself sufficiently to sit up and look about him, he found his master buying a pint of ale for a labouring man who was going back with his cart in the direction of Shepperton after delivering a load. This seemed to suit Sikes, and, after another drink was pushed across the table to him, the man agreed to give them a lift.

The night was very dark. A damp mist rose from the river and the marshy ground about, and spread itself over the dreary fields. It was piercing cold, too; all was gloomy and black. Not a word was spoken, for the driver was sleepy, and Sikes was in no mood to lead him into conversation. Oliver sat huddled in a corner of the cart, bewildered with alarm and fear, and seeming to see strange objects in the gaunt trees, whose branches waved grimly to and fro, as if in some fantastic joy at the desolation of the scene.

As they passed Sunbury Church, the clock struck seven. There was a light in the ferry-house window opposite, which streamed across the road and threw into more sombre shadow a dark yew-tree with graves beneath it. There was a dull sound of falling water not far off, and the leaves of the old tree stirred gently in the night wind. It seemed like quiet music for the repose of the dead.

Sunbury was passed through, and they came again into the lonely road. Two or three miles more, and the cart stopped. Sikes alighted, took Oliver by the hand, and they once again walked on.

They turned into no house at Shepperton as the weary boy had expected, but still kept walking on, in mud and darkness, through gloomy lanes and over cold open wastes, until they came within sight of the lights of a town at no great distance. On looking intently forward, Oliver saw that the water was just below them, and that they were coming to the foot of a bridge.

Sikes kept straight on, until they were close upon the bridge, then turned suddenly down a bank upon the left.

"The water!" thought Oliver, turning sick with fear. "He has brought me to this lonely place to murder me!"

He was about to throw himself on the ground, and make one struggle for his young life, when he saw that they stood before a solitary house, all ruinous and decayed. There was a window on each side of the dilapidated entrance, and one storey above, but no light was visible. The house was dark, dismantled, and, to all appearance, uninhabited.

Sikes, with Oliver's hand in his, softly approached the low porch, and raised the latch. The door yielded to the pressure, and they passed in together.

CHAPTER 21

THROUGH THE LITTLE WINDOW

"Hallo!" cried a loud, hoarse voice, as soon as they set foot in the passage.

"Don't make such a row," said Sikes, bolting the door. "Show a glim, Toby."

"Aha, my pal!" cried the same voice. "A glim, Barney, a glim! Show the gentleman in, Barney. Wake up!"

A pair of slipshod feet shuffled hastily across the bare floor of a room, and there appeared from a door on the right hand first a feeble candle, and, next, the young man with a cold in his nose who was the waiter at the public-house on Saffron Hill.

"Bister Sikes," exclaimed Barney, with real or pretended pleasure, "cub id, sir; cub id."

"Here, you get on first," said Sikes, putting Oliver in front of him. "Quicker, or I shall tread upon your heels."

Muttering a curse upon his slowness, Sikes pushed Oliver before him, and they entered a low, dark room with a very smoky fire, two or three broken chairs, a table and a very old couch, on which, with his legs much higher than his head, a man was reposing at full length, smoking a long clay pipe. He was dressed in a smartly cut snuff-coloured coat, with large brass buttons, an orange neckerchief, a coarse, gaudy waistcoat and drab breeches. Mr Toby Crackit (for he it was) had no very great quantity of hair, either upon his head or face, but what he had was of a reddish dye, and tortured into long corkscrew curls, through which he occasionally thrust some very dirty fingers, ornamented with large, common rings. He was a trifle above the middle size, and apparently rather weak in the legs, but this did not prevent him admiring his top-boots, which he contemplated in their lofty situation with lively satisfaction.

"Bill, my boy!" said this figure, turning his head towards the door, "I'm glad to see you. I was almost afraid you'd given it up. Hallo!"

Uttering this exclamation in a tone of great surprise, as his eye rested on Oliver, Toby Crackit sat up and demanded who he was.

"The boy. Only the boy," replied Sikes, drawing a chair towards the fire.

"Wud of Bister Fagin's lads," said Barney with a grin.

"Fagin's, eh?" exclaimed Toby, looking at Oliver. "What an inwalable boy that'll make for the old ladies' pockets in chapels! His face is a fortun' to him."

"There—that's enough of that," said Sikes impatiently. "If you'll give us something to eat and drink, Barney, while we're waiting, you'll put some heart in us, or in me, at all events.

Sit down by the fire, Oliver, and rest yourself, for you'll have to go out with us again tonight, though not very far off."

Oliver looked at Sikes in mute and timid wonder, and, drawing a stool to the fire, sat with his aching head upon his hands, scarcely knowing where he was, or what was passing round him.

"Here," said Toby, as Barney placed some fragments of food and a bottle upon the table, "success to the crack!" He rose to honour the toast, and, carefully depositing his empty pipe in a corner, advanced to the table, filled a glass with spirits and and drank off its contents. Sikes did the same.

"A drain for the boy," said Toby, half-filling a wine glass. "Down with it, innocence."

"Indeed," said Oliver, looking piteously up into the man's face, "indeed, I——"

"Down with it!" echoed Toby. "Do you think I don't know what's good for you? Tell him to drink it, Bill."

"He had better!" said Sikes clapping his hand upon the pistol in his pocket. "Burn my body, if he isn't more trouble than a whole family of Dodgers. Drink it, you perwerse imp. Drink it."

Frightened by the threatening gestures of the two men, Oliver hastily swallowed the contents of the glass, and immediately fell into a violent fit of coughing, which delighted Toby Crackit and Barney, and even drew a smile from the surly Bill Sikes.

This done, and Sikes having satisfied his appetite (Oliver could eat nothing but a small crust of bread which they made him swallow), the two men laid themselves down on chairs for a short nap. Oliver retained his stool by the fire, and Barney, wrapped in a blanket, stretched himself on the floor, close outside the fender.

They slept, or appeared to sleep, for some time, nobody stirring but Barney, who rose once or twice to throw coals upon the fire. Oliver fell into a heavy doze, imagining himself straying along the gloomy lanes, or wandering about the dark churchyard, or retracing some one or other of the scenes of the past day, when he was roused by Toby Crackit jumping up and declaring it was half past one.

In an instant, the other two were on their legs, and all were actively engaged in busy preparation. Sikes and Toby enveloped their necks and chins in large dark shawls, and drew on their greatcoats. Barney, opening a cupboard, brought forth several articles, which he hastily crammed into the pockets.

"Barkers for me, Barney," said Toby Crackit.

"Here they are," replied Barney, producing a pair of pistols. "You loaded them yourself."

"All right," replied Toby, stowing them away. "Tools?"

"I've got 'em," replied Sikes.

"Keys?" inquired Toby fastening a small crowbar to a loop inside the skirt of his coat.

"Yes," rejoined his companion. "Bring them bits of timber, Barney. That's the time of day."

With these words, he took a thick stick from Barney's hands, who, having delivered another to Toby, busied himself in fastening on Oliver's cape.

"Now then," said Sikes, holding out his hand.

Oliver, who was completely dazed by the unaccustomed exercise, and the air, and the drink which had been forced upon him, put his hand mechanically into that which Sikes held out.

"Take his other hand, Toby," said Sikes. "Look outside, Barney."

Barney went to the door, and returned to announce that all was quiet. The two robbers went out with Oliver between them. Barney, having made all fast, rolled himself up as before, and was soon asleep again

It was intensely dark. The fog was much heavier than it had been in the early part of the night, and the atmosphere was so damp that, although no rain fell, Oliver's hair and eyebrows, within a few minutes after leaving the house, had become stiff with the half-frozen moisture that was floating about. They crossed the bridge, and kept on towards the lights which he had seen before. They were at no great distance off, and, as they walked pretty briskly, they soon arrived at Chertsey.

"Slap through the town," whispered Sikes. "There'll be nobody in the way tonight to see us."

Toby agreed, and they hurried through the main street of the town, which, at that late hour, was wholly deserted. A dim light shone at intervals from some bedroom window, and the hoarse barking of dogs occasionally broke the silence of the night. But there was nobody about. They had cleared the town as the church bell struck two.

Quickening their pace, they turned up a road upon the left hand. After walking about a quarter of a mile, they stopped before a detached house surrounded by a wall, to the top of which, Toby Crackit, scarcely pausing to take breath, climbed in a twinkling.

"The boy next," said Toby. "Hoist him up. I'll catch hold of him."

Before Oliver had time to look round, Sikes had caught him under the arms, and in three seconds he and Toby were lying on the grass on the other side. Sikes followed, and they stole cautiously towards the house.

And now, for the first time, Oliver, nearly mad with grief and terror, saw that housebreaking and robbery, if not murder, were the objects of the expedition. He clasped his hands together and uttered a low exclamation of horror. A mist came before his eyes, the cold sweat stood upon his ashy face, his limbs failed him, and he sank upon his knees.

"Get up!" murmured Sikes, trembling with rage and drawing the pistol from his pocket. "Get up, or I'll strew your brains upon the grass."

"Oh, for God's sake let me go!" cried Oliver. "Let me run away and die in the fields. Oh, pray, have mercy on me and do not make me steal. For the love of all the bright angels that rest in Heaven have mercy upon me!"

Sikes swore a dreadful oath and had cocked the pistol, when Toby, striking it from his grasp, placed his hand upon the boy's mouth and dragged him to the house.

"Hush," said Toby. "That won't do here. If he says another word, I'll give him a crack on the head. That makes no noise and works just as well. Here, Bill, wrench the shutter open. He'll be all right now. I've seen older hands of his age took the same way for a minute or two on a cold night."

Sikes, calling down curses upon Fagin's head for sending Oliver on such an errand, plied the crowbar vigorously, but with little noise. After some delay, and some assistance from Toby, the shutter to which he had referred swung open on its hinges.

It was a little lattice window, about five feet and a half above the ground, at the back of the house. It belonged to a scullery or small brewing-place at the end of the passage.

The opening was so small that the members of the household had probably not thought it worth while to defend it more securely, but it was large enough to admit a boy of Oliver's size, nevertheless. Bill soon dealt with the fastening of the lattice window, and it soon stood wide open also.

"Now listen, you young limb," whispered Sikes, drawing a dark lantern from his pocket, and throwing the glare full on Oliver's face. "I'm going to put you through there. Take this light, go softly up the steps straight afore you, and along the little hall to the street-door. Unfasten it, and let us in."

"There's a bolt at the top you won't be able to reach," said Toby. "Stand upon one of the hall chairs. There are three there, Bill, with a jolly large blue unicorn and gold pitch-fork on 'em, which is the old lady's arms."

"Keep quiet, can't you?" replied Sikes with a threatening look. "The room door is open, is it?"

"Wide," replied Toby, after peeping in to satisfy himself. "They always leave it open with a catch, so that the dog may walk up and down when he feels wakeful. Ha! Ha! Barney got him away with a bone tonight. So neat!"

Although Toby Crackit was scarcely whispering, and laughed without noise, Sikes, with an oath, commanded him to be silent, and get to work. Toby obeyed, by first producing his lantern and placing it on the ground, then by planting himself firmly with his head against the wall beneath the window, and his hands upon his knees, so as to make a step on his back. This was no sooner done, than Sikes, climbing upon him, put Oliver gently through the window with his feet first, and, without leaving hold of his collar, planted him safely on the floor inside.

"Take this lantern," said Sikes, looking into the room. "You see the stairs afore you?"

Oliver, more dead than alive, gasped out, "Yes." Sikes, pointing to the street door with the pistol-barrel, whispered to him that he was within shot all the way, and that, if he hesitated, he would fall dead that instant.

"It's done in a minute," said Sikes, in the same low whisper. "Directly I leave go of you, do your work. Hark!"

"What's that?" whispered the other man.

They listened intently.

"Nothing," said Sikes, releasing his hold of Oliver. "Now!"

In the short time he had had to collect his senses, the boy

had firmly resolved that, whether he died in the attempt or not, he would make one effort to dart upstairs from the hall, and alarm the family. Filled with this idea, he advanced at once, but stealthily.

"Come back!" suddenly cried Sikes aloud. "Back! Back!"

Scared by the sudden breaking of the dead stillness of the place, and by a loud cry which followed it, Oliver let his lantern fall and knew not whether to advance or fly.

The cry was repeated—a light appeared—a vision of two terrified half-dressed men at the top of the stairs swam before his eyes—a flash—a loud noise—smoke—a crash somewhere, but where, he knew not—and he staggered back.

Sikes had disappeared for an instant, but he was up again, and had him by the collar before the smoke had cleared away. He fired his own pistol after the men, who were already retreating, and dragged the boy up.

"Clasp your arm tighter," said Sikes as he drew him through the window. "Give me a shawl here. They've hit him. Quick! How the boy bleeds!"

Then came the loud ringing of a bell, mingled with the noise of fire-arms, and the shouts of men, and the sensation of being carried over uneven ground at a rapid pace. And then the noises grew confused in the distance, and a cold, deadly feeling crept over the boy's heart, and he saw or heard no more.

CHAPTER 22

MRS CORNEY ENTERTAINS

The night was bitter cold. The snow lay on the ground, frozen into a hard thick crust, so that only the heaps that had drifted into by-ways and corners were affected by the sharp wind that howled around them and caught the snow savagely up in clouds, and, whirling it into a thousand misty eddies, scattered it in the air.

Such was the weather out of doors when Mrs Corney,

the matron of the workhouse where Oliver Twist was born, sat herself down before a cheerful fire in her own little room, and glanced complacently at a small round table, on which stood a tray ready laid for tea. As she glanced from the table to the fireplace, where the smallest of all possible kettles was singing a small song in a small voice, her inward satisfaction evidently increased—so much so, indeed, that Mrs Corney smiled.

"Well!" said the matron, leaning her elbow on the table, and looking reflectively at the fire, "I'm sure we have all on us a great deal to be grateful for! A great deal if we did but know it. Ah!"

Mrs Corney shook her head mournfully, as if regretting the stupidity of those workhouse inmates who did *not* know it, and thrusting a silver spoon (private property) into a two-ounce tin tea-caddy, proceeded to make the tea.

Unfortunately for her peace of mind, however, the black tea-pot, being very small and easily filled, ran over while Mrs Corney was moralising, and the water slightly scalded Mrs Corney's hand.

"Drat the pot!" said the worthy matron, setting it down very hastily on the hob, "a little stupid thing, that only holds a couple of cups! What use is it of, to anybody? Except," said Mrs Corney, pausing, "except to a poor desolate creature like me. Oh dear!"

With these words, the matron dropped into her chair, and, once more resting her elbow on the table, thought of her solitary fate. The small teapot, and the single cup, had awakened in her mind sad recollections of Mr Corney (who had not been dead more than five-and-twenty years), and she was overpowered.

"I shall never get another!" said Mrs Corney peevishly, "I shall never get another like him."

She had poured out and was just tasting her first cup, when she was disturbed by a soft tap at the room-door.

"Oh, come in with you!" said Mrs Corney sharply. "Some of the old women dying, I suppose. They always die when I'm at meals. Don't stand there, letting the cold air in, don't. What's the matter now, eh?"

"Nothing, ma'am, nothing," replied a man's voice.

"Dear me!" exclaimed Mrs Corney in a much sweeter tone, "is that Mr Bumble?"

"At your service, ma'am," said Mr Bumble, who had been stopping outside to rub his shoes clean, and to shake the snow off his coat, and who now made his appearance, bearing the cocked hat in one hand and a bundle in the other. "Shall I shut the door, ma'am?"

The matron modestly hesitated to reply, lest there should be anything improper in holding an interview with Mr Bumble behind closed doors. Mr Bumble, taking advantage of the hesitation, and being very cold himself, shut it without permission.

"Hard weather, Mr Bumble," said Mrs Corney.

"Hard indeed, ma'am," replied the beadle. "Bad for the parish, ma'am. We have given away, Mrs Corney, we have given away a matter of twenty quartern loaves and a cheese and a half, this very blessed afternoon, and yet them paupers are not contented."

"Of course not. When would they be?" said the matron, sipping her tea.

"When indeed, ma'am!" rejoined Mr Bumble. He started to unpack his bundle. "This is the port wine, ma'am, that the board ordered for the infirmary; real, fresh, genuine port wine, only out of the cask this forenoon; clear as a bell and no sediment." There were two bottles. Having held the first bottle up to the light, and shaken it well to test its excellence, Mr Bumble placed them both on top of a chest of drawers, folded up the wrapping, and took up his hat as if to go.

"You'll have a very cold walk, Mr Bumble," said the matron.

"It blows, ma'am," replied Mr Bumble, turning up his coat-collar, "enough to cut one's ears off."

The matron looked from the little kettle to the beadle, who was moving towards the door, and bashfully inquired whether—whether he wouldn't take a cup of tea?

Mr Bumble instantaneously turned back his collar again, laid his hat and stick upon a chair, and drew another chair up to the table. As he slowly seated himself, he looked at the matron. She fixed her eyes upon the little tea-pot. Mr Bumble coughed, and slightly smiled.

Mrs Corney rose to get another cup and saucer from the closet. As she sat down, her eyes encountered those of the gallant beadle; she blushed and applied herself to the task of making his tea. Again Mr Bumble coughed—louder this time than he had coughed yet.

"Sweet, Mr Bumble?" inquired the matron, taking up the sugar-basin.

"Very sweet indeed, ma'am," replied Mr Bumble. He fixed his eyes on Mrs Corney as he said this, and if ever a beadle looked tender, Mr Bumble was that beadle at that moment.

The tea was made, and handed in silence. Mr Bumble, having spread a handkerchief over his knees to keep the crumbs of a piece of buttered toast that went with it off his breeches, began to eat and drink, sighing deeply from time to time as he did so.

"You have a cat, ma'am, I see," said Mr Bumble, glancing at one who, in the centre of her family, was basking before the fire; "and kittens, too, I declare!"

"I am so fond of them, Mr Bumble, you can't think," replied the matron. "They're *so* happy, *so* frolicsome, and *so* cheerful, that they are quite companions for me."

"Very nice animals, ma'am," replied Mr Bumble approvingly, "so very domestic."

"Oh yes!" rejoined the matron with enthusiasm, "so fond of their home, too, that it's quite a pleasure, I'm sure."

"Mrs Corney, ma'am," said Mr Bumble slowly, and marking the time with his teaspoon, "I mean to say this, ma'am, that any cat or kitten that could live with you, ma'am, and *not* be fond of its home, must be a ass, ma'am."

"Oh, Mr Bumble!" protested Mrs Corney.

"It's of no use disguising facts, ma'am," said Mr Bumble slowly, flourishing the teaspoon in a dignified manner which made him doubly impressive. "I would drown it myself, with pleasure."

"Then you're a cruel man," said the matron gaily, as she held out her hand for the beadle's cup, "and a very hard-hearted man, besides."

"Hard-hearted, ma'am?" said Mr Bumble. "Hard?" Mr Bumble gave up his cup without another word, squeezed Mrs Corney's little finger as she took it, and, inflicting two open-handed slaps upon his laced waistcoat, gave a mighty sigh, and hitched his chair a little morsel farther from the fire.

It was a round table, and this brought him nearer Mrs Corney, who had been sitting opposite him. He continued moving his chair little by little, until finally the two chairs touched, and, when they did so, Mr Bumble stopped.

Mrs Corney said nothing, and handed Mr Bumble another cup of tea.

"Hard-hearted, Mrs Corney?" said Mr Bumble, stirring his tea and looking up into the matron's face. "Are *you* hard-hearted, Mrs Corney?"

"Dear me!" exclaimed the matron, "what a very curious question from a single man. What can you want to know for, Mr Bumble?"

The beadle drank his tea to the last drop, finished a piece of toast, whisked the crumbs off his knees, wiped his lips and deliberately kissed the matron.

"Mr Bumble!" cried Mrs Corney in a whisper, for the fright was so great that she had quite lost her voice. "Mr Bumble, I shall scream!" Mr Bumble made no reply, but, in a slow and dignified manner, put his arm round the matron's waist.

As Mrs Corney had stated her intention of screaming, she would no doubt have done so, but for a hasty knocking at the door, which was no sooner heard than Mr Bumble darted to the wine bottles and began dusting them with great violence, while the matron, recovering her voice, sharply demanded who was there.

"If you please, mistress," said a withered old female inmate, putting her head in at the door, "old Sally is a-going fast."

"Well, what's that to me?" angrily demanded the matron. "I can't keep her alive, can I?"

"No, no, mistress," replied the old woman. "Nobody can, she's far beyond the reach of help. But she's troubled in her mind and she says she has got something to tell you, which you must hear. She'll never die quiet till you come, mistress."

Mrs Corney, grumbling exceedingly, muffled herself in a thick shawl and briefly requested Mr Bumble to stay till she came back, lest anything particular should occur. Bidding the messenger walk fast, and not be all night hobbling up the stairs, she followed her from the room with a very bad grace, scolding all the way.

Mr Bumble's conduct, on being left to himself, was rather odd. He opened the closet, counted the teaspoons, weighed the sugar-tongs, closely inspected a silver milk-pot to ascertain

D

that it was of the genuine metal, and, having satisfied his curiosity on these points, put on his cocked hat corner-wise and danced gravely four times round the table. Having gone through this very extraordinary performance, he took off the cocked hat again, and, spreading himself before the fire with his back towards it, seemed to be making an exact list in his head of Mrs Corney's furniture.

CHAPTER 23

THE OLD WOMAN TELLS HER SECRET

The old woman tottered along the passages and up the stairs, and, being at length compelled to pause for breath, she gave the light into the hand of her mistress, and remained behind to follow as she might while the matron made her way to the room where the sick woman lay.

It was a bare garret-room, with a dim light burning at the farther end. There was another old woman watching by the bed, and the parish apothecary's apprentice was standing by the fire, making a toothpick out of a quill.

"Cold night, Mrs Corney," said this young gentleman, as the matron entered.

"Very cold indeed, sir," replied the mistress in her most civil tones, and dropping a curtsey as she spoke.

"You should get better coals out of your contractors," said the apothecary's deputy, breaking a lump on the top of the fire with the rusty poker; "these are not at all the sort of thing for a cold night."

"They're the board's choosing, sir," returned the matron. "The least they could do would be to keep us pretty warm, for our places are hard enough."

The conversation was here interrupted by a moan from the sick woman.

"Oh," said the young man, turning his face towards the bed, as if he had previously quite forgotten the patient, "it's all U.P. there, Mrs Corney."

"It is, is it, sir?" said the matron.

"If she lasts a couple of hours, I shall be surprised," said the apothecary's apprentice, intent upon the toothpick's point. "It's a break-up of the system altogether. Is she dozing, old lady?"

The attendant stooped over the bed to look, and nodded.

"Then perhaps she'll go off in that way, if you don't make a row," said the young man. "Put the light on the floor. She won't see it there."

The attendant did as she was told, shaking her head meanwhile, as if to say that the woman would not die so easily. Having done so, she resumed her seat by the side of the old woman who had fetched the matron, and who had by this time returned. The mistress, with an expression of impatience, wrapped herself in her shawl and sat at the foot of the bed.

The apothecary's apprentice, having completed the manufacture of the toothpick, planted himself in front of the fire and made good use of it for ten minutes or so; then, apparently growing rather bored, he wished Mrs Corney joy of her job and took himself off on tiptoe.

When they had sat in silence for some time, the two old women rose from the bed and, crouching over the fire, held out their withered hands to catch the heat. The flames threw a ghastly light on their shrivelled faces and made their ugliness appear terrible as, in this position, they began to talk in low voices.

"Did she say any more, Anny, dear, while I was gone?" inquired the messenger.

"Not a word," replied the other. "She was restless, but I held her hands, and she soon dropped off."

"Did she drink the hot wine the doctor said she was to have?" demanded the first.

"I tried to get it down," rejoined the other, "but her teeth were tight set, and she clenched the mug so hard that it was as much as I could do to get it back again, so I drank it, and it did me good!"

Looking cautiously round, to make sure they were not overheard, the two old hags cowered nearer the fire, and chuckled heartily.

"I mind the time," said the first speaker, "when she would have done the same, and made rare fun of it afterwards."

"Ay, that she would," rejoined the other. "She had a merry heart."

The matron, who had been impatiently watching until the dying woman should awaken from her stupor, now joined them by the fire, and sharply asked how long she was to wait.

There was a movement from the bed, and they saw that the patient had raised herself upright and was stretching her arms towards them.

"Who's that?" she cried in a hollow voice.

"Hush, hush," said one of the women, stooping over her. "Lie down, lie down!"

"I'll never lie down again alive!" said the woman, struggling. "I *will* tell her! Come here. Nearer! Let me whisper in your ear."

She clutched the matron by the arm, and, forcing her into a chair by the bedside, was about to speak, when, looking round, she caught sight of the two old women bending forward in the attitude of eager listeners.

"Turn them away," said the old woman drowsily. "Make haste! Make haste!"

Paying no heed to their protests, the matron pushed the two old crones from the room, closed the door, and returned to the bedside.

"Now listen to me," said the dying woman aloud, as if making a great effort to revive one hidden spark of energy. "In this very room—in this very bed—I once nursed a pretty young creature, that was brought into the house with her feet cut and bruised with walking, and all soiled with dust and blood. She gave birth to a boy and died. Let me think— what was the year again?"

"Never mind the year," said the matron impatiently; "what about her?"

"Ay," murmured the sick woman, relapsing into her former drowsy state, "what about her?—what about—I know!" she cried, jumping fiercely up, her face flushed and her eyes starting from her head. "I robbed her, so I did! She had only just died when I stole it!"

"Stole what, for Heaven's sake?" cried the matron, with a movement as if she would call for help.

"*It!*" replied the woman, laying her hand over the matron's mouth. "The only thing she had. She needed clothes to keep her warm, and food to eat, but she had kept it safe and had it round her neck. It was gold, I tell you! Rich gold, that might have saved her life!"

"Gold!" echoed the matron, bending eagerly over the woman as she fell back. "Go on, go on—yes—what of it? Who was the mother? When was it?"

"She charged me to keep it safe," replied the woman with a groan, "and trusted me because I had cared for her. I stole it in my heart when she first showed it me, and if the child is dead now, the blame is on me. They would have treated him better, if they had known it all!"

"Known what?" asked the matron. "Speak!"

"The boy grew so like his mother," said the woman, rambling on, and not heeding the question, "that I could never forget it when I saw his face. Poor girl, poor girl. She was so young, too. Such a gentle lamb. Wait. There's more to tell. I have not told you all, have I?"

"No, no," replied the matron, bending her head to catch the words as they came faintly from the dying woman. "Be quick, or it may be too late!"

"The mother," said the woman, making a more violent effort than before, "the mother, when she knew she was dying, whispered in my ear that if her baby was born alive and thrived, the day might come when it would not feel so much disgraced to hear its poor young mother named, and she prayed that Heaven would raise up some friends who wouid take pity upon her poor desolate child thrown on the mercy of this troubled world."

"The boy's name?" demanded the matron.

"They *called* him Oliver," replied the woman feebly. "The gold I stole was——"

"Yes, yes—what?" cried the other.

She was bending eagerly over the woman to hear her reply, but drew back instinctively as she sat up once and fell back lifeless on the bed.

"Stone dead!" said one of the old women, hurrying in as soon as the door was opened.

"And nothing to tell after all," rejoined the matron, walking carelessly away.

The two old cronies, to all appearances, too busily occupied to make any reply, were left alone, hovering about the body.

CHAPTER 24

A SINISTER VISITOR

While these things were passing in the country workhouse, Fagin sat in the old den—the same from which Oliver had been removed by Nancy—brooding over a dull, smoky fire. He held a pair of bellows upon his knee, but he was not using them. He had fallen into deep thought, and with his arms folded on them, and his chin resting on his thumbs, gazed with unseeing eyes at the rusty bars.

At the table behind him sat the Artful Dodger and Charley Bates, intent upon a game of cards. It being a cold night, the Dodger wore his hat, as, indeed, he often did indoors. He also held a clay pipe between his teeth, which he only removed for a brief space when he wished to drink from a quart pot upon the table, which stood ready filled with gin and water for the convenience of the company.

The Dodger was winning as usual, when he suddenly put his cards face downwards on the table.

"Hark!" he cried, looking up, "I heard the tinkler." Catching up the light, he crept softly upstairs. He returned in a minute with a man in a coarse smock-frock, who, after casting a hurried glance round the room, pulled off a large muffler which had concealed the lower portion of his face, and disclosed, all haggard, unwashed and unshaven, the features of flash Toby Crackit.

"Alone!" cried the old man, turning pale.

"How are you, Faguey?" said Toby. "Pop that shawl in a safe place, Dodger, so that I may know where to find it when I cut. That's the time of day!"

With these words, he pulled up the smock-frock and, winding it round his middle, drew a chair to the fire and placed his feet upon the hob.

"See there, Faguey," he said, pointing disconsolately to his top-boots, "not a drop of blacking since you know when. But don't look at me in that way, man. All in good time.

I can't talk about business till I've ate and drank; so produce the food, and let's have a quiet fill-out for the first time these three days!"

Fagin motioned to the boys to place what eatables there were, upon the table, and, seating himself opposite the hungry house-breaker, waited impatiently while he ate and drank. Toby continued until he could eat no more, then, ordering the boys out of the room, he closed the door, mixed a glass of spirits and water, and composed himself for talking.

"First and foremost, Faguey," said Toby, "how's Bill?"

"What!" screamed the old man, starting from his seat.

"Why, you don't mean to say——" began Toby, turning pale.

"Mean?" cried Fagin, stamping furiously on the ground. "Where are they? Sikes and the boy! Where are they? Where have they been? Where are they hiding? Why have they not been here?"

"The crack failed," said Toby faintly.

"I know it," replied Fagin, tearing a newspaper from his pocket and pointing to it. "What more?"

"They fired and hit the boy. We cut over the fields at the back with him between us—straight as the crow flies—through the hedge and ditch. Alive or dead, that's all I know about him."

The old man stopped to hear no more, but, uttering a loud yell, and twining his hands in his hair, rushed from the room, and from the house.

He went straight to Nancy's.

"Now," muttered the old man, as he knocked at the door, "if there is any deep play here, I shall have it out of you, my girl, cunning as you are."

A woman came to the door and said that Nancy was in her room. Fagin crept softly upstairs and entered it without knocking. Nancy was alone, lying with her head upon the table and her hair straggling over it.

"She has been drinking," thought the old man coolly, "or perhaps she is only miserable." He turned to close the door and the noise aroused the girl. She eyed his crafty face narrowly, as she inquired whether there was any news, and as she listened to the recital of Toby Crackit's story. When it was concluded, she sank into her former attitude, but spoke not a word. She pushed the candle impatiently away, and once or twice, as she feverishly changed her position, shuffled her feet upon the ground, but this was all.

During the silence, Fagin looked restlessly about the room for signs that Sikes might secretly have returned. Apparently satisfied with his inspection, he coughed once or twice and attempted to open a conversation, but the girl heeded him no more than if he had been made of stone. At length he made another attempt, and, rubbing his hands together, said, in his most pleasant tone, "And where should you think Bill is now, my dear?"

The girl moaned out some half-heard reply, that she could not tell. She seemed to be crying.

"And the boy, too," said Fagin, straining his eyes to catch a glimpse of her face. "Poor leetle child! Left in a ditch, Nancy; only think!"

"The child," said Nancy suddenly looking up, "is better where he is than among us; and if no harm comes to Bill from it, I hope he lies dead in the ditch, and that his young bones may rot there."

"What?" cried the old man in amazement.

"Yes, I do," returned the girl, meeting his gaze. "I shall be glad to have him away from my eyes, and to know that the worst is over. I can't bear to have him about me. The sight of him turns me against myself, and all of you."

"Pooh!" said Fagin scornfully. "You're drunk."

"Am I?" cried the girl bitterly. "It's no fault of yours if I am not! You'd never have me anything else, if you had your will, except now. It doesn't suit you now, does it?"

"No," rejoined Fagin furiously, "it does not. That boy's worth hundreds of pounds to me. Am I to lose it through the whims of a drunken gang that I could whistle away the lives of? With six words I can get Sikes hanged. Besides, I'm bound to another, a born devil that has the power to——"

Panting for breath, the old man stammered for a word, then realised that he had said too much, and sank into a chair. After a short silence, he ventured to look round at his companion and appeared somewhat relieved to see her in the same listless attitude from which he had first roused her.

"Nancy, dear," croaked Fagin in his usual voice. "Did you mind me, dear?"

"Don't worry me now, Fagin," replied the girl, raising her head languidly. "If Bill has not done it this time, he will another. He has done many a good job for you, and will do many more when he can, and when he can't, he won't, so no more about that."

"Regarding this boy, my dear?" said Fagin, rubbing the palms of his hands nervously together.

"The boy must take his chance with the rest," interrupted Nancy hastily, "and I say again, I hope he is dead, and out of harm's way, and out of yours—that is, if Bill comes to no harm. And if Toby got clear off, Bill's pretty sure to be safe, for Bill's worth two of Toby any time."

"And about what I was saying, my dear?" observed Fagin, keeping his glistening eyes steadily upon her.

"You must say it all over again, if it's anything you want me to do," rejoined Nancy; "and if it is, you had better wait until tomorrow. The drink makes me stupid."

Somewhat relieved in his mind, Fagin turned his face homeward, leaving Nancy asleep, with her head upon the table.

It was within an hour of midnight. The weather being dark, and piercing cold, he had no temptation to loiter. The sharp wind that scoured the streets seemed to have cleared them of people, for few people were about, and they were, to all appearance, hastening fast home. It blew from the right quarter for the old man, however, and straight before it he went, trembling and shivering, as every gust drove him violently on his way.

He had reached the corner of his own street, and was already fumbling in his pocket for the door-key, when a dark figure emerged from deep shadow, and, crossing the road, glided up behind him.

"Fagin!" whispered a voice close to his ear.

"Ah!" said the old man, turning quickly round, "is that——"

"Yes," interrupted the stranger. "I have been lingering here these two hours. Where the devil have you been?"

"On *your* business, my dear," replied Fagin, glancing uneasily at his companion, and slackening his pace as he spoke. "On *your* business."

"Oh, of course!" said the stranger with a sneer. "Well, and what's come of it?"

"Nothing good," said the old man.

"Nothing bad, I hope?" said the stranger, stopping short and turning a startled look on his companion.

Fagin shook his head, and was about to reply when the stranger, interrupting him, motioned to the house, before which they had by this time arrived, remarking that he had better say what he had to say under cover, for his blood was chilled with standing about so long, and the wind blew through him.

Fagin looked as if he could have willingly excused himself from taking home a visitor at that time of the night, and, indeed, muttered something about having no fire; but his companion insisting, he unlocked the door, and requested him to close it softly while he got a light.

"It's as dark as the grave," said the man, groping forward a few steps. "Make haste!"

"Shut the door," whispered Fagin from the end of the passage. As he spoke, it closed with a loud noise.

"That wasn't my doing," said the other man, feeling his way. "The wind blew it to, or it shut of its own accord, one or the other. Look sharp with the light, or I shall knock my brains out against something in this confounded hole."

Fagin stealthily descended the kitchen stairs. After a short absence, he returned with a lighted candle, and the information that Toby Crackit was asleep in the back room below, and that the boys were in the front one. Beckoning the man to follow him, he led the way upstairs.

"We can say the few words we've got to say in here, my dear," said the old man, throwing open a door on the first floor; "and as there are holes in the shutters, and we never show lights to our neighbours, we'll set the candle on the stairs. There!"

With those words, Fagin, stooping down, placed the candle on an upper flight of stairs, exactly opposite to the room door.

This done, he led the way into the apartment, which had nothing in it except a broken armchair, and an old couch or sofa without covering which stood behind the door. Upon this piece of furniture, the stranger sat himself with the air of a weary man, and, the old man drawing up the armchair opposite, they sat face to face. It was not quite dark; the door was ajar, and the candle outside threw a feeble reflection on the opposite wall.

They talked for some time in whispers. It seemed that Fagin

was defending himself against some angry remarks of the stranger, whom he addressed as Monks.

"I tell you," said Monks. "It was badly planned. Why not have kept him here among the rest, and made a sneaking, snivelling pickpocket of him at once? In time he would have been caught, convicted, and sent safely out of the kingdom, perhaps for life."

"Whose turn would that have served, my dear?" inquired Fagin.

"Mine," replied Monks.

"But not mine," replied Fagin. "He might have become of use to me. When there are two parties to a bargain, it is only reasonable that the interests of both should be considered, is it not, my good friend?"

"What then?" demanded Monks.

"I saw it was not easy to train him up as a thief," replied Fagin, "he was not like other boys, living on the streets as best they could."

"Curse him, no!" muttered the man, "or he would have been deep in it long ago."

"I had no hold upon him to make him worse," went on Fagin, anxiously watching his companion's face. "I had nothing to frighten him with, which we always must have in the beginning or we labour in vain. What could I do? Send him out to pick pockets with the Dodger and Charley? We had enough of that at first, my dear. I trembled for us all."

"*That* was not my doing," remarked Monks.

"No, no, my dear," said the old man. "And I don't quarrel with it now, because if it had never happened, you would never have seen the boy and discovered it was him you were looking for. Well I got him back for you by means of Nancy, and then *she* takes his side."

"Throttle *her*!" said Monks impatiently.

"Why, it's not convenient to do that just now, my dear," replied Fagin smiling, "and beside, it's not our custom, or one of these days I might be glad to have it done. I know what these girls are, Monks. As soon as the boy begins to harden, she'll care no more for him than a block of wood. If he's still alive, that is."

"What's that?" cried Monks springing to his feet.

"What?" said Fagin, clutching his arm. "Where?"

"Yonder!" replied the man, glaring at the opposite wall.

"The shadow! I saw the shadow of a woman in a cloak and bonnet pass along the wainscot like a breath!""

Fagin released his arm, and they rushed tumultuously from the room. The candle, wasted by the draught, was standing where it had been placed. It showed them only the empty staircase, and their own white faces. They listened intently; a profound silence reigned throughout the house.

"It's your fancy," said Fagin, taking up the light and turning to his companion.

"I'll swear I saw it!" replied Monks, trembling. "It was bending forward when I saw it first, and when I spoke, it darted away."

Fagin glanced contemptuously at the pale face of his companion, and, telling him he could follow if he pleased, ascended the stairs. They looked into all the rooms; they were cold, bare and empty. They descended into the passage, and thence into the cellars below. The green damp hung upon the low walls; the tracks of the snail and slug glistened in the light of the candle, but all was still as death.

"What do you think now?" said Fagin, when they had regained the passage. "Besides ourselves, there's not a creature in the house except Toby and the boys, and they're safe enough. See here!"

As a proof of the fact, Fagin drew forth two keys from his pocket, and explained that when he first went downstairs, he had locked them in, to prevent any intrusion on the conference.

Monks appeared satisfied and presently he uttered several very grim laughs, confessing that it could only have been his excited imagination. As it had turned one o'clock, they did not renew their conversation. Monks slunk away into the darkness and Fagin drew forth yet another key and locked the street door.

CHAPTER 25

MR BUMBLE PROPOSES

Mr Bumble had recounted the teaspoons, re-weighed the sugar-tongs, made a closer inspection of the milk-pot, and made a thorough examination of the furniture down to the very horse-hair seats of the chairs, and had repeated each process full half-a-dozen times, before he began to think that it was time for Mrs Corney to return. One thought leads to another, and as there were no signs of Mrs Corney's approach, it occurred to Mr Bumble that it would be an innocent and virtuous way of spending the time, if he were further to satisfy his curiosity by a quick look inside Mrs Corney's chest of drawers.

Having listened at the keyhole to assure himself that nobody was approaching the room, Mr Bumble pulled out three long drawers in turn, and discovered various garments of good fashion and texture, carefully preserved between two layers of old newspapers, speckled with dried lavender. Inside the right-hand corner drawer, he found a small padlocked box which, being shaken, gave forth a pleasant sound as of the chinking of coin.

Mr Bumble returned with a stately walk to the fireplace, spread himself again with his back to the fire, and said with a grave and determined air, "I'll do it!"

Footsteps were heard outside, and Mrs Corney, hurrying into the room, threw herself in a breathless state on a chair by the fireside. Covering her eyes with one hand, she placed the other over her heart and gasped for breath.

"Mrs Corney," said Mr Bumble, stooping over the matron, "what is it, ma'am?"

"Oh, Mr Bumble!" cried the lady, "I have been so dreadfully put out!"

"Put out, ma'am?" exclaimed Mr Bumble. "I know, it's those wicious old women."

"It's dreadful to think of!" said the lady, shuddering.

"Then *don't* think of it, ma'am," rejoined Mr Bumble.

"I can't help it," whispered the lady.

"Then take something, ma'am," said Mr Bumble soothingly. "A little of the wine?"

"Not for the world!" replied Mrs Corney. "I couldn't—oh! The top shelf in the right-hand corner—oh!"

Mr Bumble rushed to the closet and, snatching a pint green-glass bottle from the shelf, filled a tea-cup with its contents and held it to the lady's lips.

"I'm better now," said Mrs Corney, falling back in her chair after drinking half of it.

Mr Bumble raised his eyes piously to the ceiling in thankfulness, and, bringing them down again to the brim of the cup, lifted it to his nose.

"Peppermint," said Mrs Corney in a faint voice, smiling gently on the beadle as she spoke. "Try it. There's a little—a little something else in it."

Mr Bumble tasted the medicine with a doubtful look, smacked his lips, took another taste, and put the cup down empty.

"It's very comforting," said Mrs Corney.

"Very much so indeed, ma'am," said the beadle. As he spoke, he drew a chair beside the matron and tenderly inquired what had happened to distress her.

"Nothing," replied Mrs Corney. "I am a foolish, weak creetur."

"Not weak, ma'am," retorted Mr Bumble, drawing his chair a little closer. "Are you a weak creetur, Mrs Corney?"

"We are all weak creeturs," said Mrs Corney.

"So we are," said the beadle, removing his left arm from the back of Mrs Corney's chair, where it had previously rested, to Mrs Corney's apron-string, round which it gradually became entwined.

"This is a very comfortable room, ma'am," said Mr Bumble, looking round. "Another room, and this, ma'am, would be a complete thing."

"It would be too much for one," murmured the lady.

"But not for two, ma'am," rejoined Mr Bumble softly, "Eh, Mrs Corney?" He took her hand with his free one.

Mrs Corney drooped her head modestly and released her

110

hand to get at her pocket handkerchief, but, as if she were not thinking, replaced it in that of Mr Bumble.

"The board of governors allow you coals, don't they, Mrs Corney?" inquired the beadle, affectionately pressing her hand.

"And candles," replied Mrs Corney, slightly returning the pressure.

"Coals, candles and house-rent free," said Mr Bumble. "Oh, Mrs Corney, what a Angel you are!" Mr Bumble seized Mrs Corney in his arms, and imprinted a passionate kiss upon her nose.

"Such perfection!" exclaimed Mr Bumble rapturously. "You know that Mr Slout is worse tonight, my fascinator?"

"Yes," replied Mrs Corney bashfully.

"He can't live a week, the doctor says," continued Mr Bumble. "He is the master of this establishment; his death will cause a wacancy; that wacancy must be filled up. Oh, Mrs Corney, what a prospect this opens! What an opportunity for a jining of hearts and housekeepings!"

Mrs Corney sobbed.

"The little word?" said Mr Bumble. "The one little, little, little word, my blessed Corney?"

"Ye-ye-yes!" sighed the matron.

"Once more," said the beadle, "compose your darling feelings for only one more. When is it to come off?"

Mrs Corney twice attempted to speak, and twice failed. At length, summoning up courage, she threw her arms around Mr Bumble's neck, and said that she would marry him as soon as he pleased and that he was "a irresistible duck."

They celebrated with another teacupful of the peppermint mixture, and, while they were doing this, Mrs Corney told Mr Bumble about the death of the old woman, but, in spite of his curiosity, gave him no details and did not explain why she had seemed agitated.

Mr Bumble did not press her, but suggested he could call at Mr Sowerberry's on his way home, and ask the undertaker to send someone up in the morning. Having exchanged a long and affectionate embrace with his future partner, he left the building with a light heart and bright visions of his future promotion, and this served to occupy his mind until he reached the shop of the undertaker.

And now that we have accompanied him so far on his road

home and have made all necessary preparations for the old woman's funeral, let us set on foot a few inquiries after young Oliver Twist, and discover whether he be still lying in the ditch where Toby Crackit left him.

CHAPTER 26

OLIVER IS RESCUED

"Wolves tear your throats!" muttered Sikes, grinding his teeth. "I wish I was among some of you; you'd howl the hoarser for it." He rested the wounded boy across his bended knee, and turned his head for an instant, to look back at his pursuers.

He could see little in the mist and darkness, but the loud shouting of men vibrated through the air, and the barking of the neighbouring dogs, roused by the sound of the alarm bell, resounded in every direction.

"Stop, you white-livered hound!" cried the robber, shouting after Toby Crackit, who, making the best use of his long legs, had started to run.

Toby, not sure if he was in range of Sike's pistol, came reluctantly back.

"Bear a hand with the boy," cried Sikes, "quick."

At this moment, the noise grew louder. The men who were giving chase were already climbing the gate of the field in which they stood, and a couple of dogs were some paces in front of them.

"It's all up, Bill!" cried Toby. "Drop the kid and show 'em your heels." Preferring the chance of being shot by his friend to the certainty of being captured by his enemies, Toby Crackit fairly turned tail, and darted off at full speed.

Sikes clenched his teeth, took one look around, threw over Oliver the cape in which he had been hurriedly muffled, ran along the front of the hedge, as if to distract the attention of his pursuers from the spot where the boy lay, paused for a second before another hedge which met it at right angles, and, whirling his pistol high into the air, cleared it at a bound, and was gone.

"Ho, ho, there!" cried a shaky voice. "Pincher! Neptune! Come here!" The dogs, who appeared as scared as their masters, readily obeyed. Three men, who were some distance into the field, stopped to take counsel together.

"My advice or, leastways, I should say my *orders* is," said the fattest man of the party, "that we go home again—now."

"I am agreeable to anything which is agreeable to Mr Giles," said a shorter man, who was very pale in the face. "Thank my stars, I know my place." His teeth chattered in his head as he spoke.

"You are afraid, Brittles," said Mr Giles.

"I ain't," said Brittles.

"You are," said Giles.

"You're a falsehood, Mr Giles," said Brittles.

"You're a lie, Brittles," said Mr Giles.

"I'll tell you what it is, gentlemen," said the third man, who had called up the dogs, "we're all afraid."

"Speak for yourself, sir," said Mr Giles, who was the palest of the three.

"So I do," replied the man. "It's natural and proper to be afraid under such circumstances. *I* am."

"So am I," said Brittles, "only there's no call to tell a man he is, so bounceably."

At this, Mr Giles at once admitted that *he* was afraid; upon which, they all three faced about and ran back again in complete agreement, until Mr Giles (who was short of breath and was burdened with a pitchfork) most handsomely insisted on stopping to make an apology for his hastiness of speech.

"But it's wonderful," said Mr Giles, when he had explained, "what a man will do when his blood is up. I should have committed murder—I *know* I should—if we'd caught one of them rascals."

Everyone agreed that this explained his own case exactly, though they were somewhat at a loss to account for the sudden cooling off.

"I know what it was," said Mr Giles, "it was the gate."

"I shouldn't wonder if it was," exclaimed Brittles, catching at the idea.

"You may depend upon it," said Giles, "that that gate

113

stopped the flow of the excitement. I felt all mine suddenly going away, as I was climbing over it."

All were agreed that it must have been the gate.

The conversation was held between the two men who had surprised the burglars, and a travelling tinker who had been sleeping in an outhouse, and who had been aroused, together with his two mongrel dogs, to join in the pursuit. Mr Giles was butler to the old lady of the mansion and Brittles was a lad-of-all-work, who, having entered her service as a mere child, was treated as a promising young boy still, although he was something past thirty.

Keeping very close together, the three men hurried back to the tree, behind which they had left their lantern, lest its light should inform the thieves in what direction to fire. Catching up the light, they made the best of their way home, at a good round trot, and, long after their dusky forms had vanished, the light might have been seen twinkling and dancing in the distance, like some kind of vapour given off by the damp and gloomy atmosphere through which it was swiftly borne.

The air grew colder as day came slowly on, and the mist rolled along the ground like a dense cloud of smoke. The grass was wet, the pathways and low places were all mud and water, the damp breath of an unwholesome wind passed over with a hollow moaning. Still Oliver lay motionless and insensible on the spot where Sikes had left him. Morning drew on apace. Objects which had looked dim and terrible in the darkness grew clearer, and gradually took shape. The rain came down, thick and fast, and pattered noisily among the leafless bushes. But Oliver felt it not as it beat against him, for he still lay stretched, helpless and unconscious on his bed of clay.

At length, a low cry of pain broke the stillness and, uttering it, the boy awoke. His left arm, roughly bandaged in a shawl, hung heavy and useless at his side. The bandage was soaked with blood. He was so weak that he could scarcely raise himself into a sitting position. When he had done so, he looked feebly round for help, and groaned with pain. Trembling in every joint from cold and exhaustion, he made an effort to stand upright, but, shuddering from head to foot, fell prostrate on the ground.

After a short return of the stupor in which he had been

so long plunged, Oliver, urged by a creeping sickness at his heart, which seemed to warn him that if he lay there, he would surely die, got upon his feet and tried to walk. His head was dizzy, and he staggered to and fro like a drunken man. But he kept up, nevertheless, and, with his head drooping on his chest, went stumbling on, hardly knowing what he was doing or where he was going.

Thus he staggered on, creeping, almost mechanically between the bars of gates or through hedge-gaps as they came in his way, until he reached a road. Here the rain began to fall so heavily that it roused him. He looked about, and saw that at no great distance there was a house which perhaps he could reach, and, summoning up all his strength for one last effort, he bent his faltering steps towards it.

As he drew nearer to this house, a feeling came over him that he had seen it before. That garden wall! On the grass inside, he had fallen on his knees last night, and asked for mercy. It was the very house that Sikes and Toby had attempted to rob. For a moment he felt such fear come over him that he was tempted to fly. Flight! He could scarcely stand, and he was in agony from his wound. Even if he had the strength, whither could he fly? He pushed against the garden gate; it was unlocked and swung open on its hinges. He tottered across the lawn, climbed the steps, knocked faintly at the door, and, his whole strength failing him, sank down against one of the pillars of the little portico.

It happened that about this time, Mr Giles, Brittles and the tinker were restoring themselves after the fatigues and terrors of the night, with tea and toast in the kitchen. It was not Mr Giles's habit to admit to too great familiarity the humbler servants, but deaths, fires and burglary make all men equals; so Mr Giles sat with his legs stretched out before the kitchen fender, leaning his left arm on the fender, while, with his right, he illustrated a detailed account of the robbery, to which his hearers (but especially the cook and house-maid, who were of the party) listened with breathless interest.

"It was about half-past two," said Mr Giles, "or I wouldn't swear it mightn't have been a little nearer three, when I woke up, and, turning round in my bed, as it might be so (here Mr Giles turned round in his chair, and pulled the corner of the table-cloth over him to imitate bed-clothes), I fancied I heerd a noise."

At this point of the narrative, the cook turned pale and asked the housemaid to shut the door: who asked Brittles, who asked the tinker, who pretended not to hear.

"—Heerd a noise," continued Mr Giles. "I says at first, 'This is your fancy,' and was composing myself off to sleep, when I heerd the noise again, distinct."

"What sort of a noise?" asked the cook.

"A kind of busting noise," replied Mr Giles, looking round him.

"More like the noise of rubbing an iron bar on a nutmeg-grater," suggested Brittles.

"It was, when *you* heerd it," rejoined Mr Giles, "but at this time, it had a busting sound. I turned down the clothes," continued Mr Giles, rolling back the table-cloth, "sat up in bed, and listened."

The cook and housemaid together exclaimed "Lor!" and drew their chairs closer to each other.

"I heerd it now, quite apparent," resumed Mr Giles. " 'Somebody', I says, 'is forcing of a door or window; what's to be done? I'll call up that poor lad Brittles, and save him from being murdered in his bed; or his throat,' I says, 'may be cut from his right ear to his left, without his knowing it.' "

Here all eyes were turned upon Brittles, who fixed his upon the speaker, and stared at him with his mouth wide open, and a face of extreme horror.

"I got the loaded pistol that I always have by my bed at night," continued Mr Giles, "woke Brittles, and we took a dark lantern that was standing on Brittles's table, and groped our way downstairs in the pitch dark—as it might be so."

Mr Giles had risen from his seat, and taken two steps with his eyes shut, to accompany his description with appropriate action, when he started violently, in common with the rest of the company, and hurried back to his chair.

The cook and housemaid screamed.

"It was a knock," said Mr Giles, appearing perfectly calm. "Open the door, somebody."

Nobody moved.

"It seems a strange sort of thing, a knock coming at such a time in the morning," said Mr Giles, surveying the pale faces which surrounded him, and looking very blank himself, "but the door must be opened. Do you hear, somebody?"

There was no reply. Brittles would not look at him, and

the tinker pretended that he had fallen asleep. The women were out of the question.

"If Brittles would rather open the door in the presence of witnesses," said Mr Giles after a short silence, "I am ready to be one of them."

"So am I," said the tinker, appearing to wake up suddenly.

Brittles gave in on these terms, and the party, being somewhat reassured by the discovery (made on throwing open the shutters) that it was now broad day, took their way upstairs, with the dogs in front. The two women, who were afraid to stay below, brought up the rear.

On the word of command of Mr Giles, Brittles opened the door, and the group, peering with frightened faces over each other's shoulders, saw nothing more frightening than poor Oliver Twist, speechless and exhausted, who raised his eyes to them in a silent plea for pity.

"A boy!" exclaimed Mr Giles. He seized Oliver by one leg and one arm (fortunately not the broken limb) lugged him straight into the hall, and deposited him at full length on the floor.

"Here he is!" bawled Giles, calling in a state of great excitement up the staircase. "Here's one of the thieves, ma'am! Here's a thief, miss! Wounded, miss! I shot him, miss."

The two women-servants ran upstairs to carry the news that Mr Giles had captured a robber, but in the midst of all the noise and commotion, there was heard a sweet female voice, which quelled it in an instant.

"Giles!" whispered the voice from the stairhead.

"I'm here, miss," replied Mr Giles. "Don't be frightened, miss; I ain't much injured. He didn't make a very desperate resistance, miss! I was too much for him."

"Hush!" replied the young lady. "You frighten my aunt as much as the thieves did. Is the poor creature much hurt?"

"Wounded desperate, miss," replied Giles with calm satisfaction.

"He looks as if he was a-going, miss," bawled Brittles, anxious not to be left out. "Wouldn't you like to come and look at him, miss, in case he should?"

"Hush, pray; there's a good man!" rejoined the lady. "Wait quietly only one instant, while I speak to Aunt."

With a footstep as soft and gentle as the voice, the speaker tripped away. She soon returned with instructions that the wounded person was to be carried carefully upstairs to Mr Giles's room, and that Brittles was to saddle the pony at once, and ride to Chertsey, from which place he was to despatch with all speed a constable and a doctor.

"Won't you take one look at him first, miss?" asked Mr Giles. "Just one little peep?"

"Not now, for the world," replied the young lady. "Poor fellow! Treat him kindly, Giles, for my sake!"

The old servant looked up at the speaker, as she turned away, with a glance as proud and admiring as if she had been his own child. Then, bending over Oliver, he helped to carry him upstairs, with the care and gentleness of a woman.

CHAPTER 27

THE DOCTOR IS CALLED

In a handsome room, though its furniture had rather the air of old-fashioned comfort than of modern elegance, there sat two ladies at a well-spread breakfast table. Mr Giles, dressed with scrupulous care in a full suit of black, was in dignified attendance upon them.

Of the two ladies, one was well advanced in years, but the high-backed oaken chair in which she sat was not more upright than she. The younger lady was in the lovely bloom and spring-time of womanhood. Slight and beautiful, she was not past seventeen. From time to time, the two ladies exchanged a look of tender affection, and presently the elder lady spoke.

"Brittles has been gone for over an hour, hasn't he?" she said, turning her head towards Mr Giles.

"An hour and twelve minutes, ma'am," replied Mr Giles, referring to a silver watch, which he drew forth by a black ribbon.

"He is always slow," remarked the old lady.

"Brittles always was a slow boy, ma'am," replied Mr Giles.

At that moment, a gig drove up to the garden gate, a fat gentleman jumped out, was admitted to the house and burst into the room, nearly overturning Mr Giles and the breakfast table together.

"I never heard of such a thing!" cried the fat gentleman. "You ought to be dead, positively dead with fright—in the silence of the night, too—I never heard of such a thing. Mrs Maylie and Miss Rose, what can I do for you?"

"There is a poor creature upstairs, whom Aunt wishes you to see, Dr Losberne," replied Rose.

"Ah, to be sure," replied the doctor. "That was the message. Where is he? Show me the way. I'll look in again, as I come down, Mrs Maylie. That's the little window that he got in at, eh? Well, I couldn't have believed it!" And, talking all the way, the kindly old doctor followed Mr Giles upstairs.

Dr Losberne was away for some time, and when at length he returned to the ladies, he looked very mysterious as he came into the room and closed the door carefully.

"This is a very extraordinary thing, Mrs Maylie," said the doctor, standing with his back to the door, as if to keep it shut.

"He is not in danger, I hope," said the old lady.

"Why that would *not* be an extraordinary thing under the circumstances," replied the doctor, "though I don't think he is. Have you seen this thief?"

"No," rejoined the old lady.

"Nor heard anything about him?"

"No."

"I beg your pardon, ma'am," put in Mr Giles, "but I was going to tell you about him when Dr Losberne came in."

The fact was, that after receiving great praise for his bravery, Mr Giles had not, at first, been able to bring himself to admit that he had only shot a boy.

"Rose wished to see the man," said Mrs Maylie, "but I wouldn't hear of it."

"Humph!" rejoined the doctor. "There is nothing very alarming in his appearance. Have you any objection to coming with me to see him now?"

"Certainly not, if you think it necessary. We will both come," replied Mrs Maylie.

They went upstairs all together, and Dr Losberne, entering the bedroom first, gently drew back the curtains of the bed.

Upon it, instead of the ruffian they had expected to behold, there lay a mere child, worn with pain and exhaustion and sunk into a deep sleep. His wounded arm, bound and in a splint, was crossed upon his chest; his head rested upon the other arm, which was half hidden by his long hair as it streamed over the pillow.

The good doctor held the curtain in his hand and looked on for a minute or so in silence. While he was watching the patient thus, the younger lady glided softly past, and, seating herself in a chair by the bedside, gathered Oliver's hair from his face. As she stooped over him, her tears fell upon his forehead.

The boy stirred and smiled in his sleep, as though her act of pity had awakened some pleasant dream of love and affection he had never known.

"What can this mean?" exclaimed the old lady. "This poor child can never have been the pupil of robbers!"

"My dear lady," said the doctor mournfully, "I fear it is quite possible."

"But he may have been in the power of wicked men," said Rose, "a child without parents, helpless and unprotected as I would have been if you had not taken me into your home and loved me as a mother. Dear Aunt, do not let them drag this sick child to a prison which would be the end of all hope for him. Have pity upon him, before it is too late."

"My dear love," said the old lady, taking the weeping girl in her arms, "do you think I would harm a hair of his head?"

"No, no," cried Rose, "I know that you would not."

"What can we do to save him," said the old lady, turning to Dr Losberne.

"Let me think, ma'am, let me think," said the doctor, walking up and down the room. "I'm sure I can manage that thick-headed constable downstairs. We do not *know* that the boy who came to the house for help this morning is the same boy who came as a thief through the little window. I think I can persuade him that he has not the evidence to justify him in making an arrest. I will get rid of him, and when the boy wakes, he will have to explain himself to us."

The doctor's plan succeeded, the constable went away and Oliver slept on.

It was evening when the kind-hearted doctor brought the news to Mrs Maylie and Rose that the boy was well enough to be spoken to. He was very weak from exposure and loss of blood, but was anxious to see them and could not rest quietly until he had done so.

The conference was a long one. Oliver told them all his simple history, and was often compelled to stop, by pain and lack of strength. It was a solemn thing to hear in the darkened room, the feeble voice of the sick child recounting a weary tale of evils and calamities which hard men had brought upon him.

Oliver's pillow was smoothed by gentle hands that night, and loveliness and virtue watched him as he slept. He felt calm and happy, and would not have minded if he died that night. He did *not* die, but gradually recovered under the united care of Mrs Maylie, Rose and the kind-hearted Dr Losberne. If fervent prayers be heard in Heaven, the blessings which the orphan child called down upon them sank into their souls, filling them with peace and happiness.

CHAPTER 28

A CHANCE ENCOUNTER

Oliver was ill for some time, but at length he began to get better, and was able to say sometimes, in a few tearful words, how deeply he felt the goodness of the two sweet ladies, and how ardently he hoped, when he grew strong and well again, he could serve them and prove that their kindness had not been wasted on the poor boy whom they had rescued. Only one thing troubled him: he wished that Mr Brownlow and Mrs Bedwin, who had taken such care of him, could know that he was safe.

Hearing of this, Dr Losberne promised that as soon as Oliver was well enough to bear the journey, he would take him to see them.

Oliver continued to make progress, so one morning he and Dr Losberne set out in a little carriage which belonged to Mrs Maylie.

As Oliver knew the name of the street in which Mr Brownlow resided, they were able to drive straight there. When the carriage turned into it, his heart beat so violently that he could scarcely draw his breath. They came to the house. Oliver looked up at the windows, with tears of happiness coursing down his face.

Alas! The white house was empty, and there was a notice in the window: "To Let."

"Knock at the next door," cried Dr Losberne, taking Oliver's arm in his. "What has become of Mr Brownlow, who used to live next door, do you know?"

The servant did not know, but would go and inquire. She soon returned, and said that Mr Brownlow had sold off his goods, and gone to the West Indies, six weeks before. Oliver clasped his hands and sank feebly backward.

"Has his housekeeper gone too?" inquired Dr Losberne, after a moment's pause.

"Yes, sir," replied the servant. "The old gentleman, the housekeeper, and a gentleman who was a friend of Mr Brownlow's all went together."

"Then turn towards home again," said Dr Losberne to the driver, "and don't stop to water the horses until we get out of this confounded London!"

"The book-stall keeper, sir," said Oliver. "I know the way there. See him, pray, sir! Do see him!"

"My poor boy, this is disappointment enough for one day," said the doctor. "Quite enough for both of us. If we go to the book-stall keeper's, we shall certainly find that he is dead, or has set his house on fire, or run away. No. Home again straight!"

And, in obedience to the doctor's impulse, home they went.

Oliver's disappointment was bitter, for the hope of explaining his disappearance with Mr Brownlow's money had sustained him during his many trials and helped him through his illness.

Mrs Maylie and Rose were as good to him as ever. When the weather became warmer, they left the house at Chertsey in the care of Mr Giles and another servant, and, putting the silver which Sikes had tried to steal in the bank, departed to a cottage at some distance in the country and took Oliver with them.

It was a lovely spot to which they came. The rose and

honeysuckle clung to the cottage walls, the ivy crept round the trunks of the trees, and the garden flowers perfumed the air with delicious scent. It was a happy time. Every morning Oliver went to a white-headed old gentleman for lessons, and in the afternoon he would walk with Mrs Maylie and Rose and be so happy if they wanted a flower that he could climb to reach, or had forgotten anything that he could run to fetch. In the evenings, Rose would sit at the piano and sing to them, and on Sundays they would go to church in the morning, visit some of the village people in the afternoon, and read the Bible together in the long summer evening.

In the morning, Oliver would be out early picking wild flowers for the breakfast table and fresh groundsell for Mrs Maylie's birds, and some days there was cricket on the village green. So three happy months glided away.

One day Mrs Maylie told Oliver that her son, Mr Harry, who had been staying at some great lord's house in the country, was coming to visit them, and she desired very much that Dr Losberne should share in their pleasure.

"This letter has to go, as quickly as possible, to Dr Losberne. It must be carried to the market-town, which is not more than four miles off, by the footpath over the fields, and sent from there by an express on horseback straight to Chertsey. The people at the inn will undertake to do this, and I can trust you to see it done, I know."

With these words, Mrs Maylie gave Oliver her purse, and, delighted to be of service, he started off at the best speed he could muster.

Swiftly he ran across the fields, and down the little lanes which sometimes divided them, now almost hidden by the high corn on either side, and now emerging on an open field, where the mowers and haymakers were busy at their work, nor did he stop except once or twice to recover breath until he came to the little market-place of the market town.

Here he paused, and looked about for the inn. There was a white bank, and a red brewery, and a yellow town-hall, and in one corner there was a large house, with all the wood about it painted green, before which was the sign of "The George". To this he hastened, as soon as it caught his eye.

He spoke to a postboy who was dozing under the gateway, and who, after hearing what he wanted, referred him to the ostler, who, after hearing all he had to say again, referred him to the landlord. The landlord was a tall gentleman in a blue neckcloth, a white hat, drab breeches, and boots with tops to match. He was leaning against a pump by the stable-door, picking his teeth with a silver toothpick.

This gentleman walked slowly into the bar to make out the bill, which took a long time making out, and, after it was ready and paid, a horse had to be saddled, and a man dressed, which took up ten good minutes more. At length all was ready, and, the letter having been handed up, the man set spurs to his horse, and, rattling over the uneven paving of the market-place, was out of the town, and galloping along the turn-pike road in a couple of minutes.

His task accomplished, Oliver crossed the inn-yard, and was turning out of the gateway, when he accidentally stumbled against a tall man wrapped in a cloak, who was at that moment coming out of the inn door.

"Hah!" cried the man, fixing his eyes on Oliver, and starting back. "What the devil's this?"

"I beg your pardon, sir," said Oliver. "I didn't see you coming."

"Death!" muttered the man to himself, glaring at the boy with his large dark eyes. "Who would have thought it? He'd start up from the grave to come in my way!"

"I am sorry," stammered Oliver, confused by the strange man's wild look. "I hope I have not hurt you."

"Curses on your head, boy. What are you doing here?"

He stepped forward, his fist raised, but Oliver, convinced he was dealing with a madman, turned and ran off home; and by and by he soon forgot the incident.

CHAPTER 29

FACES AT THE WINDOW

Dr Losberne arrived two days later and was soon followed by Mr Harry and Giles in a post-chaise which set them down about half a mile from the house. Oliver had gone to meet them, and, as they walked along, he glanced from time to time with much interest and curiosity at Mrs Maylie's son. He seemed about five and twenty years of age, his manner easy and likeable, and he bore a strong resemblance to his mother.

The little household spent a peaceful and happy time. Mrs Maylie and her son seemed very close, and Oliver observed that Mr Harry was constantly at the side of Rose. At other times, he and Dr Losberne would go out with Oliver, exploring the countryside, and bringing back fresh flowers for Rose and her Aunt.

Oliver was still working hard for the white-haired old gentleman, and his quick progress surprised even himself. It was while he was studying that he was greatly startled and distressed by a most unexpected occurrence.

The little room in which he was accustomed to sit, when busy at his books, was on the ground floor at the back of the house. It was quite a cottage room, with a lattice window, around which were clusters of jessamine and honeysuckle that crept over the casement and filled the place with their delicious perfume. It looked into a garden, out of which a wicket-gate opened into a small paddock; all beyond was fair meadowland and wood. There was no other dwelling near in that direction, and the view was very fine.

One beautiful evening, when the first shades of twilight were beginning to settle upon the earth, Oliver sat at his window, intent upon his books. He had been reading for some time; the day was hot and gradually, and by slow degrees, he fell asleep. That is to say, his body was asleep, but his mind was somewhere between sleeping and waking and in a kind of dream.

Oliver knew perfectly well that he was in his own little room, that his books were lying on the table before him, that the sweet air was stirring among the creeping plants outside, and yet he was asleep. Suddenly the scene changed, the air became close and confined, and he thought, with a glow of terror, that he was in Fagin's house again. There sat the hideous old man in his accustomed corner, pointing at him, and whispering to another man with his face turned away, who sat beside him.

"Hush, my dear!" he thought he heard Fagin say. "It is he, sure enough. Come away."

"He!" the other man seemed to answer. "Could I mistake him, think you? He stands in my way. He crosses my path at every turn."

The man seemed to say this with such dreadful hatred that Oliver awoke with the fear, and started up.

Good Heaven! What was that, which sent the blood tingling to his heart, and deprived him of his voice and power to move? There—there—at the window—close before him—so close that he could have almost touched him before he started back, with his eyes peering into the room, and meeting his—there stood Fagin! And beside him, white with rage or fear, or both, were the scowling features of the very man who had made to attack him in the inn-yard.

It was but an instant, a glance, a flash before his eyes, and they were gone. But they had recognised him, and he them, and their look was as firmly impressed upon his memory as if it had been deeply carved in stone and set before him from his birth. He stood transfixed for a moment, then, leaping from the window into the garden, called loudly for help.

When the inmates of the house, attracted by Oliver's cries, hurried to the spot from which they proceeded, they found him pale and agitated, pointing in the direction of the meadows behind the house, and gasping, "Fagin! Fagin!"

Mr Giles was at a loss to understand what this outcry meant, but Harry Maylie, whose mind worked more quickly, and who had heard Oliver's history from his mother, understood it at once.

"What direction did he take?" he asked, catching up a heavy stick which was standing in a corner.

"That," replied Oliver, pointing out the course the men had taken; "I missed them in an instant."

"Then they are in the ditch," said Harry. So saying, he sprang over the hedge and darted off with a speed which made it very difficult for the others to keep near him.

Giles followed him as well as he could, and Oliver followed, too, and, in the course of a minute or two, Dr Losberne, who had been out walking, and just then returned, tumbled over the hedge after them and, picking himself up with remarkable agility, sped after them, shouting all the while to know what was the matter.

On they all went, nor stopped they once to breathe, until Harry, striking off into an angle of the field indicated by

Oliver, began to search narrowly the ditch and hedge adjoining. There was no one there; not even the traces of footsteps could be seen. They widened the search to the surrounding fields, but it was in vain.

"It must have been a dream, Oliver," said Harry Maylie.

"Oh no, indeed, sir," replied Oliver, shuddering at the very thought of Fagin's face. "I saw him too plainly for that. I saw them both, as plainly as I see you now."

"Who was the other?" inquired Harry and Dr Losberne together.

"The very same man I told you of, who tried to attack me at the inn," said Oliver. "We had our eyes fixed full upon each other, and I could swear to him."

"This is strange," said Harry.

They continued the search that day and the next, and made inquiries round about, but their efforts were fruitless, and, after a few days, the affair began to be forgotten.

CHAPTER 30

HARRY MAYLIE DECLARES HIS LOVE

The little circle of people seemed content, but, although cheerful voices and merry laughter were heard in the cottage, Oliver could not fail to notice that Harry had something on his mind. He was often apart, talking with his mother, and more than once Rose appeared with traces of tears upon her face. After Dr Losberne had fixed a day for his departure to Chertsey, it seemed to get worse.

At length, one morning, when Rose was alone in the breakfast parlour, Harry Maylie entered, and, with some hesitation, begged permission to speak with her for a few moments.

They sat down; Rose was very pale.

"I—I ought to have left here before," said Harry.

"You should indeed," replied Rose. "Forgive me for saying so, but I wish you had."

"I had to see you, Rose. Have you not been happy to see me?"

"I only meant," said Rose weeping, "that I wish you had left here, so that you could turn again to high and noble tasks, to tasks well worthy of you."

"There is no task more worthy of me, than the struggle to win your heart," said the young man, taking her hand. "Rose, my own dear Rose! For years I have loved you, hoping to win my way to fame, and then come proudly home and tell you it was all done for you to share. I have not yet achieved my aim, but here and now I offer you my heart. What is your answer, dearest Rose?"

"You are kind and noble," replied Rose, "but you must try and think of me only as your old affectionate companion. I will be the truest, warmest, and most faithful friend you have, but nothing more."

There was a pause, during which Rose, who had covered her face with one hand, allowed her tears to flow. Harry still held the other hand.

"And your reasons, Rose," he said at length, in a low voice. "Is this what your heart tells you?"

"It is not," replied Rose, colouring deeply.

"Then you return my love," said Harry. "Your reason from your own lips, Rose. Let me hear it."

"You have a brilliant future," said Rose. "You have powerful and proud friends. I cannot mingle with those who might hold my own mother in scorn, nor bring disgrace or failure on the son of that dear one who has taken her place. In a word," said Rose, her voice trembling, "innocent as I am, there is a mystery about my birth, a stain upon my name. You must not become a part of this. I must bear it alone."

"If I had been less fortunate, if I had been poor, sick, helpless, would you have turned from me then?" cried Harry. "Answer me, dearest Rose."

"Yes, that would have been different," said Rose sadly. "If you had been a little, but not so far, above me, if I could have been a help and comfort to you in any humble scene of peace and retirement, and not a blot and drawback in ambitious and distinguished crowds, I should have been spared this trial. I have every reason to be happy, but then, Harry, I own I should have been happier."

"I ask one promise," said Harry. "Say within a year, but it may be much sooner, promise that I may speak to you again on this subject, for the last time."

"Let it be so," said Rose, "but I shall not change my mind. Farewell, dear Harry."

She put out her hand to him, but the young man caught her to him, kissed her on her beautiful forehead, and hurried from the room.

"And so you are resolved to be my travelling companion this morning, eh?" said the doctor, as Harry Maylie joined him and Oliver at the breakfast table. "Has any communication from the great nobs produced this sudden anxiety on your part to be done?"

"The great nobs, among who I presume you include my stately uncle, have not communicated with me at all since I have been here, nor, at this time of year, is it likely that anything would occur to cause them to ask for my presence," replied Harry.

"Well," said Dr Losberne, "they will get you into Parliament at the election before Christmas. You can be sure of that."

Harry contented himself with saying, "We'll see," and did not follow up the doctor's remarks. The poste-chaise drove up to the door shortly afterwards, and Giles coming in for the luggage, the good doctor bustled out, to see it packed.

"Oliver," said Harry Maylie in a low voice, "let me speak a word with you."

Oliver walked into the window recess, to which Mr Maylie beckoned him, much surprised at Harry's manner.

"You can write well now?" said Harry, laying his hand upon his arm.

"I hope so, sir," replied Oliver.

"I shall not be at home again, perhaps for some time. I wish you would write to me—say once a fortnight, every alternate Monday, to the General Post Office in London. Will you?"

"Oh, certainly, sir! I shall be proud to do it," exclaimed Oliver, greatly delighted at the request.

"I should like to know how my mother and Miss Maylie are," said the young man, "and you can fill up a sheet by telling me what walks you take, and what you talk about, and whether she—they I mean—seem quite happy and well. You understand me?"

E

"Oh, quite, sir, quite," replied Oliver.

"I would rather you did not mention it to them," said Harry, hurrying over his words, "because it might make my mother anxious to write to me oftener, and it is a trouble and worry to her. Let it be a secret between you and me, and mind you tell me everything! I depend upon you."

Olive, quite elated and honoured by a sense of his importance, faithfully promised to carry out those instructions, and Mr Maylie took leave of him, with many assurances of his regard and protection.

The doctor was in the chaise; Giles (who, it had been arranged, should be left behind) held the door open in his hand, and the women servants were looking on. Harry, who had said good-bye to his mother the night before, cast one slight glance at a certain latticed window, and jumped into the carriage.

"Drive on!" he cried. "Hard, fast, full gallop! Nothing short of flying will keep pace with me today!"

Behind the lattice window, shrouded by a white curtain, sat Rose.

"He seems in high spirits and happy," she said. "I feared for a time it might be otherwise. I was mistaken. I am very, very glad."

Tears are signs of gladness as well as grief, but those which crept down her face, as she sat thoughtfully at the window, seemed to tell more of sorrow than of joy.

CHAPTER 31

MRS BUMBLE ASSERTS HER RIGHTS

Mr Bumble sat in the workhouse parlour with his eyes moodily fixed on an empty grate. It was summer time. From time to time, he heaved a deep sigh and looked, if possible, gloomier than before.

Nor was Mr Bumble's gloom the only melancholy thing about him. His magnificent clothes were gone. He still wore knee-breeches, and dark cotton stockings, but they were not *the* breeches. The coat was wide-skirted, and in that respect like *the* coat, but oh, how different! The mighty cocked-hat was replaced by a modest round one. Mr Bumble was no longer a beadle, for he had married Mrs Corney, and was now master of the workhouse. Another beadle had come into power. On him the cocked-hat, gold-laced coat, and staff, had all three descended.

"And tomorrow two months it was done!" said Mr Bumble with another sigh. "It seems a age. I sold myself for six tea-spoons, a pair of sugar-tongs, and a milk-pot, with a small quantity of second-hand furniture and twenty pound in money. I went very reasonable. Cheap, dirt cheap!"

"Cheap!" cried a shrill voice in Mr Bumble's ear. "You would have been dear at any price, and dear enough I paid for you. Now then, are you going to sit snoring there all day?"

"I am going to sit here as long as I think proper, ma'am," rejoined Mr Bumble, fixing his eyes upon her, "and, although I was *not* snoring, I shall snore, gape, sneeze, laugh or cry, as the humour strikes me, such being my rights."

"*Your* rights!" sneered Mrs Bumble, with the utmost contempt.

"I said the word, ma'am," replied Mr Bumble. "The rights of a man is to command."

"And what's the rights of a woman, in the name of Good-ness?" cried the former Mrs Corney.

"To obey, ma'am," thundered Mr Bumble. "Your late, un-fortunate husband should have taught it you, and then, per-haps, he might have been alive now. I wish he was, poor man!"

Mrs Bumble, seeing at a glance that the time had come to establish which of them should be master, dropped into a chair, and, with a loud scream that Mr Bumble was a hard-hearted brute, burst into tears.

But tears were not the things to find their way to Mr Bumble's soul; his heart was waterproof. Indeed they pleased him, as being signs of weakness and, therefore, proofs of his own power. He eyed his good lady with looks of great satis-faction, and begged, in an encouraging manner, that she should cry her hardest.

"Crying opens the lungs, washes the countenance, exercises the eyes, and softens down the temper," said Mr Bumble,

131

"so cry away." He took his hat from a peg, thrust his hands into his pockets and sauntered towards the door, with much ease and waggishness depicted in his whole appearance.

Now Mrs Bumble had tried the tears, because they were less troublesome than physical assault, but she was quite prepared to try this next, as Mr Bumble was not long in discovering.

His hat was sent flying, and his wife, clasping him tightly round the throat with one hand, used the other to inflict a shower of blows upon his unprotected head. She then scratched his face and pulled his hair, and, having punished him as much as she thought necessary for the offence, pushed him over a chair, and defied him to talk about his rights again if he dared.

"Get up!" said Mrs Bumble, in a voice of command. "And take yourself away from here, unless you want me to do something desperate."

Mr Bumble was, like most bullies, also a coward, and he darted from the room without another word, leaving his wife in full possession of the field. It was too much. He decided to go out, and, boxing the ears of the boy who opened the gate for him, he walked distractedly into the street.

"All in two months!" said Mr Bumble, filled with dismal thoughts. "No more than two months ago, I was my own master, and soon she'll rule the workhouse, too, I shouldn't wonder."

He walked up one street and down another, and presently he came to a public-house whose parlour, as he gathered from a hasty peep over the blinds, was deserted, save by one solitary customer. It began to rain heavily at that moment. This decided him. Mr Bumble stepped in, and, ordering something to drink as he passed the bar, entered the room into which he had looked from the street.

The man who was seated there was tall and dark, and wore a large cloak. He looked tired and dusty, as if he had been travelling, and, having eyed Mr Bumble sideways, as he came in, seemed to pay no further attention to him.

Mr Bumble had quite dignity enough for two, supposing even that the stranger had been more familiar, so he drank his gin and water in silence and made a great show of reading the paper. He could not resist, however, stealing a look every now and then at his companion, and whenever he did so, he withdrew his eyes in some confusion, on finding that the stranger was, at that moment, stealing a look at him.

At last the stranger, in a harsh, deep voice, broke silence.

"Were you looking for me," he said, "when you peered in at the window?"

"Not that I am aware of," said Mr Bumble cautiously.

"I have seen you before, I think," said the stranger. "You were differently dressed at that time, and I only passed you in the street, but I should know you again. You were beadle here once, were you not?"

"I was," said Mr Bumble, in some surprise, "parish beadle."

"Just so," rejoined the other. "What are you now?"

"Master of the workhouse," said Mr Bumble impressively. "Master of the workhouse, young man."

The stranger walked to the door and closed it, the window being already shut.

"Now listen to me," he said. "I came down to this place today to find you out, and by one of those chances which the devil throws in the way of his friends sometimes, you walked into the very room I was sitting in, while you were uppermost in my mind. I want some information from you. I don't ask you to give it for nothing, slight as it is. Take that to begin with."

As he spoke, he pushed a couple of gold coins across the table to his companion, carefully, as though unwilling that the chinking money should be heard outside. When Mr Bumble had carefully examined the coins to see that they were genuine, and had put them, with much satisfaction, in his waistcoat pocket, the stranger went on:

"Carry your memory back—let me see—twelve years last winter."

"It's a long time," said Mr Bumble. "Very good. I've done it."

"The scene, the workhouse."

"Yes."

"And the time, night."

"Yes."

"A boy was born."

"A many boys," observed Mr Bumble, shaking his head despondently.

"I speak of one," said the stranger. "A meek-looking, pale-faced boy who was apprenticed down here to a coffin-makers. I wish he had made his coffin, and screwed his body in it! He ran away to London, as was supposed."

"Why, you mean Oliver! Young Oliver Twist!" said Mr Bumble. "I remember him, of course. There wasn't an obstinator young rascal——"

"It's not of him I want to hear. I've heard enough of him," said the stranger. "It's of a woman, the hag that nursed his mother. Where is she?"

"She died last winter," said Mr Bumble.

The man did not speak, but appeared lost in thought, as if he did not know whether to be relieved or disappointed by the information. At length he observed that it was no great matter, and rose, as if to depart.

But Mr Bumble was cunning enough, and he at once realised that his wife was in possession of some secret which might make money for them. He well remembered the night of old Sally's death, as it was the same evening that he had proposed to Mrs Corney, and although she had not taken him into her confidence, he had heard enough to know that it had to do with something which had occurred during old Sally's attendance as workhouse nurse upon the young mother of Oliver Twist.

Remembering all this, he informed the stranger, with an air of mystery, that one woman had been alone with old Sally shortly before she died, and that she might, possibly, be able to help him.

"How can I find her?" said the stranger, thrown off his guard, and plainly showing that all his fears (whatever they were) were aroused afresh by this news.

"Only through me," rejoined Mr Bumble.

"When?" cried the stranger hastily.

"Tomorrow," said Mr Bumble.

"At nine in the evening," said the stranger, producing a scrap of paper, and writing down a little-known address by the water-side. "At nine in the evening, bring her to me there. I needn't tell you to be secret. It's your interest."

With these words, he led the way to the door, and, remarking that their roads were different, he departed.

On glancing at the address, Mr Bumble observed that it contained no name. The stranger had not gone far, so he went after him to ask it.

"What do you want?" cried the man, turning round and
134

scowling as Mr Bumble touched him by the arm. "Are you following me?"

"Only to ask a question," said the other, pointing to the scrap of paper. "What name am I to ask for?"

"Monks!" rejoined the man, and strode hastily away.

CHAPTER 32

MRS BUMBLE TELLS A STORY

It was a dull, close, overcast summer evening. The clouds, which had been threatening all day, spread out in a dense and sluggish mass of vapour, already yielded large drops of rain, and seemed to herald a violent thunder storm, when Mr and Mrs Bumble, turning out of the main street of the town, directed their steps towards a scattered little colony of ruinous houses, distant from it some mile and a half or thereabouts, and erected on a low unwholesome swamp, bordering upon the river.

They were both wrapped in old and shabby outer garments which might perhaps serve the double purpose of protecting them from the rain and sheltering them from the notice of others.

They walked quickly and soon arrived at a collection of hovels, some hastily built with loose bricks, others of old worm-eaten ship-timber, jumbled together without any attempt at order or arrangement, and planted, for the most part, within a few feet of the river's bank.

In the heart of this cluster of huts, and skirting the river, which its upper stories overhung, stood a large building, formerly used as a factory of some kind, but long since gone to ruin, and it was before this building that the couple paused, as the first peal of distant thunder reverberated in the air, and the rain commenced pouring violently down.

"The place should be somewhere here," said Bumble, consulting a scrap of paper he held in his hand.

"Hullo there!" cried a voice from above.

Following the sound, Mr Bumble raised his head and saw a man looking out of a half-door on the second storey.

"Stand still a minute," cried the voice. "I'll be with you directly." The head of the man disappeared, and the door closed.

"Is that the man?" asked Mrs Bumble.

Mr Bumble nodded.

"Then mind what I told you," said the matron, "and be careful to say as little as you can, or you'll betray us at once."

Mr Bumble was beginning to look as if he wished they hadn't come, when Monks appeared through a small door near which they stood and beckoned them inwards.

Bestowing something half-way between a smile and a frown upon his two companions, and again beckoning them to follow him, he led them to a room on an upper floor, from which a ladder led to another floor of warehouses above. He led the way up this ladder and, hastily closing the window-shutter of the room into which it led, lowered a lantern which hung at the end of a rope and pulley passed through one of the heavy beams in the ceiling, and which cast a dim light upon an old table and three chairs that were placed beneath it.

"Now," said Monks, when they had all three seated themselves, "the sooner we come to our business, the better for all." He thrust his hand into a side-pocket, and, producing a canvas bag, counted out twenty-five gold sovereigns on the table, and pushed them over to the woman.

"Now," he said, "gather them up, and when this cursed peal of thunder, which I feel is coming up to break over the house-top, is gone, let's hear your story."

The thunder, which seemed in fact much nearer, and to shiver and break almost over their heads, having subsided, Monks, raising his face from the table, bent forward to listen to what the woman should say. The faces of the three nearly touched, as the two men leant over the small table in their eagerness to hear, and the woman also leant forward so that they could catch her whisper. The sickly rays of the suspended lantern falling directly upon them made their faces look pale and ghastly against the surrounding gloom and darkness.

"When this woman, that we called old Sally, died," the matron began, "she and I were alone."

"Was there no one by?" asked Monks, in the same hollow

whisper, "no sick wretch or idiot in some other bed? No one who could hear, and might, by possibility, understand?"

"Not a soul," replied the woman; "we were alone. *I* stood alone beside the body when death came over it."

"Good," said Monks, regarding her attentively. "Go on."

"She spoke of a young creature," resumed the matron, "who had brought a child into the world some years before, not merely in the same room, but in the same bed in which Old Sally herself then lay dying. The child was Oliver Twist, and as soon as the mother was dead, the nurse stole from her something which she had begged her with her last breath to keep for him."

"She sold it?" cried Monks, with desperate eagerness. "Did she sell it? Where? When? To whom? How long before?"

"She said that she had," replied the matron, "but after she died, I found a scrap of paper in her hand. It was a pawn ticket, and the next day I redeemed the pledge."

"Where is it now?" asked Monks quickly.

"*There*," replied the woman. And, as if glad to be relieved of it, she hastily threw upon the table a small kid bag scarcely large enough for a French watch, which Monks, pouncing upon, tore open with trembling hands. It contained a little gold locket in which were two locks of hair and a plain gold wedding-ring.

"It has the word 'Agnes' engraved on the inside," said the woman. "There is a blank left for the surname, and then follows the date, which is within a year before the child was born. I found out that."

"And this is all?" said Monks, after a close and eager scrutiny of the contents of the little packet.

"All," replied the matron.

Mr Bumble drew a long breath, as if he were glad to find that the story was over, and no mention made of taking the five-and-twenty pounds back again, and now he took courage to wipe off the perspiration which had been trickling over his nose, unchecked, during the whole of the previous conversation.

"I know nothing of the story, beyond what I can guess at," said his wife, addressing Monks after a short silence, "and I want to know nothing, for it's safer not. But may I ask you two questions, may I?"

"You may ask," said Monks, with some show of surprise, "but whether I answer or not is another question."

"Is that what you expected to get from me?" demanded the matron.

"It is," replied Monks. "The other question?"

"What you propose to do with it? Can it be used against me?"

"Never," rejoined Monks, "nor against me, either. See here!"

He suddenly wheeled the table aside, and, pulling an iron ring in the floor, threw back a large trap-door, which opened close at Mr Bumble's feet and caused him to step back quickly.

The water, swollen by the heavy rain, was rushing rapidly on below, and all other sounds were lost in the noise of its plashing and eddying against the green and slimy supports of the building.

Monks picked up the little packet, and, tying it to a leaden weight, which had formed part of some pulley and was lying on the floor, dropped it into the stream. It fell straight and true as a die, cleaved the water with a faint splash, and was gone.

The three, looking into each other's faces, seemed to breathe more freely.

"There!" said Monks, closing the trap-door, which fell heavily back into its former position. "That is the last of it, and so farewell. Keep your counsel as you wish to keep your lives, and get away from here as fast as you can."

CHAPTER 33

A SECRET CONVERSATION

On the evening following the visit of Mr and Mrs Bumble to Monks on business, Bill Sikes, awakening from a nap, drowsily growled forth an inquiry what time of night it was. He was in a new room, but in the same quarter of town and at no great distance from his former lodgings.

He seemed to have come down in the world. The room was small and badly-furnished, and was lit only by one small window in the shelving roof, overlooking a close and dirty lane. His general state seemed to be one of extreme poverty, and he himself looked thin and wasted.

The housebreaker was lying on the bed, wrapped in his white great-coat by way of dressing-gown. He wore a soiled nightcap, and had a stiff black beard of a week's growth. The dog sat at the bedside, now eyeing his master with a wistful look, and now pricking his ears and uttering a low growl, as some noise in the street, or in the lower part of the house, attracted his attention. Seated by the window was Nancy, busily engaged in patching an old waistcoat. She looked pale, thin and hungry.

"Not long gone seven," she said in reply to his question. "How do you feel tonight, Bill?"

"As weak as water," replied the sick man with a curse. "Here, lend us a hand, and let me get off this thundering bed, anyhow."

Illness had not improved his temper, for, as the girl raised him up and led him to a chair, he muttered various curses on her awkwardness, and struck her.

"Why, you don't mean to say you'd be hard upon me to-night, Bill," said the girl, laying her hand on his shoulder, while a tear trembled in her eye.

"No?" said Bill. "Why not?"

"Such a number of nights," said the girl, with a touch of woman's tenderness, "such a number of nights as I've been patient with you, nursing and caring for you, as if you had been a child, and this the first time I've seen you like yourself. You wouldn't have struck me if you'd thought of that, now would you?"

"Well then," rejoined Bill, "I wouldn't. Why, damme now, how the girl whines!"

"It's nothing," said Nancy, throwing herself into a chair. "Don't you mind me." Being really weak and exhausted, however, she dropped her head over the back of the chair, and fainted.

Not knowing very well what to do, Bill called for assistance.

"What's the matter here, my dear?" said Fagin, looking in.

"Lend a hand to the girl, can't you?" replied Sikes impatiently. "Don't stand chattering and grinning at me!"

With an exclamation of surprise, Fagin hastened to Nancy's assistance, while the Artful Dodger, who had followed the old man into the room, hastily deposited on the floor, a bundle which he had been carrying, and, snatching a bottle from the grasp of Charley Bates, who came close at his heels, uncorked it in a twinkling with his teeth and poured a portion of its contents down the patient's throat, previously taking a taste himself to prevent mistakes.

"Give her a whiff of fresh air with the bellows, Charley," said the Dodger, "and you slap her hands, Fagin, while Bill undoes the petticuts."

Their united efforts were soon successful. Nancy slowly recovered her senses, and, staggering to a chair by the bedside, hid her face upon the pillow, leaving Bill to confront the newcomers in some astonishment.

"Why, what evil wind has blown you here?" he asked Fagin.

"No evil wind at all, my dear, for evil winds blow nobody any good, and I've brought something good with me, that you'll be glad to see. Dodger, my dear, open the bundle, and give Bill the little trifles that we spent all our money on this morning."

The Dodger obediently untied his bundle, which was of large size, and formed of an old tablecloth, and handed the food it contained one by one to Charley Bates, who placed them on the table with various expressions of admiration for their excellence.

Finally he produced, from one of his big pockets, a full-sized wine bottle, carefully corked, while the Dodger, at the same instant, poured out a wine-glassful of raw spirits from the bottle *he* carried, which Sikes tossed down his throat without a moment's hesitation.

"Ah!" said Fagin, rubbing his hands with great satisfaction. "You'll do, Bill; you'll do now."

"Do!" exclaimed Sikes. "I might have been done for, twenty times over, afore you'd have done anything to help me. What do you mean by leaving me in this state, three weeks and more, you false-hearted wagabond?"

"I've been out of town, Bill, on a job," replied Fagin meekly.

"Oh yes, on a job!" said Bill scornfully. "If it hadn't been for the girl, I might have died."

"There now, Bill," protested Fagin, eagerly catching at the word. "If it hadn't been for the girl! Who but poor old Fagin was the means of your having such a handy girl about you?"

"He says true enough there," said Nancy. "Let him be. Let him be."

"All right, I'll let you be," said Bill, "but I must have some money from you tonight."

"I haven't a single coin about me," replied Fagin.

"Then you've got lots at home," retorted Sikes, "and I must have some from there. Tonight."

"Well, well," said Fagin with a sigh, "I'll send the Artful round presently."

"You won't do nothing of the kind," rejoined Sikes, "Artful's a deal too Artful and would lose his way or forget to come or anything for an excuse, if you put him up to it. Nancy shall go and fetch it, to make all sure, and I'll lie down and have a snooze while she's gone."

After a great deal of haggling and squabbling, Fagin beat down the amount of the required loan from five pounds to three pounds four shillings and sixpence, protesting on his solemn oath that that would only leave him eighteenpence to keep house with, and Sikes sullenly remarked that if he couldn't get any more, he must be content with that.

Fagin then returned homeward, accompanied by the boys and Nancy. They found Toby Crackit just about to leave.

"Has nobody been, Toby?" asked Fagin.

"Not a living leg," answered Toby. "It's been as dull as swipes." He yawned and, inquiring after Sikes, took up his hat to go.

"Dodger! Charley!" said Fagin. "It's time you were at work. It's near ten and nothing done yet."

In obedience to this hint, the boys, nodding to Nancy, took up their hats again and left the room.

"Now," said Fagin, when they had left the room, "I'll go and get you that cash, Nancy. This is only the key of a little cupboard where I keep a few odd things the boys get, my dear. I never lock up my money, for I've got none to lock up, my dear. It's a poor trade, Nancy, and no thanks, but I'm fond of seeing the young people about me, and I bear it all; I bear it all. Hush!" he said, hastily concealing the key in his breast-pocket. "Who's that? Listen!"

The girl, who was sitting at the table with her arms folded, appeared in no way interested at the arrival, or to care whether the person, whoever he was, came or went, until the murmur of a man's voice reached her ears. The instant she caught the sound, she tore off her bonnet and shawl with the rapidity of lightning, and thrust them under the table. Fagin turning round immediately afterwards, she affected a drowsy voice, and said how hot it was.

"Bah!" whispered Fagin, as though annoyed by the interruption; "it's the man I expected before; he's coming downstairs. Not a word about the money while he's here, Nance. He won't stop long. Not ten minutes, my dear."

Laying his skinny forefinger upon his lip, Fagin carried a candle to the door, as a man's step was heard upon the stairs outside. He reached it at the same moment as the visitor, who, coming hastily into the room, was close upon the girl before he observed her.

It was Monks.

"Only one of my young people," said Fagin, observing that Monks drew back on seeing a stranger. "Don't move, Nancy."

The girl drew closer to the table, and, glancing at Monks carelessly, withdrew her eyes, but as he turned his towards Fagin, she stole another look, so keen and searching, and full of purpose, that if anyone else had been watching, he could hardly believe the two looks came from the same person.

"Any news?" inquired Fagin.

"Yes," said Monks with a smile. "Let me have a word with you."

Nancy made no offer to leave the room, so Fagin, perhaps fearing she might say something about the money if he tried to get rid of her, pointed upward, and took Monks out of the room. It sounded, by the creaking of the boards, as if they were ascending to the second storey.

Before the sound of their footsteps had ceased to echo through the house, the girl had slipped off her shoes, and, drawing her gown loosely over her head, and muffling her arms in it, stood at the door, listening with breathless interest. The moment the noise ceased, she glided from the room, ascended the stairs with incredible softness and silence, and was lost in the gloom above.

The room remained deserted for a quarter of an hour or more; the girl glided back with the same unearthly tread, and, immediately afterwards, the two men were heard descending. Monks went at once into the street, and Fagin crawled upstairs again for the money. When he returned, the girl was adjusting her shawl and bonnet, as if preparing to be gone.

"Why, Nance," exclaimed the old man, starting back as he put down the candle, "how pale you are!"

"Pale?" echoed the girl, shading her eyes with her hands, as if to look steadily at him.

"Quite horrible. What have you been doing to yourself?"

"Nothing that I know of, except sitting in this close place for I don't know how long and all," replied the girl carelessly. "Let me get back now, there's a dear."

With a sigh for every piece of money, Fagin counted the amount into her hand. They parted without more conversation, merely exchanging a "good night".

When Nancy got into the open street, she sat down upon the doorstep, and seemed, for a few minutes, wholly bewildered and unable to pursue her way. She shook her head helplessly, wrung her hands and burst into tears.

It might be that her tears relieved her, or that she felt there was nothing she could do at the time, but presently she arose and, hurrying on, soon reached the dwelling where she had left the house-breaker.

If she showed any excitement, Sikes did not observe it, being still partly asleep, but the lynx-eyed Fagin would have realised at once by her manner that she was on the eve of some bold and hazardous undertaking.

As the day closed in, she sat by him, watching until he should drink himself asleep again. There was an unusual paleness in her cheek, and a fire in her eye, that even Sikes observed with astonishment.

Being weak from fever, he was lying in bed taking hot water with his gin to render it less fiery, and had pushed his glass towards Nancy to be refilled for the third or fourth time, when these symptoms first struck him.

"Why, burn my body!" said the man, raising himself on his hands as he stared the girl in the face. "You look like a corpse come to life again. What's the matter?"

"Matter?" replied the girl. "Nothing. Why do you look at me so hard for?"

"I tell you what it is," said Sikes. "If you haven't caught the fever, and got it comin' on, now, there's something more than usual in the wind, and something dangerous, too. You're not a-going to – No, damme, you wouldn't do that!"

"Do what?" asked the girl.

"There ain't," said Sikes, fixing his eyes upon her, and muttering the words to himself, "there ain't a stauncher-hearted gal going, or I'd have cut her throat three months ago. She's got the fever coming on; that's it."

Thus reassuring himself, Sikes drained his glass to the bottom, and then, with many grumbling oaths, called for his medicine. Nancy jumped up at once, poured it quickly out, but with her back towards him, and held the glass to his lips while he drank off the contents.

She sat by him while he dozed until he fell into a deep and heavy sleep and lay as one in a coma.

"The laudanum has taken effect at last," murmured the girl, as she rose from the bedside. "I may be too late, even now."

She hastily dressed herself in her bonnet and shawl, looking fearfully round from time to time, as if, despite the sleeping draught, she expected every moment to feel the pressure of Sike's heavy hand upon her shoulder; then, stooping softly over the bed, she kissed the robber's lips, and then, opening and closing the room-door with noiseless touch, hurried from the house.

CHAPTER 34

NANCY SEEKS HELP FOR OLIVER

About an hour later, Nancy arrived at a family hotel in a quiet but handsome street near Hyde Park.

As the brilliant light of the lamp which burnt before its door guided her to the spot, the clock struck eleven. She had been hurrying before, but now loitered for a few paces, as though uncertain whether to advance. The sound of the clock decided her, and she stepped into the hall.

The porter's seat was vacant. She looked round with an air of uncertainty and advanced towards the stairs.

"Now, young woman," said a smartly-dressed female, looking out from a door behind her, "who do you want here?"

"A lady who is stopping in this house—Miss Maylie," said Nancy.

Looking at her appearance with some contempt, the female summoned a manservant who asked her name.

"No name," said Nancy, "but I must see the lady."

The man looked at her doubtfully, but went upstairs with the message. Nancy remained pale and almost breathless until he returned and said she was to walk upstairs.

Nancy followed him with trembling limbs to a small antechamber, lighted by a lamp from the ceiling. Here he left her, and retired.

A light step was heard; Rose appeared and greeted her kindly.

"I am the person you inquired for," said Rose. "Tell me why you wished to see me."

The sweet voice and gentle manner took Nancy completely by surprise, and she burst into tears.

"Oh, lady, lady!" she said, clasping her hands passionately before her face, "if there was more like you, there would be fewer like me—there would—there would!"

"Sit down," said Rose, "and tell me how I can help you. I shall be glad to do so, if I can—I shall indeed. Sit down."

"Let me stand, lady," said the girl, still weeping, "and do not speak to me so kindly until you know me better. It is growing late. Is that door shut?"

"Yes," said Rose, retreating a few steps, as if to be nearer assistance in case she should require it. "Why?"

"Because," said Nancy, "I am about to put my life, and the lives of others, in your hands. I am the girl that dragged little Oliver back to old Fagin's, on the night he went out from the house in Pentonville."

"You!" said Rose.

"Me, wretched creature as I am," said Rose, "but tonight I have stolen away from those who would surely murder me, if they knew I had been here, to tell you what I have overheard. Do you know a man named Monks?"

"No," said Rose.

"He knows you," replied the girl, "and knew you were here, for it was by hearing him tell the place that I found you out."

145

"I never heard the name," said Rose.

"Then he goes by that name only when he is with us," said Nancy, "which I more than thought before. Some time ago, and soon after Oliver was put into your house on the night of the robbery, I—suspecting this man—listened to a conversation held between him and Fagin in the dark. I found out, from what I heard, that Monks had seen Oliver accidentally with two of our boys on the day we first lost him, and had known him directly to be the same child that he was watching for, though I couldn't make out why. A bargain was struck with Fagin, that if Oliver was got back, he should have a certain sum of money and he was to have more for making Oliver a thief, which this Monks wanted for some purpose of his own."

"For what purpose?" asked Rose.

"He caught sight of my shadow on the wall as I listened, in the hope of finding out," said Nancy, "and there are not many people besides me that could have got out of their way in time to escape discovery. But I did, and I saw him no more until last night."

"And what occurred then?"

"I'll tell you, lady. Last night he came again. Again they went upstairs, and I, wrapping myself up so that my shadow should not betray me, again listened at the door. The first words I heard Monks say were these: "So the only proofs of the boy's identity lie at the bottom of the river, and the old hag that received them from the mother is rotting in her coffin. They laughed about this, and Monks, getting very wild, said that though he had got Oliver's money safely now, he'd rather have had it by Oliver going in for a life of crime and finally getting hanged, which Fagin could easily manage, after having made a good profit out of him first. That way his young brother would be out of his father's will for good."

"His brother!" exclaimed Rose.

"Those were his words," said Nancy, glancing uneasily round, as she had scarcely ceased to do since she began to speak, for a vision of Sikes haunted her perpetually. "And more. When he spoke of you and the other lady, and said that Heaven or the devil had worked against him in sending Oliver into your hands, he said that even that was some comfort, for you would give thousands and hundreds of thousands of pounds, if you had them, to know who Oliver really was."

"We must act at once," said Rose. "There is a gentleman in the next room, to whom you must repeat your story. Will you come with me?"

"I must go back," said Nancy. "There is a man who works for Fagin, a desperate man, but one I love, who does not know I am here. If I told others what I have told you, he would be taken with the rest of them, and would be sure to die. He is the boldest and has been so cruel!"

"Stay here," said Rose. "We could put you in a place of safety. It is madness to go back."

"I must go back," answered the girl. "I believe I would go back to him if I knew that I was to die by his hand at last."

"But your secret!" cried Rose. "How can we help Oliver?"

"Tell it to a gentleman you can trust, and seek his advice," said the girl.

"But where can I find you?" asked Rose. "I must be able to find you."

"Will you promise to come alone, or with only the other person to whom you tell the secret, and I shall not be watched or followed home?" asked Nancy.

"I promise you solemnly," answered Rose.

"Every Sunday night, from eleven until the clock strikes twelve," said the girl without hesitation, "I will walk on London Bridge if I am alive."

She moved hurriedly towards the door.

"You will," said Rose, "take some money which will make it possible for you to live honestly—at all events until we meet again?"

"Not a penny," said Nancy. "God bless you, sweet lady, and send as much happiness on your head as I have brought shame on mine."

With a sob, she hastened away, and Rose Maylie sank into a chair and wondered if she had been dreaming.

CHAPTER 35

OLIVER AND MR BROWNLOW ARE REUNITED

Rose sat for a long time wondering what to do, and finally decided that she would have to seek the help of Harry. Tears came to her eyes as she thought of him. Perhaps, by this time, he had learnt to forget her, and to be happier away. To add to her difficulty, she yearned to help Nancy while still keeping her confidence, but her love for Oliver meant that she must act to save him. She decided to wait a few hours while she thought of a plan.

Rose passed a sleepless night, and, after considering all next day, she came to the same conclusion that she *must* consult Harry.

She had taken up her pen to write to him, and laid it down again fifty times without writing the first word, when Oliver, who had been walking in the streets with Mr Giles as a bodyguard, entered the room in breathless haste and near to tears in his excitement.

"I have seen Mr Brownlow," cried Oliver, "the gentleman who was so good to me. He was getting out of a coach. He didn't see me, and I trembled so much I couldn't speak to him, but after he had gone into a house, Giles asked for me whether he lived there, and they said he did. Look here," said Oliver, opening a scrap of paper, "here it is; here's where he lives—I'm going there at once! Oh, dear me, dear me! What shall I do when I come to see him and hear him speak again!"

Rose read the address, which was Craven Street in the Strand, and very soon decided to make use of the discovery.

"Quick," she said, "tell them to fetch a hackney coach, and be ready to go with me. I will just tell my aunt that we are going out for a hour, and I will be ready as soon as you are."

In little more than five minutes, they were on their way to Craven Street. When they arrived there, Rose left Oliver in the coach, under the pretence of preparing the old gentleman to receive him, and, sending up her card by the servant, requested to see Mr Brownlow on very pressing business. The servant soon returned to beg that she would walk upstairs, and, following him into an upper room, Miss Maylie was presented to an elderly gentleman of kindly appearance, wearing a bottle-green coat, who rose with great politeness as she came towards him.

"My dear young lady," said Mr Brownlow, "pray be seated. What can I do for you?"

"I shall surprise you very much, I have no doubt," said Rose, "but you once showed great kindness and goodness to a very dear young friend of mine, and I am sure you will take an interest in hearing of him again."

"Indeed!" said Mr Brownlow.

"Oliver Twist, you knew him as," replied Rose.

Astonished, the old gentleman drew his chair nearer. "Tell me about him," he said. "Against my will, I was forced to believe the boy had betrayed his trust."

"He is a child of a noble nature and warm heart," said Rose, and she proceeded to relate in a few words all that had befallen Oliver since he left Mr Brownlow's house.

"His only sorrow," added Rose, "was in not being able to explain to you, who had been so kind to him, what had happened."

"I knew Grimwig was wrong about him!" exclaimed Mr Brownlow, jumping up. "Where is my dear boy?"

"He is waiting in a coach at the door," said Rose.

Mr Brownlow hurried downstairs, and soon returned with Oliver. Then he sent for Mrs Bedwin.

The old housekeeper answered the summons with all haste, and, dropping a curtsey at the door, waited for orders.

"Why, you get blinder every day, Bedwin," said Mr Brownlow rather testily.

"Well, that I do, sir," replied the old lady. "People's eyes, at my time of life, don't improve with age, sir."

"I could have told you that," rejoined Mr Brownlow, "but put on your glasses, and see if you can't find out what you were wanted for, will you?"

The old lady began to rummage in her pocket for her spectacles. But Oliver's patience was not proof against this new trial, and, yielding to his first impulse, he sprang into her arms.

"God be good to me!" cried the old lady, embracing him; "it is my innocent boy!"

"My dear old nurse!" cried Oliver.

"He would come back—I knew he would," said the old lady, "though some thought otherwise. How well he looks, and how he's grown!"

Leaving Mrs Bedwin and Oliver to compare notes, Mr Brownlow led the way into another room, and there heard from Rose the full story of her interview with Nancy, which caused him no little surprise and perplexity. Rose also explained that she had not yet taken her friend Dr Losberne into her confidence, as he was rather hot-headed and inclined to rush into action without proper thought.

Mr Brownlow thought that she had acted wisely, and readily undertook to hold a conference with the worthy doctor himself. It was arranged that he should call at the hotel at eight o'clock that evening, and that Rose, in the meantime, should inform her aunt of all that had occurred. Then she and Oliver returned home.

When they all met together that evening, Dr Losberne was told the whole story. He wanted to call the police at once, but Mr Brownlow pointed out that they would never get to the bottom of the mystery of Oliver's birth and regain for him his rightful inheritance, unless they could see Monks and bring him to his knees, for, as Mr Brownlow said, even if he were arrested, they had no proof against him, and, so far as they knew, he was not concerned with Sikes and the gang in any of their robberies. Besides this, they had to consider Nancy, who had put herself into extreme danger by revealing the plot against Oliver. The gang would surely bring themselves to justice in the fullness of time.

That day was Tuesday. They would therefore wait until Sunday, when Nancy could be met at the appointed place, and, in the meantime, they would say nothing to Oliver.

"I should like," said Mr Brownlow, "to call in the aid of my friend Grimwig, who is in town at present. He was mistaken in his judgement of Oliver, but he is a shrewd creature and might prove very useful to us. I should say he was bred a lawyer, but has not practised for many years."

"I have no objection to your calling in your friend, if I may call in mine," said the doctor.

"We must put it to the vote," replied Mr Brownlow. "Who may he be?"

"That lady's son, and this young lady's—very old friend," said the doctor, motioning towards Mrs Maylie, and concluding with an expressive glance at her niece.

Rose blushed deeply, but said nothing, and Harry Maylie and Mr Grimwig were accordingly added to the committee.

"We will stay in town, of course," said Mrs Maylie, "while there is the slightest chance of resolving this mystery. I am content to remain here for twelve months if necessary, for Oliver's sake, so long as you assure me that any hope remains."

"Good," said Mr Brownlow, "and later I will explain why I was not here to confirm Oliver's story, and had so suddenly left the kingdom. Come, supper is ready and Oliver is all alone in the next room."

With these words, the old gentleman gave his hand to Mrs Maylie, and escorted her into the supper-room. Dr Losberne followed, leading Rose, and the council was, for the moment, broken up.

CHAPTER 36

FAGIN DEVISES A DARK SCHEME

Skilled and cunning as she was in deceiving people when it was necessary, Nancy could not wholly conceal her unease as she thought of the step she had taken in consulting Rose. She remembered that both Fagin and Sikes had trusted her with schemes which had been hidden from all others. Vile as these schemes were, and bitter as were her feelings towards Fagin, who had led her step by step deeper and deeper into an abyss of crime and misery, from which there was no escape, still, she had no wish that he should fall at last—richly as he deserved it—by her hand.

But her mind was fixed steadily on Oliver and his interests, and she was determined not to be turned aside. Her fears for Sikes might have caused her to draw back while there was yet time, but she had insisted on her secret being kept, she had dropped no clue which could lead to his discovery, she had refused even, for his sake, to go into a place of safety to be provided by Rose, where she would find refuge from all the guilt and wretchedness that surrounded her—and what more could she do? She was resolved.

All the same, Nancy grew pale and thin even within a few days. She became absorbed in her thoughts, and took little heed of the conversations of those around her.

It was Sunday night, and the bell of the nearest church struck the hour. Sikes and Fagin were talking, but they paused to listen. The girl looked up from the low seat on which she crouched, and listened too. Eleven.

"An hour this side of midnight," said Sikes, raising the blind to look out and returning to his seat. "Dark and heavy it is, too. A good night for business, this."

"Ah!" replied Fagin. "What a pity, Bill, my dear, that there's none quite ready to be done."

"You're right for once," replied Sikes gruffly. "It is a pity, for I'm in the humour, too."

Fagin sighed, and shook his head despondingly.

"We must make up for lost time when we've got things arranged. That's all I know," said Sikes.

"That's the way to talk, my dear," replied Fagin, venturing to pat him on the shoulder. "It does me good to hear you."

"Does you good, does it?" cried Sikes. "Well, so be it."

"Ha! Ha! Ha!" laughed Fagin, as if he were relieved by an apparently amiable remark. "You're like yourself tonight, Bill. Quite like yourself."

"I don't feel like myself when you lay that withered old claw on my shoulder, so take it away," said Sikes, casting off Fagin's hand.

"It makes you nervous, Bill—reminds you of being caught, does it?" said Fagin, determined not to be offended.

"Reminds me of being nabbed by the devil," returned Sikes, "unless he was your father, which I shouldn't wonder at a bit."

Fagin offered no reply to this compliment, but, pulling Sikes by the sleeve, pointed his finger towards Nancy, who, while they were talking, had put on her bonnet, and was now leaving the room.

"Hallo!" cried Sikes. "Nance. Where's the gal going to at this time of night?"

"Not far."

"What answer's that?" returned Sikes. "Where are you going?"

"I say, not far."

"And I say where?" retorted Sikes. "Do you hear me?"

"I don't know where," replied the girl.

"Then I do," said Sikes, more in the spirit of obstinacy than because he had any real objection to the girl going where she pleased. "Nowhere. Sit down."

"I'm not well. I told you that before," rejoined Nancy. "I want a breath of air."

"Put your head out of the winder," replied Sikes.

"There's not enough there," said the girl. "I want it in the street."

"Then you won't have it," replied Sikes. With that, he rose, locked the door, took the key out, and, pulling her bonnet from her head, flung it up to the top of an old cupboard.

"There," said the robber. "Now stop quietly where you are, will you?"

Nancy turned very pale. Then, sitting herself down on the floor before the door, she said earnestly, "Bill, let me go; you don't know what you are doing. You don't indeed. For only one hour—do—do!"

"Cut my limbs off one by one!" cried Sikes, seizing her roughly by the arm, "if I don't think the gal's stark raving mad. Get up."

"Not till you let me go—not till you let me go. Never, never!" screamed the girl. Sikes looked on for a minute, watching his opportunity, and, suddenly pinioning her hands, dragged her, struggling and wrestling with him by the way, into a small room adjoining, where he sat himself on a bench, and, thrusting her into a chair, held her down by force. She struggled and implored by turns until twelve o'clock had struck, and then, wearied and exhausted, ceased to resist him. Warning her, with many oaths, to make no more attempts to go out that night, Sikes left Nancy to recover and rejoined Fagin.

"Whew!" said the housebreaker, wiping the perspiration from his face. "What a precious strange gal that is!"

"You may say that, Bill," replied Fagin thoughtfully. "You may say that."

"What did she take it into her head to go out tonight for, do you think?" asked Sikes. "Come, you should know her better than me. What does it mean?"

"Hush!" whispered Fagin, as Nancy returned to the room, her eyes swollen and red, and sat down in her usual place.

Fagin took up his hat and bade them good night. He paused when he reached the room-door, and looking round, asked if somebody would light him down the dark stairs.

"Light him down," said Sikes, who was filling his pipe. "It's a pity he should break his neck himself, and disappoint the hangman. Show him a light."

Nancy followed the old man downstairs with a candle. When they reached the passage, he laid his finger on his lip, and, drawing close to the girl, said in a whisper, "What is it, Nancy, dear?"

"What do you mean?" replied the girl in the same tone.

"The reason of all this," replied Fagin. "If *he*——" he pointed with his skinny fore-finger up the stairs—"is so hard with you (he's a brute, Nance, a brute-beast), why don't you——"

"Well?" said the girl, as Fagin paused with his mouth almost touching her ear, and his eyes looking into hers.

"No matter just now. We'll talk of this again. You have a friend in me, Nance, a staunch friend. I have the means at hand quiet and close. If you want revenge on one that treats you like a dog—worse than his dog, for he humours him sometimes—come to me. He is the mere hound of a day, but you know me of old, Nance."

"I know you well," replied the girl, without emotion. "Good night."

Fagin walked towards his own house, intent upon the thoughts that were working within his brain. He was beginning to wonder if Nancy, wearied of the housebreaker's brutality, had become attached to another man. Her altered manner, her repeated absences from home alone, her lack of interest now in the gang and, added to these, her desperate impatience to leave the house at a certain hour—all these things combined to support this theory. If she *had* another man, he would be a valuable recruit with such an assistant as

Nancy, and must (so Fagin told himself) be enrolled in the gang without delay.

There was another, and a darker object to be gained. Sikes knew too much; he was a ruffian without loyalty, and he could certainly kill or wound a rival.

"With a little persuasion," thought Fagin, "she might agree to poison him. Such things have been done before, and for the same reasons. That would be Sikes, the dangerous villain whom I hate, gone, perhaps a more useful man in his place, and my influence over Nancy, with my knowledge of her crime, unlimited."

But perhaps she would shrink from a plot to take the life of Sikes

"How," thought Fagin, as he slunk homeward, "can I increase my influence with her? What new power can I acquire over her?"

If he kept watch, discovered whom Nancy was meeting, and threatened to tell Sikes (of whom she stood in fear), she might be made to fall in with his schemes in order to save herself.

"It can be done," said Fagin to himself. "She dare not refuse me then. Not for her life, she dare not. I'll have you yet, Bill!"

He cast back a dark look, and a threatening motion of the hand, towards the spot where he had left the bolder villain, and went on his way, grasping his tattered garment in his bony hands and wrenching at it, as though there were a hated enemy crushed with every motion of his fingers.

CHAPTER 37

ON LONDON BRIDGE

The church clocks chimed three quarters past eleven, as two figures emerged on London Bridge. One, which advanced with a swift and rapid step, was that of a woman who looked eagerly about her, as though she were expecting to meet somebody, the other figure was that of an old man, who slunk along in the deepest shadow he could find, and, at some distance, kept pace with her, stopping when she stopped, and, as she moved again, creeping stealthily on, but never passing her. Thus they crossed the bridge from the Middlesex to the Surrey shore, but apparently not seeing the person whom she had come to meet, the woman suddenly turned back. Her follower was not thrown off his guard, however, but slipped into one of the alcoves on the bridge and hid himself as far as he could, while she passed by on the opposite pavement. When she was about the same distance in advance as she had been before, he slipped quietly out, and followed her again. At nearly the centre of the bridge, she stopped. The man stopped too.

It was a very dark night. The day had been unfavourable, and at that hour and place there were few people stirring. Those people who were still out hurried quickly past, very possibly without seeing, but certainly without noticing, either the woman or the old man who kept her in view.

A mist hung over the river, deepening the red glare of the fires that burnt upon the small craft moored off the different wharfs, and rendering darker and more indistinct the murky buildings on the banks. The old smoke-stained storehouses on either side rose heavy and dull from the dense mass of roofs and gables, and frowned sternly upon water too black to reflect even their lumbering shapes. The tower of old Saint Saviour's Church, and the spire of Saint Magnus, so long the giant warders of the ancient bridge, were visible in the gloom, but the forest of shipping below bridge, and the thickly scattered spires of churches above were nearly all hidden from sight.

The girl had taken a few restless turns to and fro—closely watched meanwhile by her hidden observer—when the heavy bell of St Paul's tolled for the death of another day. Midnight had come upon the crowded city.

The hour had not struck two minutes when a young lady, accompanied by a grey-haired gentleman, alighted from a hackney carriage within a short distance of the bridge, and, having dismissed the vehicle, walked straight towards it. They had scarcely set foot upon its pavement, when the girl started, and immediately made towards them.

The lady and her companion walked onward, looking about them as if they hardly expected to be met, when she suddenly came up to them.

156

"Not here," said Nancy hurriedly. "I am afraid to speak to you here. Come away—out of the public road—down the steps yonder."

As she uttered these words, and indicated with her hand the direction in which she wished them to proceed, the watcher slipped from his hiding place, gained the steps ahead of them, unobserved, and began to descend.

These stairs are a part of the bridge; they consist of three flights. Just below the end of the second, going down, the stone wall on the left terminates in an ornamental pilaster or column facing towards the Thames. At this point, the lower steps widen, so that a person turning that angle of the wall is necessarily unseen by any others on the stairs who chance to be above him, if only a step. The watcher looked hastily round when he reached this point, and, as there seemed no better place for concealment, and, the tide being out, there was plenty of room, he slipped aside with his back to the pilaster, and there waited, pretty certain that they would come no lower, and that even if he could not hear what was said, he could follow them again with safety. Presently he heard the sound of footsteps, and directly afterwards of voices almost close at his ear. He shrank back against the wall and, scarcely breathing, listened attentively.

"This is far enough," said a voice, which evidently belonged to the gentleman. "I will not allow the young lady to go any further. For what purpose can you have brought us to this strange place? Why not have let me speak to you up above where it is light, and there is movement, instead of bringing us to this dark and dismal hole?"

"I told you before," replied Nancy, "that I was afraid to speak to you there. I don't know why it is," said the girl, shuddering, "but I have such a fear and dread upon me to-night that I can hardly stand."

"A fear of what?" asked the gentleman, who seemed to pity her.

"I scarcely know of what," replied the girl. "I wish I did. Horrible thoughts of death, and a fear that has made me burn as if I was on fire, have been upon me all day."

"Speak to her kindly," said the young lady to her companion. "Poor creature! She seems to need it."

"You were not here last Sunday night," said the gentleman.

"I couldn't come," replied Nancy. "I was kept in by force."

"By whom?"

"The man that I told the young lady of before."

"He did not suspect anything, I hope," said the gentleman.

"No," replied the girl, shaking her head. "It's not very easy for me to leave him unless he knows why. I couldn't have seen the lady when I did, if I hadn't given him a drink of laudanum before I came away."

"Did he awake before you returned?" inquired the gentleman.

"No, and neither he nor any of them suspect me."

"Good," said the gentleman. "Now listen to me."

"I am ready," replied the girl, as he paused for a moment.

"This young lady," the gentleman began, "has told me and some friends who can be trusted, what you told her a fortnight ago. I confess to you that at first I wondered if you could be relied upon, but now I firmly believe we can trust you."

"You can," said the girl earnestly.

"Very well," said the gentleman. "I will now tell you that we plan to obtain the secret from this man Monks, but if we fail, *if* we fail, you must deliver up the Jew."

"Fagin!" cried the girl, drawing back.

"The man must be delivered up by you," said the gentleman.

"I will not do it! I will never do it!" replied Nancy. "Devil that he is, and worse than devil as he has been to me, I will never do that."

"You will not?" said the gentleman who seemed fully prepared for this answer.

"Never!" returned the girl.

"Tell me why."

"Because," said the girl firmly, "bad life as he has led, I have led a bad life, too—we all have. But none of them would turn upon me, bad as they are, and I will not turn upon them."

"Then," said the gentleman, "put Monks into my hands, and leave him to me to deal with."

"What if he turns against the others?"

"I promise you that in that case, if the truth is forced from him, there the matter will rest. The others shall go free."

"And if you do not succeed?"

"Then," said the gentleman, "this Fagin shall not be brought to justice without your consent."

"Have I the lady's promise for that?" asked Nancy.

"You have," replied Rose, "my true and faithful pledge."

"Monks would never learn how you knew what you do?" said the girl, after a short pause.

"Never," replied the gentleman. "We shall make certain of it."

"I have been a liar, and among liars from a little child," said the girl after another interval of silence, "but I will take your words."

In a low voice, so that the listener could barely hear what she said, Nancy now began to describe by name and situation the public house where Monks was often to be found, and then she went on to describe the man himself.

"He is tall," said the girl, and a strongly made man, but not stout. He has a lurking walk and, as he walks, constantly looks over his shoulder, first on one side, and then on the other. He is dark and looks much older than his years. He can't be more than six or eight and twenty. I have found out some of this from people at the public house I tell you of, for I have only seen him twice, and both times he was covered up in a long cloak. I think that's all I can give you to know him by. Stay, though," she added. "Upon his throat, so high that you can see a part of it below his neckerchief when he turns his face, there is——"

"A broad red mark, like a burn or scald?" cried the gentleman.

"How's this?" said the girl. "You know him!"

The young lady uttered a cry of surprise, and for a few moments they were so still that the listener heard him mutter, "It must be he!"

There was another silence and the gentleman spoke again.

"You have given us most valuable assistance, young woman. What can I do to serve you?"

"Nothing," replied Nancy.

"You will not persist in saying that," rejoined the gentleman kindly. "Think now. Tell me."

"Nothing, sir," said Nancy, weeping. "You can do nothing to help me. I am past all hope indeed."

"You put yourself beyond all hope," said the gentleman. "Let us take you to a place of safety. You need never return to your old life. Be rid of your old associates. Quit your old haunts for ever while you have the chance!"

"She will be persuaded now," cried the young lady. "She hesitates, I'm sure."

"I fear not, my dear," said the gentleman.

"No, sir, I do not hesitate," replied Nancy. "I am chained to my old life. I loathe and hate it now, but I cannot leave it. I have gone too far to turn back." She looked hastily round. "This fear comes over me again. I must go home."

"It is useless," said the gentleman with a sigh. "She is in danger, staying here."

"This purse," cried the young lady. "Take it for my sake, that you may have some resource in an hour of need and trouble."

"No!" replied the girl. "I have not done this for money. Give me something that you have worn: I should like to have something—no, no, not a ring—your gloves or handkerchief—anything that I can keep, as having belonged to you, sweet lady. There. Bless you! God bless you. Good night, good night!"

The listener heard the sound of retreating footsteps, and the voices ceased.

The figures of the young lady and her companion soon afterwards appeared upon the bridge. They stopped at the summit of the stairs.

"Hark!" cried the young lady, listening. "Did she call? I thought I heard her voice."

"No, my love," replied Mr. Brownlow, looking sadly back. "She has not moved, and will not till we are gone."

Rose Maylie lingered, but the old gentleman drew her arm through his, and led her away. As they disappeared, Nancy sank down nearly at her full length upon one of the stone stairs, and poured out the anguish of her heart in bitter tears.

After a time, she rose, and, with feeble and tottering steps, ascended to the street. The listener remained motionless for some minutes afterwards, and, having made sure, with many cautious glances round him, that he was unobserved, crept shivering from his hiding place, and returned, stealthily and in the shadow of the wall, in the same manner as he had descended. Then he made for home as fast as his old legs would carry him.

CHAPTER 38

NANCY PAYS THE PRICE

When he reached his lair, Fagin sat for a long time crouched over a cold hearth, wrapped in an old torn coverlet. It was nearly daybreak, and although he had been out for several hours in the night, he had not yet slept. His scheme for taking revenge on Sikes through Nancy had been overthrown; the girl had dared to confide in strangers, and, in spite of what he had heard her say, he was certain she would betray him. The fear of detection, ruin and death kindled a fierce and deadly rage as every evil thought and blackest purpose lay working at his heart.

He sat without changing his attitude in the least, or appearing to take the smallest heed of time, until his quick ear seemed to be attracted by a footstep in the street.

"At last," he muttered, wiping his dry and fevered mouth. "At last!"

The bell rang gently as he spoke. He crept upstairs to the door, and presently returned accompanied by a man muffled to the chin, who carried a bundle under one arm. Sitting down and throwing back his outer coat, the man displayed the burly frame of Sikes.

"There!" he said, laying the bundle on the table. "Take care of that, and do the most you can with it. It's been trouble enough to get. I thought I should have been here three hours ago."

Fagin laid his hand upon the bundle, and, locking it in the cupboard, sat down again without speaking. But he did not take his eyes off the robber for an instant during this action, and now they sat over against each other, face to face, he looked fixedly at him, with his lips quivering so violently, and his face so pale and distorted, that the housebreaker unconsciously drew back his chair, and surveyed him with a look of real affright.

F

"What now?" cried Sikes. "What do you look at a man so for?"

Fagin raised his right hand, and shook his trembling forefinger in the air, but his passion was so great that the power of speech was for the moment gone.

"Damme!" said Sikes, feeling inside his coat with a look of alarm. "He's gone mad. I must look to myself here."

"No, no," rejoined Fagin, finding his voice. "It's not—you're not the person, Bill. I've no—fault to find with you."

"Oh, you haven't, haven't you?" said Sikes, looking sternly at him, and ostentatiously passing a pistol into a more convenient pocket. "That's lucky—for one of us. Which one that is, don't matter."

"I've got something to tell you, Bill," said Fagin, drawing his chair nearer, "that will make you worse than me."

"Aye?" returned the robber with an incredulous air. "Tell away! Look sharp, or Nance will think I'm lost."

"Lost!" cried Fagin. "She has pretty well settled that in her own mind, already."

Sikes looked bewildered and then angry. He seized the old man by the coat collar and shook him soundly.

"Speak, will you?" he said, "or if you don't, it shall be because I'll strangle you. Open your mouth and say what you've got to say in plain words. Out with it, you thundering old cur, out with it!"

"Suppose someone," continued Fagin, "was to blow upon us all, first seeking out the right folks for the purpose, and then having a meeting with 'em in the street to describe our likenesses, every mark that they might know us by and where we could be caught. What then? What would you do?"

"What then?" replied Sikes with a tremendous oath. "I'd grind his skull under the iron heel of my boot into as many grains as there are hairs upon his head."

"What if *I* did it?" cried Fagin almost in a yell. "*I*, that know so much, and could hang so many besides myself!"

"I don't know," replied Sikes, clenching his teeth and turning white at the mere suggestion. "I'd do something in the jail that would get me put in irons, and if I was tried along with you, I'd fall upon you with them in the open court, and beat your brains out afore the people. I should have such strength," muttered the robber, bending his brawny arm, "that I could smash your head as if a loaded waggon had gone over it."

"You would?"

"Would I!" said the housebreaker. "Try me."

"If it was Charlie, or the Dodger, or Bet, or——"

"I don't care who," replied Sikes impatiently. "Whoever it was, I'd serve them the same."

"I'm very tired, Bill," said Fagin. "I've been out all night, watching for *her* so long—watching for *her*, Bill."

"What do you mean?" asked Sikes, drawing back. "Who are you talking about?"

"About NANCY," said Fagin, clutching Sikes by the wrist, as if to prevent his leaving the house before he had heard enough. "I followed her to London Bridge where she met two people. Two people, a gentleman and a lady that she had gone to of her own accord before, who asked her to give up all her pals, and Monks first of all, which she did—and to describe him, which she did, and to say what house it was we met at, which she did—and where it could best be watched from, which she did—and what time the people went there, which she did. She did all this. She told it all, every word without a threat, without a murmur, and then they asked her why she hadn't come the Sunday before, as she promised. She said she couldn't, because she was forcibly kept at home by Bill, the man she had told them of before. She said she couldn't very easily get out of doors unless he knew where she was going to, and so the first time she went to see the lady, she gave him a drug to make him sleep."

"Hell's fire!" cried Sikes, breaking fiercely away. "Let me go!"

Flinging the old man from him, he rushed from the room, and darted wildly and furiously up the stairs.

"Bill, Bill!" cried Fagin, following him hastily. "A word, only a word."

The housebreaker would not have waited, but he was unable to open the door, and was twisting the key violently when Fagin came panting up.

"Let me out," said Sikes. "Don't speak to me! it's not safe. Let me out, I say!"

"Hear me speak a word," rejoined Fagin, laying his hand upon the lock. "You won't be——"

"Well?" replied the other.

"You won't be—too—violent, Bill?"

The day was breaking, and there was light enough for the

men to see each other's faces. They exchanged one brief glance; there was a fire in the eyes of both, which could not be mistaken.

"I mean," said Fagin, "not too violent for safety. Be crafty, Bill, and not too bold."

Sikes made no reply, but, pulling open the door, of which Fagin had turned the lock, dashed into the silent streets. Fagin crept back up the stairs, as a young boy, who had followed them down, shrank back unseen among the shadows.

Without one pause, or moment's consideration, without once turning his head to right or left, Sikes held on his head-long course, nor muttered a word, nor relaxed a muscle, until he reached his own door. He opened it softly with a key, strode lightly up the stairs, and, entering his own room, double-locked the door, and, lifting a heavy table against it, drew back the curtain of the bed.

The girl was lying, half-dressed, upon it. He had roused her from her sleep, for she raised herself with a hurried and startled look.

"Get up!" said the man.

"It *is* you, Bill!" cried the girl, with an expression of pleasure at his return.

"It is," was the reply. "Get up."

There was a candle burning, but the man hastily drew it from the candlestick and hurled it under the grate. Seeing the faint light of early day outside, the girl rose to draw back the curtain.

"Let it be," said Sikes, thrusting his hand before her. "There's light enough for what I've got to do."

"Bill," said the girl, in a low voice of alarm, "why do you look like that at me?"

The robber sat regarding her for a few seconds. His eyes were staring, and he was breathing heavily. Then, grasping her by the head and throat, he dragged her into the middle of the room and, looking once towards the door, placed his heavy hand upon her mouth.

"Bill, Bill!" gasped the girl, wrestling and twisting her head with the strength of mortal fear—"I—I—won't scream or cry —not once—hear me—speak to me—tell me what I have done!"

"You know what you have done, you she-devil!" returned
164

the robber. "You were watched tonight; every word you said was heard."

"Then spare my life for the love of Heaven, as I spared yours," rejoined the girl, clinging to him. "Bill, dear Bill, you cannot have the heart to kill me. Think of all I have given up, only this night, for you. For God's sake stop before you spill my blood! I have been true to you, upon my soul I have!"

The man struggled violently to release his arms, but those of the girl were clasped round his, and tear her as he would, he could not tear them away.

"Bill," cried the girl, striving to lay her head upon his breast, "the gentleman and that dear lady offered me a place of safety if I would leave you, and repent my way of life. I would not leave you, Bill—I told them—— Could not we both repent and lead new lives far from this dreadful place?"

The housebreaker freed one arm and grasped his pistol. The certainty of immediate detection if he fired, flashed across his mind even in the midst of his fury, and he beat it twice, with all the force he could summon, upon the upturned face that almost touched his own.

She staggered and fell, nearly blinded with the blood that rained down from a deep gash in her forehead, but, raising herself with difficulty on her knees, drew from her bosom a white handkerchief.—Rose Maylie's own—and, holding it up in her folded hands, as high towards Heaven as her feeble strength would allow, breathed one prayer for mercy to her Maker.

It was a ghastly figure to look upon. The murderer, staggering backward to the wall, and shutting out the sight with his hand, seized a heavy club and struck her down.

CHAPTER 39

SIKES ON THE RUN

Of all bad deeds that, under cover of the darkness, had been committed within wide London's bounds since night hung over it, that was the worst. Of all the horrors that rose with an ill scent upon the morning air, that was the foulest and most cruel.

The sun—the bright sun, that brings back not light alone, but new life and hope and freshness to man—burst upon the city in clear and radiant glory. Through costly-coloured glass and paper-mended window, through cathedral dome and rotten crevice, it shed its equal ray. It did. He tried to shut it out, but it would stream in. If the sight had been a ghastly one in the dull morning, what was it now in all that brilliant light?

He had not moved; he had been afraid to stir. At one time, he threw a rug over the body, but it was worse to fancy the eyes, and imagine them moving towards him, than to see them glaring upward as if watching the reflection of the pool of blood that quivered and danced in the sunlight on the ceiling. He had plucked the blanket off again. And there was the body —mere flesh and blood, no more—but such flesh, and so much blood!

He struck a light, kindled a fire and burnt the club. He washed himself and rubbed his clothes; there were spots that would not be removed, but he cut the pieces out and burnt them as well. How those stains were dispersed about the room! The very feet of the dog were bloody.

All this time he had never once turned his back upon the body, no, not for a moment. Such preparations completed, he moved backward towards the door, dragging the dog with him, lest he should soil his feet anew and carry new evidences of the crime into the streets. He shut the door softly, locked it, took the key, and left the house.

He crossed over, and glanced up at the window, to be sure that nothing was visible from the outside. There was the curtain still drawn, which she would have opened to admit the light she never saw again. It lay nearly under there. *He* knew that. God, how the sun poured down upon the very spot!

The glance was instantaneous. It was a relief to have got free of the room. He whistled on the dog and walked rapidly away.

He went through Islington, strode up the hill at Highgate on which stands the stone in honour of Whittington, turned down to Highgate Hill, unsteady of purpose, and uncertain where to go, struck off to the right again almost as soon as he began to descend it, and, taking the foot-path across the fields, skirted Caen Wood, and so came out on Hampstead Heath. Traversing the hollow by the Vale of Health, he mounted the opposite bank, and, crossing the road which joins the villages of Hampstead and Highgate, made along the remaining portion of the heath to the fields at North End, in one of which he laid himself down under a hedge and slept.

Soon he was up again and away—not far into the country, but back towards London by the high-road—then back again— then over another part of the same ground as he had already traversed—wandering up and down in fields, and lying on the slopes of ditches to rest, and starting up to make for some other spot, and do the same, and ramble on again.

Where could he go, that was near and not too public? Hendon. That was a good place, not far off, and out of most people's way. Thither he directed his steps, but when he got there, all the people he met—the very children at the doors— seemed to view him with suspicion. Back he turned again, without the courage to purchase bite or drop, though he had tasted no food for many hours, and once more he lingered on the Heath, uncertain where to go.

He wandered over miles and miles of ground, and still came back to the old place. Morning and noon had passed, and the day was on the wane, and still he rambled to and fro, and up and down, and round and round, and still lingered about the same spot. At last he got away, and shaped his course for Hatfield.

It was nine o'clock at night, when the man, quite tired out, and the dog, limping and lame from the unaccustomed exercise, turned down the hill by the church of the quiet village, and, plodding along the little street, crept into a small public-house, whose scanty light had guided them to the spot. There was a fire in the tap-room, and some country-labourers were drinking before it. They made room for the stranger, but he sat down in the furthest corner, and ate and drank alone, or rather with his dog, to whom he cast a morsel of food from time to time. He slept a little and, when the inn closed, paid his reckoning and set off again.

With no set purpose, he turned back up the town, and, getting out of the glare of the lamps of a stage-coach that was standing in the street, was walking past, when he recognised the mail from London, and saw that it was standing at the little post-office. He almost knew what was to come, but he crossed over and listened.

The guard was standing at the door, waiting for the letter-bag. A man dressed like a gamekeeper came up at the moment, and he handed him a basket which lay ready on the pavement.

"That's for your people," said the guard. "Now, look alive in there, will you. Damn that 'ere bag; it warn't ready night afore last. This won't do, you know!"

"Anything new up in town, Ben?" asked the gamekeeper, drawing back to the window-shutters, the better to admire the horses.

"No, nothing that I knows on," replied the man, pulling on his gloves. "Corn's up a little. I heard talk of a murder, too, down Spitalfields way, but I don't reckon much upon it."

"Oh, that's quite true," said a gentleman inside, who was looking out of the window. "And a dreadful murder it was."

"Was it, sir?" rejoined the guard, touching his hat. "Man or woman, pray, sir?"

"A woman," replied the gentleman. "It is believed the murderer has gone to Birmingham, but they'll have him yet, for the officers are out, and by tomorrow night there'll be a cry all through the country."

"Now, Ben," said the coachman impatiently.

"Damn that 'ere bag," said the guard; "are you gone to sleep in there?"

"Coming!" cried the office keeper, running out.

"Coming," growled the guard. "Ah, and so's the young woman of property that's going to take a fancy to me, but I don't know when. Here, give hold. All ri-ight!"

The horn sounded a few cheerful notes, and the coach was gone.

Sikes remained standing in the street, apparently unmoved by what he had just heard, and agitated by no stronger feeling than a doubt where to go. At length he went back again, and took the road which leads from Hatfield to St Albans.

He went on doggedly, left the town behind him, and plunged into the solitude and darkness of the road.

There was a shed in a field he passed presently that offered shelter for the night. Before the door were three tall poplar trees, which made it very dark within, and the wind moaned

168

through them with a dismal wail. Here he stretched himself close to the wall—but not to sleep.

For now a vision came before him. Nancy's staring eyes appeared in the midst of the darkness, light in themselves, but giving light to nothing. There were but two, but they were everywhere. If he shut out the sight, there came the room, with every well-known object, each in its accustomed place. The body was in *its* place, and its eyes were as he saw them when he stole away. He got up and rushed into the field outside. The eyes were behind him. He re-entered the shed and shrank down once more, sweating, and trembling in every limb. The eyes were there, before he had laid himself by the wall.

He left the shed and walked till he almost dropped upon the ground, then lay down in a lane and had a long, but broken and uneasy sleep. He wandered on again, not knowing what to do, and oppressed with the fear of another solitary night.

Suddenly he took the desperate resolution of going back to London.

"There's somebody to speak to there, at all events," he thought. "A good hiding-place, too. They'll never expect to nab me there. Why can't I lie by for a week or so, and, forcing money from Fagin, get abroad to France? Damme, I'll risk it."

He acted upon this impulse without delay, and, choosing the most lonely roads, began his journey back, resolved to lie concealed within a short distance of the city, and entering at dusk by a roundabout route, to go straight to that part of it in which he had decided to hide.

The dog, though. If any description of him were out, it would not be forgotten that the dog was missing, and had probably gone with him. This might lead to his arrest as he passed along the streets. He resolved to drown him, and walked on, looking about for a pond, picking up a heavy stone and tying it to his handkerchief as he went.

The animal looked up into his master's stern face and instinct told him something was wrong. He skulked a little further in the rear than usual, and cowered as he came more slowly along. When his master halted at the brink of a pool, and looked around to call him, he stopped outright.

"Do you hear me call? Come here!" cried Sikes.

The animal came up from the very force of habit, but, as

Sikes stooped to attach the handkerchief to his throat, he uttered a low growl and backed away.

"Come·back!" said the robber.

The dog wagged his tail, but moved not. Sikes made a running noose and called him again.

The dog advanced, retreated, paused an instant, turned and scoured away at his hardest speed.

The man whistled again and again, and sat down and waited, in the expectation that he would return. But no dog appeared, and at length he resumed his journey.

CHAPTER 40

THE TRUTH IS OUT

The twilight was beginning to close in, when Mr Brownlow alighted from a hackney-coach at his own door, and knocked softly. The door being opened, a sturdy man got out of the coach and stationed himself on one side of the steps, while another man, who had been seated on the box, dismounted too, and stood upon the other side. At a sign from Mr Brownlow, they helped out a third man, and, taking him between them, hurried him into the house. This man was Monks.

They walked in the same manner up the stairs without speaking, and Mr Brownlow, going ahead, led the way into a back-room. At the door of this apartment, Monks, who had ascended with evident reluctance, stopped. The two men looked to the old gentleman as if for instructions.

"He knows the alternative," said Mr Brownlow. "If he hesitates or moves a finger without permission, drag him into the streets, call for the aid of the police and have him arrested as a criminal."

"How dare you kidnap me in the streets and cause these dogs to bring me here. How dare you call me a criminal?" cried Monks, looking from one to the other of the men who stood beside him.

"You have been free to go all along," said Mr Brownlow.

"Let him go. There, sir. You are free, but I warn you that the instant you set foot in the street, that instant will I have you arrested on a charge of fraud and robbery."

"Is—is there no other way?" said Monks, hesitating.

"None, for I speak for the interests of others—others whom you have deeply wronged," said Mr Brownlow. "If you wish for mercy, go and sit down in that chair. It has waited for you two whole days."

Monks looked at the old gentleman with an anxious eye, but observing the severity and determination of his expression, walked into the room, and, shrugging his shoulders, sat down.

"Lock the door on the outside," said Mr Brownlow to the attendants, "and come when I ring."

The men obeyed, and the two were left alone together.

"This is pretty treatment, sir," said Monks, throwing down his hat and cloak, "from my father's oldest friend."

"It is because of that friendship," said Mr Brownlow, "that I am moved to deal gently with you now. Yes, Edward Leeford, for that is your real name. Your father's only sister died on the very morning she was to have become my young wife. He was still a boy, and my broken heart clung to him from that day forth, through all his trials and errors till he died."

"What has the name to do with it?" asked the other, looking with wonder at the old gentleman, who appeared to be in the grip of a strong emotion. "What is the name to me?"

"Nothing," replied Mr Brownlow, "nothing to you. But it was *hers,* and even at this distance of time brings back to me, an old man, the glow and thrill which I once felt, only to hear it mentioned. I am glad you have changed it—very—very."

"This is all mighty fine," said Monks after a long silence, during which he had jerked himself in sullen defiance to and fro, and Mr Brownlow had sat, shading his face with his hand. "But what do you want with me?"

"You have a brother," said Mr Brownlow, rousing himself at last.

"I have no brother," replied Monks. "I was an only child."

"You have a brother, and that is why, in your alarm, you came with me, when I whispered his name in your ear. Not a full brother, but a brother none the less."

"My parents were separated," said Monks. "I was their only child, and I went with my mother."

"True," said Mr Brownlow, "your mother soon forgot her

171

young husband, and he, in his loneliness, made new friends."

"This is all nothing to me," said Monks.

"I shall interest you by and by," said Mr Brownlow. "These new friends were a naval officer retired from active service, whose wife had died some half-a-year before, and left him with two children. They were both daughters, one a beautiful girl of nineteen, and the other a mere child of two or three years old. Your father was accepted as part of the family; he fell in love with the eldest daughter, a sweet and innocent girl, and, although he was not free, the end of the first year found him solemnly promised to that daughter, the first and only love of an innocent girl."

"Your tale is of the longest," said Monks, moving restlessly in his chair.

"It is a true tale of grief and trial and sorrow, young man," returned Mr Brownlow, "and such tales usually *are* long. If it were one of unmixed joy and happiness, it would be very brief. Eventually a rich relation died and left his money to your father. He had died in Rome, leaving his affairs in great confusion, so that your father had to go there. He went, was seized with mortal illness there, and was followed, the moment the news reached her, by your mother, his separated wife, who took you with her. He died the day after arrival, leaving no will—*no will*—so that the whole property fell to her and to you."

Monks was now listening with a face of intense eagerness, though his eyes were not directed towards the speaker. As Mr Brownlow paused, he changed his position with the air of one who had experienced a sudden relief, and wiped his hot face and hands.

"Before your father went abroad, and he passed through London on his way," said Mr Brownlow slowly, and fixing his eyes upon the other's face, "he came to me."

"I never heard of that," interrupted Monks in a tone of disagreeable surprise.

"He came to me, and left with me, among some other things, a picture—a portrait painted by himself—a likeness of the girl he loved—which he did not wish to leave behind, and could not take with him on his hasty journey to Rome. He talked in a wild, distracted way, was full of anxiety and remorse because he had wronged her, and told me that he intended to sell all the property, settle money on you and your mother and leave the country with the one who meant everything to him in life. He promised to write to me and tell me all, and to see me once again for the last time before he left. Alas! *That* was the last time. I had no letter, and I never saw him more."

"When I heard no more," went on Mr Brownlow, "I feared something might have happened to him, and I sought out the family, to offer the poor girl a home, but I found they had settled such small debts as there were and left the place by night. Why or whither, none can tell."

Monks drew his breath yet more freely, and looked round with a smile of triumph.

"When your brother," said Mr Brownlow, drawing nearer to the other's chair, "when your brother, a feeble, ragged, neglected child was cast in my way by a stronger hand than chance, and rescued by me from a life of crime——"

"What?" cried Monks.

"Yes, by me," said Mr Brownlow. "I see that your fellow conspirator Fagin did not tell you that. When Oliver was rescued by me, then, and lay recovering from illness in my house, his strong resemblance to this picture I have spoken of, struck me with astonishment. Even when I first saw him in all his dirt and misery, there was a lingering expression on his face that came upon me like a glimpse of some old friend flashing on one in a vivid dream. I need not tell you that he was forcibly taken back to Fagin before I knew his history——"

"Why not?" asked Monks hastily.

"Because you know it well."

"You—you can't prove anything against me," stammered Monks. "I defy you to do it."

"We shall see," returned the old gentleman, with a searching glance. "I lost the boy, and no efforts of mine could recover him. Your mother being dead, I knew that you alone could solve the mystery if anybody could, and as, when I last heard of you, you were in the West Indies, I made the voyage. I found that you had left there months before and were supposed to be in London, but no one could tell me where. I returned, and have been looking for you ever since. I paced the streets by night and day, but, until two hours ago, all my efforts were fruitless, and I never saw you for an instant."

"And now you do see me," said Monks, rising boldly, "and

you accuse me of fraud and robbery on the strength of a fancied resemblance in a young boy to a painting by a dead man of his mistress. Brother! You don't even know that they had a child; you don't even know that."

"I did not," replied Mr Brownlow, rising too, "but within the last fortnight I have learnt it all. You have a brother and you know him. What is more, your mother destroyed a will she found in which your father left his property to the child who was likely to be born while he was in Rome. The child was born, and accidentally encountered by you some years later when your suspicions were aroused by his likeness to your father. You went to the workhouse where he was born. You discovered that a certain Mrs Bumble had the proofs of his birth and parentage. You obtained these and destroyed them, and, in your own words to your accomplice Fagin, *'the only proofs of the boy's identity lie at the bottom of the river, and the old hag that received them from the mother is rotting in her coffin.'* You were heard, Edward Leeford, and the girl who, at the risk of her life, told me the true story, has suffered a violent death. You are morally responsible for her murder, although you had no hand in it."

"No, no," cried Monks, "I had no hand in that. I was trying to find out the cause when you overtook me. I thought it was a common quarrel."

"It was, in part, because she told me of the secret plot between you and Fagin to deny Oliver his inheritance, and keep him in a life of crime. Now that I have told you all I know, will you reveal the whole story?"

"Yes, I will."

"Set your hand to a statement of truth and facts, and repeat it before witnesses?"

"That I promise, too."

"You must also, remembering your father's will, give Oliver the money to which he is entitled. After that, you may go where you please. In this world, you and he need meet no more."

While Monks was pacing up and down with dark and evil looks, thinking about this proposal and wondering how he could avoid doing it, but at the same time torn by fear, the door was hurriedly unlocked, and a gentleman (Dr Losberne) entered the room in violent agitation.

"The man will be taken," he cried. "He will be taken to-night."

"The murderer?" asked Mr Brownlow.

"Yes, yes," replied the other. "His dog has been seen lurking about some old haunt, and it is likely that his master will return there under cover of darkness. Spies are hovering about in every direction. I have spoken to the men who seek him, and they tell me he cannot escape. A reward of a hundred pounds is proclaimed by Government tonight."

"I will give fifty more," said Mr Brownlow, "and proclaim it with my own lips upon the spot, if I can reach it. Where is Mr Maylie?"

"Harry? As soon as he had seen this man here, safe in a coach with you, he hurried off to where he heard this," replied the doctor, "and, mounting his horse, sallied forth to join the others in their search, at some place in the outskirts agreed upon between them."

"Fagin," said Mr Brownlow, "what of him?"

"When I last heard, he had not been taken, but he will be, or is taken by this time. They're sure of him."

"Have you made up your mind?" asked Mr Brownlow, in a low voice, to Monks.

"Yes," he replied. "You—will not give me up?"

"I will not. Remain here till I return. It is your only hope of safety."

They left the room, and the door was again locked.

"What have you done?" asked the doctor in a whisper.

"All that I could hope to do and even more. The whole villainous plot has been laid bare, and will be admitted in writing and signed. Write and appoint the evening after to-morrow, at seven, for the meeting. We shall be down there a few hours before, but shall require rest, especially the young lady, who *may* have greater need of firmness than either you or I can quite foresee just now. But my blood boils to avenge this poor murdered creature. Which way have they taken?"

"Drive straight to the Police Office and you will be in time," replied Dr Losberne. "I will remain here."

The two gentlemen hastily separated, each in a fever of excitement wholly uncontrollable.

CHAPTER 41

SIKES IS CORNERED

Near to that part of the Thames by which the church at
Rotherhithe stands, there exists the filthiest, the strangest, the
most extraordinary of the many places that are hidden in
London, wholly unknown, even by name, to the great mass of
its inhabitants.

To reach this place, the visitor has to penetrate through
a maze of close, narrow and muddy streets, thronged by the
roughest and poorest of waterside people, and made up mainly
of cheap shops, overflowing warehouses and tottering houses
which seem about to fall down as he passes.

In such a neighbourhood, beyond Dockhead in the Borough
of Southwark, stands Jacob's Island, surrounded by a muddy
ditch six or eight feet deep and fifteen or twenty wide when
the tide is in, once called Mill Pond, but known in the days
of this story as Folly Ditch. It is a creek or inlet from the
Thames, and can always be filled at high water by opening
the sluices at the Lead Mills from which it took its old name.
Wooden bridges span it at intervals.

Rotting houses line it on either side, and, in the upper room
of one of these, the back of which overlooked the ditch, there
were sitting two men who, regarding each other now and then
with anxious looks, sat for some time in profound and gloomy
silence. One of these was Toby Crackit, and the other a robber
of fifty years whose nose had been almost beaten in in some
old scuffle, and whose face bore a frightful scar most probably received on the same occasion. This man was an old
associate of Fagin's, who had been sentenced to be transported. He had returned in secret, and, therefore, went always
in fear of his life. His name was Kags.

Turning presently to Toby, who appeared to have lost all
his devil-may-care swagger, he spoke of what was uppermost
in both their minds.

"When was Fagin took, then?"

"Just at dinner-time—two o'clock this afternoon. I think Charley knows something. If he gives evidence, Fagin will swing, by God."

"What about the Artful?"

"Oh, he didn't know nothink about it. He got nabbed two weeks ago with a silver snuff box on him. He'll most likely be transported."

"And Bet, what happened to her?"

"Poor Bet! She went to see the Body, to identify it," replied Toby, "and she went off mad, screaming and raving, and beating her head against the boards, so they put a straight-jacket on her and took her to hospital—and there she is."

While the two men sat again in silence with their eyes fixed upon the floor, a pattering noise was heard upon the stairs, and Sikes's dog bounded into the room. They ran to the window, downstairs, and into the street. The dog had jumped in at an open window; he made no attempt to follow them, nor was his master to be seen.

"What's the meaning of this?" said Toby, when they had returned. "He can't be coming here. I—I—hope not."

"If he was coming here, he'd have come with the dog," said Kags, stooping down to examine the animal, who lay panting on the floor. "Here! Give us some water for him; he has run himself faint."

"Where can he have come from?" exclaimed Toby. "He's been to the other dens, of course, and finding them filled with strangers come on here, where he's been many a time and often. But where can he have come from first, and how comes he here alone without the other?"

"He"—(neither of them called the murderer by his old name)—"He can't have made away with himself. What do you think?" said Kags.

Toby shook his head.

"If he had," said Kags, "the dog 'ud want to lead us away to where he did it. No. I think he's got out of the country and left the dog behind. He must have given him the slip somehow."

This solution, appearing the most probable one, was adopted as the right one. The dog, after drinking up all the water down to the last drop, crept under a chair and coiled himself to sleep, without more notice from anybody.

It being now dark, the shutter was closed, and a candle lighted and placed upon the table. The terrible events of the last two days had made a deep impression on both of them, increased by the danger and uncertainty of their own position. They drew their chairs closer together, starting at every sound. They spoke little, and that in whispers, and were as silent and awe-stricken as if the remains of the murdered woman lay in the next room.

They had sat thus some time, when suddenly was heard a hurried knocking at the door below.

"Young Bates," said Kags, looking angrily round to check the fear he felt himself.

The knocking came again. No, it wasn't he. He never knocked like that.

Crackit went to the window and, shaking all over, drew in his head. There was no need to tell who it was; his pale face was enough. The dog, too, was on the alert in an instant, and ran whining to the door.

"We must let him in," said Crackit, taking up the candle.

"Isn't there any help for it?" asked the other man in a hoarse voice.

"None. He *must* come in."

"Don't leave me in the dark," said Kags, taking down a candle from the chimney-piece, and lighting it with such a trembling hand that the knocking was twice repeated before he had finished.

Crackit went down to the door, and returned followed by a man with the lower part of his face buried in a handkerchief, and another tied over his head under his hat. He drew them slowly off. Blanched face, sunken eyes, hollow cheeks, beard of three days growth, wasted flesh, short thick breath; it was the very ghost of Sikes.

He laid a shaking hand upon a chair which stood in the middle of the room, and sat down.

Not a word had been exchanged. He looked from one to another in silence, and they would not meet his eye, but sat with eyes cast down, gazing at the floor.

"How came that dog here?" asked Sikes at last.

"Alone. Three hours ago."

"Tonight's paper says that Fagin's took. Is it true, or a lie?"

"True."

178

They were both silent again.

"Damn you both!" said Sikes, passing his hand across his forehead. "Have you nothing to say to me?"

There was an uneasy movement, but nobody spoke.

"You that keep this house," said Sikes, turning his face to Crackit, "do you mean to give me up, or to let me lie here till this hunt is over?"

"You may stop here, if you think it safe," returned Toby, after some hesitation.

Sikes carried his eyes slowly up the wall behind him, rather trying to turn his head than actually doing it, and said, "Is—it—the body—is it buried?"

They shook their heads.

"Why isn't it?" he retorted, with the same glance behind him. "What do they keep such ugly things above ground for? Who's that knocking?"

Crackit intimated, by a motion of his hand as he left the room, that there was nothing to fear, and came back immediately with Charley Bates behind him. Sikes sat opposite the door, so that the moment the boy entered the room he saw him.

"Toby," said the boy, falling back, as Sikes turned his eyes towards him, "why didn't you tell me this downstairs?"

There had been something so tremendous in the shrinking off of the other two, that the wretched man was willing to seek the favour even of this lad. Accordingly he nodded, and made as though he would shake hands with him.

"Let me go into some other room," said the boy, retreating still farther.

"Charley!" said Sikes, stepping forward. "Don't you—don't you know me?"

"Don't come nearer me," answered the boy, still retreating, and looking with horror in his eyes upon the murderer's face. "You monster!"

The man stopped half-way, and they looked at each other, but Sikes's eyes sank gradually to the ground.

"Witness you two," cried the boy, still shaking his clenched fist, and becoming more and more excited as he spoke. "Witness you two—I'm not afraid of him—if they come here after him, I'll give him up *and* tell what I heard. He may kill me for it if he likes, or if he dares, but, if I am here, I'll give him up. I'd give him up if he was to be boiled alive. Murder! Help! Down with him!"

Shouting and waving his arms, the boy actually threw himself single-handed upon the strong man, and, in the intensity of his energy and the suddenness of his surprise, brought him heavily to the ground.

The two spectators seemed quite stupefied. They offered no interference, and the boy and man rolled on the ground together, the boy heedless of the blows showered upon him, clutching tighter and tighter in the garments about the murderer's breast, and never ceasing to call for help with all his might.

The conquest, however, was too unequal to last long. Sikes had him down, and his knee was on his throat, when Crackit pulled him back with a look of alarm, and pointed to the window. There were lights gleaming below, voices in loud and earnest conversation, the tramp of hurried footsteps—endless they seemed in number—crossing the nearest wooden bridge. One man on horseback seemed to be among the crowd, for there was the noise of hoofs rattling on the uneven pavement. The gleam of lights increased, the footsteps came more thickly and noisily on. Then came a loud knocking at the door, and then a hoarse murmur from such a multitude of angry voices as would have made the boldest flinch.

"Help!" shrieked the boy in a voice that rent the air. "He's here! Break down the door!"

"In the King's name," cried the voices outside, and the hoarse cry arose again, but louder.

"Break down the door!" screamed the boy. "I tell you they'll never open it. Run straight to the room where the iight it. Break down the door!"

Strokes thick and heavy rattled upon the door and lower window shutters as he ceased to speak, and a loud huzzah burst from the crowd, giving the listener, for the first time, some adequate idea of its immense extent.

"Open the door of some place where I can lock this screeching Hell-babe," cried Sikes fiercely, running to and fro, and dragging the boy now as easily as if he were an empty sack. "That door. Quick!" He flung him in, bolted it, and turned the key. "Is the downstairs door fast?"

"Double-locked and chained," replied Crackit, who, with Kags, still remained quite helpless and bewildered.

"The panels—are they strong?"

"Lined with sheet-iron."

"And the windows, too?"

"Yes, and the windows."

"Damn you!" cried the desperate ruffian, throwing up the sash and menacing the crowd. "Do your worst! I'll cheat you yet!"

Of all the terrific yells that ever fell on mortal ears, none could exceed the cry of the infuriated throng. Some shouted to those who were nearest to set the house on fire; others roared to the officers to shoot him dead. Among them all, none showed such fury as the man on horseback, who, throwing himself out of the saddle, and bursting through the crowd as if he were parting water, cried, beneath the window, in a voice that rose above all others, "Twenty guineas to the man who brings a ladder."

The nearest voices took up the cry, and hundreds echoed it. The people waved to and fro in the darkness beneath like a field of corn moved by an angry wind, and joined from time to time in one loud furious roar.

"The tide," cried the murderer, as he staggered back into the room, and shut the faces out, "the tide was in as I came up. Give me a rope, a long rope. They're all in front. I can drop into the Folly Ditch, and clear off that way. Give me a rope, or I shall do two more murders, and then kill myself."

The panic-stricken men pointed to where such articles were usually kept; the murderer, hastily selecting the longest and strongest cord, hurried up to the house-top.

All the windows in the rear of the house had been long ago bricked up, except one small one in the room where the boy was locked, and that was too small even for him to squeeze his body, but he never ceased to call through it, telling those outside to guard the back. Thus, when the murderer emerged at last on the house-top by the door in the roof, a loud shout proclaimed the fact to those in front, who immediately began to pour round, pressing upon each other in an unbroken stream.

He planted a board, which he had carried up with him for the purpose, so firmly against the door, that it would be a matter of great difficulty to open it from the inside, and, creeping over the tiles, looked over the low parapet.

The water was out, and the ditch a bed of mud.

The crowd had been hushed during these few moments, watching his movements and not sure of his purpose, but the instant they realised it and knew it was defeated, they raised a cry of triumphant note to which all their previous shouting had been whispers.

"They have him now," cried a man who was watching from one of the little wooden bridges over the ditch. "Hurrah!"

"I will give fifty pounds," cried an old gentleman near him, "to the man who takes him alive. I will remain here, till he comes to ask for it."

There was another roar. At this moment the word was passed among the crowd that the door was forced at last, and that the man who had first called for the ladder had mounted into the room which led to the roof. People who had been at windows or on the little bridges poured into the streets pushing and crushing those who were already there, all of them panting with impatience to get near the door, and look upon the criminal as the officers brought him out.

The man had shrunk down under the ferocity of the crowd, but all at once he sprang upon his feet, determined to make one last effort for his life by dropping into the ditch, and, at the risk of being stifled by the mud, endeavouring to creep away in the darkness and confusion.

Roused into new strength and energy, for he could hear the people inside the house, he set his foot against the stock of chimneys, fastened one end of the rope tightly and firmly round it, and with the other made a strong running noose, by the aid of his hands and teeth, almost in a second. He could let himself down by the cord to within a less distance of the ground than his own height, and had his knife ready in his hand to cut it then and drop.

At the very instant when he brought the loop over his head before slipping it beneath his armpits, the murderer, looking behind him on the roof, threw his arms above his head, and uttered a yell of terror.

"Nancy's eyes!" he cried in an unearthly screech.

Staggering as if struck by lightning, he lost his balance and tumbled over the parapet. The noose was on his neck. It ran up with his weight, tight as a bowstring, and swift as the arrow it speeds. He fell for five and thirty feet. There was a sudden jerk, a terrific convulsion of the limbs, and there he hung, with the open knife clenched in his stiffening hand.

The old chimney quivered with the shock, but stood it bravely. The murderer swung lifeless against the wall, and the boy, thrusting aside the dangling body which obscured his view, called to the people to come and take him out, for God's sake.

A dog, which had lain concealed till now, ran backwards and forwards on the parapet with a dismal howl, and collecting himself for a spring, jumped for the dead man's shoulders. Missing his aim, he fell into the ditch, turning completely over as he went, and, striking his head against a stone, dashed out his brains.

CHAPTER 42

OLIVER LEARNS OF HIS HERITAGE

The events narrated in the last chapter were only two days old, when Oliver found himself, at three o'clock in the afternoon, in a travelling carriage rolling fast towards the town where he was born. Mrs Maylie and Rose and Mrs Bedwin and good Dr Losberne were with him, and Mr Brownlow followed in a post-chaise accompanied by one other person whose name had not been mentioned.

They did not talk about the death of Sikes, for the ladies and Oliver had not yet been informed of it, and they were all rather silent, thinking of the information concerning Oliver which Mr Brownlow had forced from Monks, and knowing that the purpose of their visit was to uncover, if possible, the rest of the mystery.

As they approached the town, and at length drove through its narrow streets, Oliver became quite agitated. There was Sowerberry's the undertaker's, just as it used to be, only smaller and less imposing in appearance than he remembered it—there were all the well-known shops and houses, with almost every one of which he had some slight incident connected. There was the workhouse, the dreary prison of his youthful days, with its dismal windows frowning on the street —there was the same lean porter standing at the gate, at sight of whom Oliver shrank back, and then laughed at himself for being so foolish, then cried, then laughed again—there were scores of faces at the doors and windows that he knew quite well—there was nearly everything as if he had left it but yesterday, and all his recent life had been but a happy dream. But it was real enough. They drove straight to the door of the chief hotel, and here was Mr Grimwig, all ready to receive them, and not offering to eat his head, no, not once. There was dinner prepared, and there were bedrooms ready, and everything was arranged as if by magic.

Mrs Maylie and Rose were sitting with Oliver after dinner, wondering if anything was going to happen that evening, when Dr Losberne and Mr Grimwig entered the room, followed by Mr Brownlow and a man whom Oliver almost shrieked with surprise to see; for they told him it was his brother, and it was the same man he had met at the market town, and seen looking in with Fagin at the window of his little room. Monks cast a look of hate, which, even then, he could not conceal, at the astonished boy, and sat down near the door. Mr Brownlow, who had papers in his hand, walked to a table near which Rose and Oliver were seated.

"This is a painful task," said he, "but your statement, which you signed in London before many gentlemen, must be repeated here. We must have it from your own lips, and you know why."

"Go on," said Monks, turning away his face. "Quick. I have almost done enough, I think. Don't keep me here."

"This child," said Mr Brownlow, drawing Oliver to him, "is your half-brother, the son of your father, my dear friend Edward Leeford, by poor young Agnes Fleming, who died in giving him birth. Oliver was born in this town, was he not?"

"In the workhouse of this town," was the sullen reply. "You have the story there." He pointed impatiently to the papers as he spoke.

"You must tell it here, too," said Mr Brownlow, looking round upon the listeners.

"Listen then! You!" returned Monks. "His father, being taken ill in Rome, was joined by his wife, my mother, from whom he had long been separated, who went from Paris and took me with her—to look after his property, not to look after him, for she had no great affection for him, nor he for her. He knew nothing of us, for his senses were gone, and he slumbered on till next day, when he died. Among the papers in his desk were two, dated on the night his illness first came on, directed to yourself;" he looked at Mr Brownlow; "and enclosed in a few short lines to you, with an instruction on the cover of the package that it was not to be forwarded till after he was dead. One of these papers was a letter to this girl, Agnes, the other a will."

"What of the letter?" asked Mr Brownlow.

"The letter?—a sheet of paper confessing his sorrow and praying to God to help her. He had told the girl that some secret mystery preventing him marrying her just then, but that all would be explained one day. So she had gone on patiently trusting him, until she trusted too far. When he wrote, it was only a few months before the birth of their baby. He told her all he had meant to do for her and the baby and prayed her forgiveness, for all the guilt was his. He reminded her of the day he had given her the little locket and the ring with her Christian name engraved upon it, and a space for his surname, which he had hoped to add later. He prayed her to keep it, and wear it next her heart, as she had always done. He wrote the same over and over again, as if he was out of his mind. I believe he was."

"The will," said Mr Brownlow, as Oliver's tears fell fast. Monks was silent.

"The will," said Mr Brownlow, speaking for him, "was in the same spirit as the letter. He talked of miseries which his wife had brought upon him, of the wickedness of you, his only son, who had been trained to hate him, and left you and your mother sufficient income for life. The bulk of his property he divided into two equal portions—one for Agnes Fleming, and the other for their child, if it should be born alive and ever come of age. If it were a girl, it was to inherit the money unconditionally, but if a boy, only if, before he came of age, he should never have stained his name with any public act of dishonour, meanness, cowardice or crime. He did this to mark his confidence in the mother, and his strong belief that the child would share her gentle heart and noble nature. If this were not so, then the money would come to you, for if his two sons were equal in wickedness, then you had the first claim on his money."

"My mother," said Monks boldly, "did what a woman should have done. She burnt this will. The letter to the girl never reached its destination, but she kept it and other proofs in case they ever tried to lie about what had happened, and she took care to tell the girl's father about his daughter. Wretched with shame, he fled with his children into a remote corner of Wales, and here, no great while afterwards, he was found dead in his bed. The girl had left her home in secret, some weeks before; he had searched for her on foot in every town and village near: it was on the night when he returned home, certain that she had destroyed herself, to hide her shame and his, that his old heart broke."

There was a short silence here, until Mr Brownlow continued the story.

"Years after this," he said, "this man's mother came to me. At the age of eighteen, he had left her, robbed her of jewels and money, gambled, forged and, having squandered the money, fled to London, where he fell in with the lowest outcasts. She knew she was dying when she came to me, and wanted him back. We made inquiries and searches which were unsuccessful for a time, but finally we found him, and he went back with her to France."

"There she died," said Monks, "after a lingering illness, and, on her death-bed, she bequeathed these secrets to me. She was certain the girl had not destroyed herself, and that a boy had been born who would prove a threat to me. I swore to her, if ever he crossed my path, to hunt him down; never to let him rest; to pursue him with the unrelenting hatred that I deeply felt, and to avenge that insulting will by dragging him, if I could, to the very gallows-foot. She was right. He came in my way at last. I began well, and, but for babbling women, I would have finished as I began!"

As the villain folded his arms tight together, and cursed softly under his breath, Mr Brownlow turned to the terrified group beside him, and explained that Fagin, who was an accomplice of Monks, had a large reward for keeping hold of Oliver, and this explained the visit to the cottage, when Oliver saw the faces of Monks and Fagin at the window.

"The locket and ring?" said Mr Brownlow, turning to Monks.

"I bought them from the man and woman I told you of, who stole them from the nurse, who stole them from the body of the girl," answered Monks without raising his eyes. "You know what became of them."

Mr Brownlow merely nodded to Mr Grimwig, who disappeared and shortly returned, pushing in Mrs Bumble, and dragging her unwilling husband after him.

"Do my hi's deceive me!" cried Mr Bumble with pretended enthusiasm, "or is that Oliver? Oh, O-li-ver, if you know'd how I've been a-grieving for you——"

"Hold your tongue, fool," murmured Mrs Bumble.

"Do you know that person?" inquired Mr Brownlow, pointing to Monks.

"No," replied Mrs Bumble flatly.

"Perhaps *you* don't?" said Mr Brownlow, addressing her husband.

"I never saw him in all my life," said Mr Bumble.

"Nor sold him anything, perhaps?"

"No," replied Mrs Bumble.

"You never had, perhaps, a certain gold locket and ring?" said Mr Brownlow.

"Certainly not," replied the matron. "Why are we brought here to answer such nonsense as this?"

Again Mr Brownlow nodded to Mr Grimwig, and again that gentleman disappeared, to return this time with two palsied old women, who shook and tottered as they walked.

"You shut the door the night old Sally died," said the foremost one, raising her hand and addressing Mrs Bumble. "You couldn't shut out the sound, though, nor stop up the holes in that door."

"No, no," said the other, looking round her and wagging her toothless jaws. "No, no, no."

"We heard old Sally try to tell you what she'd done, and saw you take a paper from her hand, and watched you, too, next day, to the pawnbroker's shop," said the first.

"Yes," added the second, "and it was a locket and gold ring. We found out that, and saw it given you. We were there. Oh, we were there!"

"Would you like to see the pawnbroker himself?" asked Mr Grimwig, with a motion towards the door.

"No," replied the matron. "If he"—she pointed to Monks—"has been coward enough to confess, as I see he has, and you have sounded all these old women till you found the right ones, I have nothing more to say. I *did* sell them, and they're where you'll never get them. What then?"

"Nothing," replied Mr Brownlow, "except that it remains for us to take care that neither of you is employed in a situation of trust again. You may leave the room."

"I hope," said Mr Bumble, looking miserably about him as Mr Grimwig disappeared with the two old women, "I hope that this unfortunate little circumstance will not deprive me of my post at the workhouse."

"Indeed it will," replied Mr Brownlow. "You may make up your mind to that, and think yourself well off besides."

"It was all Mrs Bumble. She *would* do it," urged Mr Bumble, first looking round to make sure that his partner had left the room.

"That is no excuse," replied Mr Brownlow. "You were present when the trinkets were destroyed, and indeed are the more guilty of the two in the eye of the law; for the law supposes that your wife acts under your direction."

"If the law supposes that," said Mr Bumble, squeezing his hat emphatically in both hands, "the law is a ass—a idiot. If that's the eye of the law, the law is a bachelor, and the worst I wish the law is, that his eye may be opened by experience—by experience." Mr Bumble fixed his hat on very tight, and, putting his hands in his pockets, followed his wife downstairs.

"Young lady," said Mr Brownlow, turning to Rose, "give me your hand. Do you know this young lady, sir?"

"Yes," replied Monks.

"I never saw you before," said Rose faintly.

"I have seen you often," returned Monks.

"The father of the unhappy Agnes—Oliver's mother—had *two* daughters," said Mr Brownlow. "What was the fate of the other—the child?"

"The child," said Monks. "When her father, who seemed to be hiding some tragic secret, died among strangers, leaving no clue by which friends or relatives could be traced—the child was taken by some poor cottagers, who assumed there was some shameful mystery about its birth, but reared it as their own. There she lived a wretched life, until a widow lady, residing then at Chester, saw the girl by chance, and, having heard from the cottagers her supposed history, pitied her, and took her home. She remained with this lady and was happy, as my mother, who had tracked her down, told me later. We lost sight of

188

her two or three years ago, and I saw her no more until a few months back."

"Do you see her now?"

"Yes, leaning on your arm."

"But still my adopted niece," cried Mrs Maylie, folding the fainting girl in her arms. "Still my dearest child. I would not lose her now, for all the treasures of the world. My sweet companion, my own dear girl!"

"The only friend I ever had," cried Rose, clinging to her. "The kindest, best of friends. My heart will burst. I cannot bear all this."

"But see, my love," said Mrs. Maylie, "remember who this is who waits to clasp you in his arms—your nephew, Oliver."

"I'll never call you aunt," cried Oliver, throwing his arms about her neck, "but sister, my own, dear sister."

Oliver and Rose were a long, long time alone. A soft tap at the door at length announced that someone was outside. Oliver opened it, slipped away, and gave place to Harry Maylie.

"I know it all," he said, taking a seat beside the lovely girl. "There was *no* mystery about your birth, and nothing of which you might be ashamed. Will you not now change your mind, my dearest Rose?"

"But how can I leave the dear one who saved me from a life of poverty and suffering? I owe her everything," said Rose, bursting into tears.

"When I left you last," said Harry, "I made up my mind to leave the rich and powerful society in which I moved in the hope that you and I could share a quiet and simple life together. I have done so. My old acquaintances look coldly on me now, but there are smiling fields and waving trees in England's richest countryside, and by one village church—mine, Rose, my own!—there stands a rustic dwelling which you can make me prouder of than all the hopes I have given up, were there a thousand of them. This is *my* rank and position now, and here, at your feet, I lay it down."

Mr Grimwig and Mr Brownlow waited a most unreasonable time for their supper that night, and neither Mrs Maylie, nor the young clergyman, nor Rose (who all came in together), could offer a word of excuse.

189

CHAPTER 43

THE END OF THE STORY

The fortunes of those who have figured in this tale are nearly closed, and can be related in a few and simple words.

Before three months had passed, Rose and Harry were married in his own little church, and, on the same day, accompanied by Mr Giles and Brittles, entered into possession of their new and happy home. Mrs Maylie went with them, to enjoy a tranquil old age with the two people she loved most in the world.

It was found that the amount of money which Monks still held, would, if it were equally divided between himself and Oliver, amount to little more than three thousand pounds each. Under the terms of his father's will, Oliver could have taken the whole, but Mr Brownlow, wishing to give the elder son one further chance, proposed that they should share the money, and Oliver joyfully agreed. Monks took the money, and went to the New World where, having quickly squandered it, he fell into his old ways, was imprisoned for fraud, fell ill and died far from home. His old accomplice, Fagin, was convicted, on the evidence of Charley Bates, of plotting the death of Nancy, and was hung. Charley himself, appalled by Sikes's crime, began to wonder if an honest life was not, after all, the best. He left the city and, after many struggles and some suffering, became the merriest young cattle-farmer in Northamptonshire. Dodger, who had been transported to Australia for theft, was eventually freed and established himself as a trader. The rest of Fagin's gang broke up, and was seen no more in city streets.

Mr Brownlow adopted Oliver, and they and Mrs Bedwin went to live within a mile of the parsonage house. Mr Grimwig and Dr Losberne often came to visit, and in that peaceful village lived a group of people whose condition approached as nearly one of perfect happiness as can ever be known in this changing world.

Within the altar of the old village church there stands a white marble tablet, which bears but one word, "Agnes", and I believe that the shade of Agnes sometimes hovers round that solemn nook. And I believe that Oliver knows it too, and is glad.

Oliver Twist

BBC TV adaptation

Cast list

Agnes	Lysette Anthony
Bumble	Godfrey James
William	Spencer Rheault
Tom	Felix Yates
Little Oliver	Scott Funnell
Gamfield	Simon Watkins
Sowerberry	Raymond Witch
Charlotte	Carys Llewellyn
Noah	Julian Firth
Oliver	Ben Rodska
Monks	Pip Donaghy
Dodger	David Garlick
Bill Sikes	Michael Attwell
Fagin	Eric Porter
Charley	Nicholas Bond-Owen
Nancy	Amanda Harris
Barney	Christian Rodska
Mr Brownlow	Frank Middlemass
Mrs Corney	Miriam Margolyes
Toby Crackit	Christopher Driscoll
Giles	David King
Brittles	Terry Molloy
Martha	Janet Henfrey
Anny	Beryl Cooke
Rose	Lysette Anthony
Dr Losberne	David McKail
Harry	Dominic Jephcott